once

THE METCALF-ROOKE AWARD:

2006 Patricia Young for *Airstream*
      (Short-fiction)

2007 Kathleen Winter for *boYs*
      (Short-fiction)

2008 Rebecca Rosenblum for *Once*
      (Short-fiction)

once

(stories)

REBECCA ROSENBLUM

BIBLIOASIS

FIRST EDITION

Library and Archives Canada Cataloguing in Publication

Rosenblum, Rebecca, 1978–
        Once : stories / Rebecca Rosenblum.

ISBN 10: 1-897231-49-0
ISBN 13: 978-1-897231-49-4

        I. Title.

PS8635.O65O53 2008   C813'.6   C2008-904001-5

Edited by John Metcalf & Leon Rooke.

Cover image by Marta Chudolinska from
the graphic novel *Back and Forth*.

PRINTED AND BOUND IN CANADA

Dedicated to
Gerald, Barbara, and Ben Rosenblum

Contents

ContEd

EVA'S PLACE IS BUSIEST IN THE EVENINGS – lots of fried cheese and ass-grabbing near midnight. We're supposed to close at one, but drunk people are hard to scatter. It's good tips, and I got used to sloppy pub scenes when I hung around with Riley, my ex. I just don't like getting home so late there's not enough time for sleeping, cooking, errands, let alone reading. *Tax Answers* is boring, but I understand if I concentrate. When I'm tired, I wind up staring at the same page until I fall asleep. The book cost $60.

By the time I get to the campus I have ten minutes to find the classroom. I meant to stop and eat. I meant to look calm and smart, not confused and late. The Continuing Education people sent me a map that I can't follow, a little notebook, a ruler, a pen, all printed with *ContEd*. As I walk, I keep thinking ContEd isn't a real word. My feet hurt and the interconnected buildings make no sense; when I look out a window I'm across the street from where I started.

I only notice the room number because a man with red-blond hair is closing the door. "Oh," I call so he'll wait. I feel like if I get there before the door closes, I'm not really late. I try to catch his eye and smile, but he's not paying attention. He's got loafers on, too, shinier than mine.

There's about thirty desks and orange plastic chairs, mainly taken. I don't look at anyone, just push towards the only empty seat – in the far corner, of course – *sorryexcusemesorry*. The man in loafers stands at the front, tossing a piece of chalk. He's got serious glasses, serious loafers, but a soft pink mouth, and a shaving cut on his chin.

"Welcome, everyone, to Introductory Tax Preparation, an opportunity to learn about your own taxes as well as move towards becoming a professional tax preparer, a fascinating career. I'm Barton Denby, and I'm a tax guy, and . . . well, it's a fascinating career. Now, you can all introduce yourselves, and then we'll do a quick quiz to see what skill level we're working with. Ummm, could you start . . ." He kind of just waves at the left side of the room, but a cute Asian girl with tiny pigtails answers.

"Hi, Mr. Denby. I'm Ling. Last year we got audited and my husband sent me here to make sure that *never* happens again." She grins and bounces her crossed leg.

"Just Barton, please. This is ContEd, we're all adults." He says ContEd like it's a real word.

"I'm Jeff, and I'm a bank teller. Um, yeah." Jeff seems nervous for someone who talks for work, shuffling his lace-ups under his desk. Then again, I'm nervous too. It didn't occur to me that I'd have talk in front of everyone. I thought I could just listen, do the homework, see how it goes.

"I'm Marina. I've been a stay-at-home mom for twenty-three years, and now I'd like to get into the exciting world of business." Marina keeps looking at her long navy dress, touching it. It must be the best thing she owns.

"I'm Stevey. My EI says I gotta retrain for something. I used to do carpet-cleaner rentals." Stevey's shirt has a name tag that says *Lou*, and he's wearing dirty white sneakers with the laces undone.

It's my turn. In high school math, I usually got 60s, but that was without ever trying. Riley said I was too smart for homework, or even to go to class. When I paid attention, it seemed easy. "I'm Isobel. I used to be good at math."

The quiz is hard. I only brought my ContEd pen, so I have to cross out mistakes, which looks awful. We mark ourselves since the quiz doesn't count, but I still feel stupid.

I get 74%, and then someone asks if class is over. The teacher looks surprised, but he says yes. It's nearly nine when I get on the streetcar and open the box of leftovers Eva gave me. Beautiful highlight-hair high-school girls glare across the aisle when I get rice on the floor. This whole night felt like high school. But that was a long time ago, and back then I didn't even really care.

At home, I take off my shoes before I turn on the lights. Blood rushes into my feet, tingling and pinging like fireworks. It feels so good I almost can't stand it. I lie on the couch and try to read the textbook, but I'm too sleepy. When the phone rings, I don't answer. When it stops, I set the alarm clock and turn off the light.

ON TUESDAY I try reading on my break. When it's raining, the only break spot is the back of the kitchen, where everyone can see you. I wish I could sit in the alley.

"That literature, Iz?" Eva asks.

Mara, another dinner-shift waitress, laughs before I can answer, which is just as well, since I haven't got one. "I always thought you were deep, Iz. That's how quiet ones are."

"It's a tax textbook."

"Oh," Mara says. She's about eight months pregnant, her belly poking out under her apron. "Why?"

I shrug. Eva slams a brick of ground beef onto the counter. "Yeah, Iz, you checking up on our honesty?" She and Mara start plucking wads of meat from the brick and weighing them on the little scale. Three ounces, roll twice in your hands, put it between two sheets of waxed paper and press it flat: tomorrow's hamburgers.

"Just seemed like . . . something to do."

"Ah, you need a boyfriend, you got too much free time, Iz."

I do need a boyfriend, but I don't even have time to get the reading done before Thursday. I wear my work blouse and a blue skirt. I'm cold and the skirt looks stupid with Docs, but I don't have gravy on me and my feet don't hurt. Much.

Barton's got a blue tie this week, but still no jacket. I wonder if he was cold on the way over, too. He has neat fingernails, no wedding ring, loafers again. I wonder if his feet hurt – shiny shoes are usually stiff, too.

"One of the most satisfying things about tax preparation is all that you can learn about human nature. You become like a confessor. People tell you *any*thing, like a doctor." I underline *confessor* in my notes. I can't imagine anyone confessing anything to me, or me being able to help. I'd like to, though.

"Questions about the intro chapter?" Stevey didn't know we were supposed to read anything. Ling couldn't find the textbook at the bookstore. Lachlan doesn't know what a "common-law partnership" is.

"Well, um, that refers to individuals in a conjugal relationship, two adults who share residence and financial resources to some degree, um, maybe kids."

"So living in sin. A man and a woman not married."

I think Barton rolls his eyes, but I'm sitting in the back again, so I can't be sure. I wasn't late this time, but everyone else sat in the same seats as before, so I did, too. "Yeah, basically. But – " Barton fists up his fingers around the chalk " – it could be a man and a woman, or two men or two women – "

"Whoa, now, Revenue Canada will count two men as a *marr*iage?" Lachlan's voice is very loud. Marina goes and shuts the door to the hallway.

"Not a, not a marriage. Partnership. And it's not Revenue Canada anymore, it's actually called Canada Revenue Agency . . . Anyother-questions?"

Lachlan raises his hand, but Barton is staring at the ceiling. For a minute we all just sit quietly. Then Marina calls, "Weren't we supposed to have a quiz?"

"Yes, right now."

I remembered to bring a pencil this week, which is good since I need to erase half of what I write down. Barton reads something called *The 48 Laws of Power* while we write. I guess teachers trust adult classes.

After the quiz, Barton shows a T4 and talks about how "non-exceptions" would fill it out. There are lots of questions, even though it's just what everybody does every April. People seem to ask stuff almost at random in this class, about pets and separate school boards and home repairs. Lachlan brings up common-law partnerships again, asking if couples can file together if they aren't married.

"Um, is that in the text? It shouldn't be in the text. You *can't* file jointly in Canada. That's an American thing." Barton plays with his chalk, making little white marks on his blue cuff and then rubbing them out.

"Well, in the States, then?"

Barton drops the chalk and he can't seem to grab it from the floor. "I only do Canadian stuff," he says from upside-down. "This class doesn't cover U.S. law."

Ling starts talking about an American TV show where accountants are also detectives. Barton finally stands up with the chalk and notices it's 9:07 and says, "We'll pick this up next week." His face is red, maybe from being upside-down.

As I walk past him towards the door, he looks up and asks, "How was the quiz?" He's shoving notes into his bag. "Easy? Hard?"

I start stacking the leftover handouts and papercut the inside of my thumb. I want to say it was easy, but he's going to mark my paper. "Hard, because I didn't finish the reading." I hand him the pages. There's blood on the edges, but he doesn't notice.

"Was there too much?" He zips his bag closed, open, closed.

"I just didn't get time. I'll catch up."

"It's not supposed to be stressful. I used to make myself crazy over tough classes. I wouldn't want to do that to you guys."

"I just want to do well."

"Just speak up when you don't understand." He holds the door open and we walk out into the hallway. "No shame in asking questions."

He thinks I'm in the same category as Stevey, who thinks cats are dependents. I duck into the ladies' room so I won't have to take the elevator with him.

EVA'S PROBABLY only about thirty-five, and Mara's younger than that, but they act like old mamas, like pretty clothes and parties are a waste of time and so is trying to be nice when you don't mean it. A few things are the same in Toronto as they were in Montreal, and one is ladies like Eva and Mara, who seem to have been born married.

They never use their husbands' names, just *he him his.* When they call *him* on the telephone they don't say hello, just start talking. Sometimes Eva and Mara come in to work with dirty hair because their husbands take really long showers. Sometimes they look in their purses and their cigarettes aren't there because the husbands are smoking them. If it weren't for their husbands, Eva and Mara would never screw anything up, ever. They are always tired but beautiful, and they made their own wedding dresses and talk to their mothers every day. They can snatch their purses back from muggers and carry three plates on each arm.

They feel bad for me, because I don't have any family in the city, because I'm a bad waitress, because I'm single. I never told them much about Riley, but somehow they figured out that there was a man in Montreal and now I'm alone. They want to help, but don't really have too many ideas.

"That guy on table fourteen was cute."

"With the little baby?"

"Yeah, but no lady friend. Single dad? You should ask him out."

Mara comes in clutching three empty coffee pots above her bump. "Yeah! Who?"

"Table fourteen."

"Oh, yeah, very cute. You can write your phone number on the back of his bill."

"I don't think that's a good idea."

"No, really, I saw it in a movie once. Or in a song, maybe, a country song?"

I couldn't do it, but they still look for men for me. It's what they've come up with.

I HAVE MONDAYS OFF, which Riley knows about, so the phone rings and rings. I used to answer sometimes, but we never had anything to say. I imagine telling him about Eva's, taxes, school. The only part I can imagine him understanding is how much my feet hurt – he works construction, when he's working. After a long shift, I feel it even in my ankles, even in my knees. Even the paper cut stings more when I'm tired.

The ringing distracts me from studying, so I go out for lunch. The Vietnamese sandwich place because it's cheap and I won't need to be waited on. I don't know what the meat on the bun is, but I get all the reading done. Then I make a summary, like the ContEd study guide said. When I get tired, I underline the headings in red. It looks smart.

A relationship of a conjugal nature, a sharing of resources. In high school, Riley gave me my own keys to his truck so I could drive myself to work after school if he ditched or got too trashed in the woods. His truck, but mine to use. By the time we'd started living together, he'd totalled the truck so bad he couldn't get it repaired, but then we split the rent. Is an apartment a resource? We lived there together a long time. Could Riley and I have been a partnership and never even known it?

Around six I go back to the counter and order another sandwich for supper. If the cashier notices that I've been there for five hours, he doesn't say. He has a hairnet, big bags under his eyes, but a nice smile, small and quiet. Is he cute? Is he smiling at me because he thinks I'm cute? How does anyone ever know? I go back to my plastic table and my books.

ON THURSDAY, we get our quizzes back. 52%. Barton just made slashes through the wrong answers, as if he trusted me to find the right ones. I did. I know home office expenses and per diems, front to back. I'm sure I aced the quiz this week. Pretty sure.

Last two classes, I was dizzy hungry by the end, so today I have a couple of Eva's baklava, free and filling. It's hard to eat something sticky and take notes at the same time, though. At the end of class, I'm still working on my first piece.

Barton wanders towards me with his eyebrows up and interested. "What's that?"

"It's baklava." His eyebrows stay high. "It's a Greek dessert, honey and nuts and pastry. Want one?" I hold out the box. I don't think I need to tell him that they're old.

"Um. Sure." He peels a pastry off the waxed paper and pops it whole into his mouth. I wouldn't have done that – I should've warned him. His eyes bug out, but no crumbs escape, no choking. I jam the box into my bag. "Have a good night, then."

He keeps chewing. His face is starting to go a bit red, but he waves as I leave.

WHEN I LEFT RILEY, it was for good. Once I'd decided, it was easy to quit my job, buy the bus ticket, pack while he was at work, go. Everybody said Toronto had cleaner streets, cleaner men, nicer weather than Montreal. That seems true, but in a year I haven't seen much. I wonder how you meet people when you don't know anyone to introduce you. I go to work and home and work. I see Toronto when the subway car bursts into the light before Broadview.

When I first got here, I didn't see the harm in letting Riley know my new number, that I'm all right, that I don't miss him. He didn't have much to say to that, or to anything, but he still calls, calls, and says nothing. Maybe it's because he loves me, but it doesn't feel like that. Still, at least someone calls.

MARA COMES IN with a stack of paper towels. The staff bathroom is really only for one person, no stalls. The lock broke ages ago, though, and waitresses aren't too polite when they're rushing. I'm just pulling my skirt over my hips, so I'm not too embarrassed. I fold my work pants into my bag.

"All dressed up for class?" Mara tries to jam the towels into the dispenser. She pushes the door up partway with her shoulder, but it's dented so she can't get it fully open. A few paper towels drift to the wet floor. "How's that going?"

"It's ok. But pretty hard, and there's some weirdos."

"Well, it *is* a whole class about taxes – what'd you expect?"

I don't want to tell her I think new people, even weirdos, are better than no people. "Barton says, when you do someone's taxes, you find out people's secrets and become a student of human nature."

"Oh." Mara jolts up suddenly and the metal door bangs back against the wall. "Aha!" She shoves the towels in. "Who's Barton?"

"The teacher." I take my hair down, but there's a dent from the elastic like a reverse halo. I put it back up.

"You call your teacher by his first name?"

"Sure. We're all adults. He's not that much older than me."

Mara's eyes snap wide. "Is he cute? Does he like Greek food?"

I pick up the soggy paper and stuff it in the trash. "He liked Eva's baklava."

"You guys shared food?" Mara makes a noise like she's cheering at a football game. "So you like him? He's cute? You should ask him out."

"Um." Another waitress, Deena, comes in and squeezes between us, already hiking up her skirt. Mara rolls her eyes and goes out and I think that's the end of it. Later, though, Eva gives me a whole box of mini-baklavas. She says that desserts are slow, these are gonna go off before they sell, but sugar and nuts don't spoil. Plus she winks.

DURING CLASS, Barton says his bosses sometimes hire his best students for tax season. "It's a good way to get started in the industry."

"Did you take a course like ours?" Ling asks dreamily.

"I'm actually – I trained as a lawyer, but then I . . . decided that my strengths lay elsewhere." He suddenly bends over and ties his shoe very carefully. Everybody's quiet. If you have to go to law school to be a real tax person, the ContEd catalogue should've said that. Barton stands up and starts talking about artistic grants.

I stay after class to give Barton the pastries. Plus, I have a list of questions for him. Mara told me men like being asked about things. So I read an article about Stephen Harper's tax plan. Actually, the article was interesting. I'd like to know the answers to my questions.

Lachlan is asking about the assignment, The Pazzi Family Tax Return. "So this Italian family has two cars and a cottage in Muskoka?"

"Yes. See, there on the handout."

"Now, but wait, though – trick assignment? Is *ev*erything declared?"

"C'mon, Lachlan, work with the info. Explore the assignment – yes, Isobel?" People mainly call me Isobel when they're reading my name tag. "You had a question?"

I don't – all the stuff I memorized about Stephen Harper has disappeared. Finally, I remember something else. "What you said about tax preparers being confessors – "

"Um, I guess I was being a bit much." He turns the projector off. "Most of the time you just take the receipts and do the math." Lachlan shuffles out.

"But what if your client doesn't trust you? What if they lie?"

"Well, Isobel, I think I can spot a liar. I try to be perceptive." IS-oh-bell – he says it very anglo – the *S* sounds like an *S*, not a *Z*. He heads out, so I have to follow. "The most important thing is that you have to keep your hands clean. Totally. The client would totally be getting you to take the fall for them if you signed off on a false return. Some people will try – well. Anyway. It's usually just dull."

"Ok." The elevator *bings*. We go in and stand in silence until the ground floor.

"Well, I'll see you next week, Isobel." He starts to walk away, then turns back. "If that answers your question, of course. Does it?"

"Sure. Um, wait." I pull the smushed box from my bag. "Since you liked that baklava, I brought you some more." The box looks like something from the garbage. He probably doesn't even remember about last week.

He takes it. "Well, thanks, Isobel. You're very sweet." He rolls his eyes.

"What?"

"Just, what a dumb joke, to say you were sweet for bringing me sweets."

"That's ok." We just stand there staring at the box until I say, "Well, bye," and go. I don't know where Barton is heading, but probably not in the same direction as me.

ON SATURDAY NIGHT, a skinny guy in a soccer shirt corners me by the coffee station. "I like the way you work. You keep your head down, don't take no guff. These assholes, they'll take advantage. You got to keep your head down."

"Yeah?" I want to put grounds in the coffee machine just to do something, even though it's past ten and this late we only do instant. "Sure." I try to smile a little sexy, with just the side of my mouth. It feels funny.

"Really, though, you're too good to be in a place like this. Where you from, really?" He's got his hand on the counter, sliding along.

"Um, Montreal. But I like it here. It's ok."

He smiles and his hand jumps up, hooks the side of my waist. Maybe it's friendly. It doesn't feel friendly.

"It's a nice place, really."

Sliding up to the bottom of my bra. "*These* kinds of assholes don't know nothing."

"What sort of asshole are you, then?" I don't smile at all, which feels a lot better.

He doesn't say anything, just marches off fast to his table and stares out the window for a while. He's sitting alone. I keep an eye on him.

I usually know better than to start a fight with a creepy guy. Fighting is a way of playing along, and you never play along with a creepy guy. When I'm settling up with a big group, I see him go marching up to Eva at the till. His steps are high-assed and angry, as if the thing happened two minutes ago instead of an hour.

I have to watch the conversation while the group in front of me tries to remember who drank what. I see the guy talking, shaking his head hard. Eva shakes her head, too. I can tell by his mouth he's raising his voice, even though I can't hear him over the music and the chatter. Eva starts to turn and he grabs her shoulder to stop her. I'm sure that's all he wants, to stop her, but you shouldn't grab someone like Eva. You shouldn't grab anyone. She shoves him back hard and he crashes into an unbussed table. He hits loud – so much noise for ten dollars worth of glasses. Eva calls one of the grillmen, Jamie, to haul him out. The guy tries to leave ahead of Jamie, but he keeps turning around to yell, so he ends up getting pulled out after all.

My group pays up and gets out fast. They give a huge tip. Probably added wrong, scared. A bunch of students.

I go apologize. "I shouldn't've . . . obviously. I'm sorry."

"What? He was a dick. And crazy, obviously. You're supposed to take that?"

"Well, yeah. But – "

"Hey! Mara said you said your teacher was cute. Are you gonna ask him out?"

It takes me a minute to switch from the creepy guy to Barton. "I don't know."

"You should. Accountant's a good job. Shows he's serious, respectable, a hard worker. And you think he's cute?"

"I – " I think about Barton's washy orange hair, his small glasses and pink mouth. Those things aren't cute. I think about his shoulders underneath his thin shirt, thick and wide. He looks like someone you could lean against and be comfortable. Is that cute? "I don't think I've ever really asked a guy out."

Eva fiddles with her order pad. "Me neither. My husband handed me a beer at a party in grade ten." Eva not knowing something feels so strange.

"Did you know all along you were going to end up marrying him?"

"No – well – I guess – I never thought about anything in the future except with him there, too. That's like knowing."

I actually don't think it is. I thought that way about Riley, but I didn't know how anything would be, that'd he drink like Saturday every night and always seem to be looking at the wall behind my head.

On Sunday, Jamie scalds his chest draining the deep fryer. Emergency room, third degree burns, waitresses throwing lamb chops on the grill – a big mess. The next night, Mara goes into labour right at the coffee station, and then on Tuesday Deena quits from all the pressure and craziness. Eva begs me to work Thursday night. I feel like I can't say no. Besides, paying the tuition has made me need the money more. I guess that's ironic.

IT'S RAINING when I leave work and I don't know where my umbrella is. My blouse soaks and clings. It might be sexy with a different bra, on a different person.

I come in early and take a seat up front. There's raindrops on my calculator, but it still turns on. Barton puts some papers on my desk, and my hair drips on them.

Barton smiles. "I – we – missed you last week. Were you sick?"

"I just had to work. What happened?"

Barton squats down next to me, arms folded on my desk. His sleeves get wet. "Just a review of GST, charitable donations, some provincial stuff. Read the dittos." He nods at the pages, and then we don't say anything for a minute. I wonder if there's a way I'm supposed to make him like me. I'm still thinking when Barton stands up and says in a talking-to-everybody voice, "Let's begin."

AFTER CLASS, Barton tries to get his umbrella over us both. "You live far, Isobel?"

"No, a bit west."

"I'll drive you. My car's just over . . . I mean, if you want?"

I think that's what I want.

Barton sees me shivering and puts the heat on. My feet itch and throb as they warm up. I don't smell wet shoes – I hope Barton can't.

The last time I was in a car was when I took a cab from the station to my new apartment, a year ago. Someone back home told me about the building. The windows were greasy and the sink made noises but it was all right. I was lucky. When I give the directions to Barton, though, he asks me if I usually go home alone this late.

"It's fine, really." I shrug. "Where do you live?"

"West . . . Etobicoke."

It takes me a minute to picture the map. "That's pretty far."

"It's easier if you drive. And it's not forever."

"Rent's cheaper farther out. I'd do it if I had a car."

He carefully pulls his elbow in when he shifts gears so he doesn't brush me. "I'm saving to buy a condo."

"Wow," I say, but he's still speaking.

"So I'm in my folks' basement until real estate gets more reasonable, you know?"

"That makes sense." I wonder how old he is. Older than me, but not that much.

"They've got a basement apartment and I can help out with . . . stuff . . . Geez, nine-thirty already. Isobel, you must be tired?"

"Well, my feet hurt. Sometimes taking off my shoes is the sexiest part of my day." I must be tired – that's a thing I think in my head, not say out loud. I can feel the blush in my neck, At least it's too dark for him to see. "Not today, though." That's worse.

"That's, um, ah, interesting. Very interesting."

I see my awning. "This is me, just . . . Here." The teenagers smoking on the stairs seem sketchier than usual. I say, "Thankyousomuch," without looking at Barton.

I hear, "Anytime," as I slide out the door. Upstairs, soaking in the shallow bathtub, I realize I didn't even give him enough time to try to kiss me, if he even wanted.

THE DAY of the final exam, my whole body aches from not sleeping and it seems like every customer has some sort of issue: not enough napkins, the wrong brand of mustard, it's cold in the ladies room, *are you sure this is diet – it doesn't taste like diet.*

I'm nervous, but as soon as I see the exam paper I feel ok. I've memorized all this, and the math isn't hard with a calculator. When I finish, everyone else is still bent over their papers. For a minute, I just watch heads, backs, arms, no faces. I wonder how everyone's doing, how they feel. I wonder if their feet hurt.

I re-check my answers until people start standing up and talking about going to some bar. I didn't know there was going to be a last-class party. Maybe I'm not invited. I put my notebook in my bag. I shouldn't be spending money anyway. "You're coming, aren't you?" Marina asks me. I guess I'm invited.

On the way over, I walk beside Barton. "How'd the test go?"

"Ok. Fine."

"Good. So you think you'll go on with tax stuff?"

"I think I could be good at it. And I want to help people."

"Isobel." He spreads his hands flat in front of him. "You have many gifts, but you need to concentrate your forces. Yeah, tax-preparers help but people don't necessarily appreciate it. You need to protect yourself . . . like at any job."

I think about Eva giving me the lunch shift that everyone fights over so I can go to class, taking tables for me when I fall behind, telling the grill guys not to yell at me.

At the pub, our waitress asks what we're celebrating.

"Wow, taxes."

It's funny to see all these classroom people under the beer-light glow. Barton's tie is looser now. I watch him sip his beer, answer Lachlan's questions about government spies, sign Stevey's EI form. Then he turns towards me. "Are you Greek, Isobel?"

"No . . ."

"The back-lah . . . back-lava? That pastry you said was Greek?"

"I'm a waitress in a Greek restaurant."

"Oh. Oh, that must be fun . . . talking to people, free food?" I can see myself reflected shiny and small in his glasses. I haven't had this beer since Montreal. It's Riley's brand, American, not my favourite but I can drink it. It smells like mid-afternoon, the old sofa we found on the curb, his voice arguing with the TV. I wonder if my phone is ringing right now.

The evening drags, but I stay. I'm covering Mara's lunch tomorrow, so I'm going to be sorry when I'm too tired to be polite when people change their orders, hate their orders, yell when they don't get what they didn't ask for. But I stay. When I get back from the bathroom, there's a chair open next to Barton. I go sit there for a while.

WE'RE THE LAST TWO, which seems good. As we leave, Barton's talking about law school, how he studied all night for exams and flunked them anyway – "Sometimes, you just want to know you won't get anything wrong, you know?" He shakes his head as if something had fallen into his hair. "I just had to re-envision my path. I'll drive you home, right?" He's already walking towards the garage.

Barton finds my street from memory. He puts the car in park and turns the key. I don't think parking out here is legal, but maybe it's late enough. He's not staying, anyway. Probably. He asks, "You have fun tonight?"

I did. I liked the bad beer and the good waitress. I liked the way all Stevey's stories ended with "that fucker," and all of Ling's with "my husband thought I was crazy." I like having someone to talk about the night with after the night is over. I start to say, "Yeah," but Barton's already talking again.

"Great night, good class, a really good group. Very positive energy." He turns towards me, seat belt still on. "How're your feet?"

I look down as if I'd forgotten they were there. "Not too bad. I got new insoles."

"For your sexy feet?" He says it too fast, like he's been waiting to say it, then laughs. Actually he just says, "Heh heh," like he's in a comic strip. He's fiddling with the gearshift now. I can see a hint of hair above his loose tie. I can see a glint of sweat on his forehead. It's a strange thought: I could kiss him if I wanted to. It'd be easy to lean over, arch my belly over the gearshift, reach my face towards his face.

He'd kiss me if I kissed him, I suddenly know it. He'd come upstairs if I let him, but he'd never ask. I could tell Mara and Eva. He could answer the phone the next time Riley called. If I wanted. But he would never lean across the gearshift. He'd let me take all the risks, make all the guesses. He's just some guy in this car.

He waits until I'm all the way on the sidewalk, just about to swing the door shut, before he reaches into his pocket for a card.

"This is . . . this is my card at the firm. I meant to pass these out at the end of class . . . You should call me about a temp position in March. You'd be a great . . . great asset."

"Thank you." I want to be sure he knows I'm not thanking him for the card. "For the ride, and the class. And everything." I shut the door.

He mouths through the window, "Night, Iz."

"Night, Barton."

Upstairs I take my shoes and socks off. My feet leave little sweat-prints on the cool tile as I cross the kitchen. The blast of freezer air feels good on my cheeks after sweating in the bar. The baklava box is damp, dinged up a little from being in my bag.

I imagine Riley sitting drunk in our old cold kitchen. I imagine Mara and her husband curled up with their tiny new baby. Then I imagine Barton getting home to his apartment in the basement of his parents' place. I take a baklava out of the box and put the card in its place, cup the pastry in my palms to thaw it. I know what Barton's kitchen looks like, because it's just like mine: the fridge and stove a funny orange from the '70s, tea towel draped over the oven handle, digital green clock on the stove. The only difference is my fridge full of Greek foods Eva gave me, things with foreign characters I found at the Chinese grocery, takeout I'm saving, everything on sale. In Barton's kitchen, I know, there is only Minute Rice, Mr. Christie's cookies, tomato sauce in cans. Nothing that's hard to pronounce, or to fit into your mouth.

Chilly Girl

ONCE THERE WAS A GIRL WHO WAS USUALLY COLD. No one liked to hold her hand. She wore toques from October to April. She ruined picnics by wanting to go home when the sun went down. She could cradle lit candles in her bare hands and never get burned. Once she was seated near a draft at a wedding banquet and her lips turned blue. Once she forgot to wear a sweater to the movies and her teeth began to chatter. Once she looked at her cup of tea and then at the man who had bought it for her at a sidewalk café and said, "I wish I could be *in* a cup of tea right now." He didn't call her again.

Once she got invited to a condo-warming party for her boss. It was July, which made her brave, so she put on her favourite dress, which was yellow and orange and pink. All those gleaming shades of warm, but the fabric was thin cotton. In rain or wind it was as good as being naked. If someone photographed her with a flash, the picture would show an outline of her bra or her sharp little nipples, depending. She took out a cardigan in case of inclement weather or photography and draped it over her arm. Then she went into the living room, where her roommate was watching a noisy Britcom. Her roommate pressed Mute when the girl came in.

"You're wearing stockings and heels."

"Yes," said the girl. She felt nervous.

"With a sundress. To a summer party."

"It's at Emmy's condo – she's probably got air-conditioning."

"You look ridiculous." Her roommate turned the volume back up and watched a lady fall into a pile of grass clippings. She was like that.

The girl slunk back into her room. She kicked off her pumps and peeled her stockings from her legs. She put sandals on her bare feet and tiptoed past her roommate out the door. She was like that.

The party was big but quiet. The girl didn't see an air-conditioning unit but she felt a whispery artificial shiver crawl over her shoulders all the same. She pulled her cardigan on over her summer dress, sad to see her colours disappear. She was fluffing her hair out of the collar when the hostess came darting up to her.

"Oh, *there* you are! I was afraid you wouldn't come."

"I'm happy to have come. It's such a nice place," said the girl.

"Oh, really? Some days, I don't know. Come with me and I'll give you a tour." The hostess took a step and then stopped. Her face flowered up a little. "But . . . could you take off your shoes? I'm sorry, we just had the floors done when we moved in and it was *such* a *thing*. You know . . ." The hostess looked miserable, like she didn't want to ask but someone had made her.

The girl looked around the living room. There were no shoes anywhere. Hairy pale feet, feet in thin nylon trouser socks, slim feet with pedicures, even stockings . . . no shoes. There could be no exceptions to this rule – someone might get stepped on, delicate naked toes under the grinding hard rubber of a heel.

The girl took off her sandals. The floor felt like icy cement, even though it was parquet. She went on the tour. She put her toes onto the blond parquet squares and walked down halls like *L*s and *T*s. The kitchen had a butcher's block in the centre covered with dishes of beans and grains. The burners were flush with the stove. The floors gleamed like an ice rink. They walked past high windows where the view pitched into the harbour. If she stood still, the girl could feel some unseen fan blowing the strands of her hair. The hostess glittered at her, the track lighting reflecting shiny and sharp off nails, teeth, eye-whites, tongue. She was lovely and sleek and her home was lovely and sleek and the girl was glad when Emmy finally left her on a couch beside the wet bar, where all her friends were sitting, too.

Her friends were glad to see her, but the people they introduced her to recoiled when they shook her icicle hand. Someone gave her a drink. The ice cubes clinked whenever the girl gestured, or trembled. She was worried her hand would freeze to the glass. She sat on the couch but the creamy beige leather was slippery and glossy and cool against her thighs through the cheap cotton of her dress.

Her friends told her that a woman named Maya, who had caramel hair and used to go out with the girl, was somewhere at the party. The girl stood up. Everyone was concerned. The girl explained that her ex-girlfriend was still her friend, but so recently ex that the friendship would be wasted right now. She thought she saw a flash, over heads and shoulders, of butter and sugar hair, and it made her stomach wobble. She walked over to the window, where she hoped that some summer might be seeping in. But no warmth could escape the street. The windows were so thick and firm that the sky beyond them looked stormy and far away. The smooth steel frames showed no clasps or hinges. They would never give, or admit any of the elements. This cold came from somewhere else, and got her anyway.

A man approached her. He wore a linen suit with the sleeves and cuffs rolled up and no shoes or socks. He was very tall and had blown-back hair, like an American. He looked happy and confident and toasty. He smiled. She smiled back, and he swept his big hand towards the window.

"How'd you like to have a view like that?"

The girl peered at his suntanned face. "I wouldn't. The waterfront looks like the end of the earth in winter, all frozen over."

The man's mouth seemed to pause in a perfect crescent before becoming real again. "Just so, just so." He wasn't looking at her anymore and sounded as though he were speaking to himself, so she made a move to walk away. Then, "Are you all right? You look . . . your fingernails are blue." He pointed at the hand holding the glass.

She could feel herself getting frozen to the spot, iced over, unable to move. She sighed in a gust. "I'm cold. I didn't know we'd have to take off our shoes." Her voice sounded like the wail of the wind. She hated that. They both looked down. Her toenails were blue, too.

His voice sounded like he were inquiring about pizza toppings over the phone. "Do you want to wear my socks?"

Her gaze snapped up from the floor to his wide mouth.

"I stuck them in my briefcase. I didn't fancy going sockfooted. Wanted to be Miami Vice, y'know? They won't match your dress, but you're welcome, if you like . . ."

She'd forgotten about her warm-coloured dress, was too cold to care about clashing, anyway. She was trapped in an igloo-condo. Her boss would ask her about it on Monday if she left early. Another sip of her rye and ginger would solidify her throat and she'd never speak again. The condo windows were sealed against the summer outside like the Arctic part of the biodome. She followed the man to the front hall. He rummaged through a pile of shoelaces and purse straps and found an old bulky brown satchel. He pulled out the socks singly, crumpled.

The socks were an electric ice, a brilliant pale blue that she'd never seen before. It was a new colour. Laid flat in her palm, they felt thick and cottony, not at all damp despite having been worn all day. She wondered if they would smell the way he looked, like a golf green in the sun, like thawed lake water . . . The man was staring at her and she realized that her face was too close to the socks, far too close to sniffing them. She felt warm colour creep into her cheeks, which was nice but she was still embarrassed as she bent down. With her head close to her smoothly shaven shins, she was able to inhale deeply but all she smelled was the baked smell of cotton, the lemon of floor polish. As she straightened, she said, "These are great socks. They are a wonderful colour."

"Thanks. I love that blue. I have a coat that shade, too. I mean – " he pressed his lips tightly for a moment " – in winter, my winter coat matches them." In the pause, he gazed at her enveloped calves and the music went silent. "They look great on you." Then, on the big German stereo in the living room, a nasal whine filtered out. "It's Elvis Costello, it's 'American Without Tears,'" he told her.

She listened and nodded. A whole minute passed before she said, "It's in waltz time. That's not so common anymore."

His lips pulled back from his teeth and his hands spread wide. "Well, then we shouldn't waste it." One arm shot straight out; the other hooked in front of him, reaching for her waist.

She stepped into his linen arms. When he whirled her into the living room the wind caught her hair again and her yellow skirt spun out around her knees and the smooth blue socks slid like blades on the polished wooden rink. The hostess passed by with a tray of flying-fish-roe canapés, looked up briefly, and altered her course so she wouldn't interrupt the dancers. Her friends widened their eyes and clutched their drinks. Maya leaned against a wall and thought about saunas.

The song ended. The man squeezed her hand and then pulled away. He had whirled her so fast that her pale skin was flushed and her heart was pulsing. She even felt a tiny drop of sweat trickle down under the collar of her sweater. She wanted to take the sweater off. She was not cold.

"I have to go," he said. He pointed towards the doorway, where three young men in suits with rolled sleeves and cuffs were standing slouched, looking impatient.

"I'll give you back your socks." She bent over and lifted up one foot.

He put a hand on her shoulder and stopped her. "It's ok. Keep them for the party, so you won't be cold."

"But how – "

"Now you'll have to find me, and I'll get to see you again." He left.

The girl had a good time at the party once she was warm. She ate canapés covered with tiny salty fish eggs and washed them down with rye and ginger, no ice. She talked and laughed, although not with Maya, who left early. And the girl asked everyone she talked to about a tall American in an expensive suit. But no one knew who that man was, not even the hostess. It was very strange. Not even the hostess.

The party ended. She went home, tiptoed past her roommate, who was watching a cartoon about amoebas, and went to bed. In the morning the girl got up and did her laundry. She put the wintry socks in the delicate cycle and dried them with a pine fabric softener. Then she rolled them into a tight ball and put the ball in the corner of her handbag.

SUMMER WAS TOO SHORT. The leaves got crunchy and the wind learned to bite. The fashion that year was for cashmere, which was petal-soft on delicate skin but let the chill run right through. The girl bought balls of 100% wool and knitted herself a thick toque and scarf. She tried to knit mittens but got stuck on the thumbs, so she wore two cashmere pairs instead.

The wind blew chunks of ice into her skin. Her eyes streamed with salt water and sad. There were Christmas lights in the window of the Indian restaurant that was supposed to be the best in the city. She opened the steamy glass door eagerly, looking forward to the meal, the peppers, the vinegar, cayenne and cinnamon. She loved vindaloo. She loved foods that made her sweat.

The waiter motioned her towards a coat rack where she could hang her fisherman's jacket, her fuzzy cardigan, her crooked scarf and tipsy hat. She stuffed everything into the sleeve of her coat and put it on a wooden hanger that looked strong enough to support it all. On the rack next to her coat was another coat. This coat was the colour of the harbour in a midday storm, or a January moon, or the heart of a flame. A coat the colour of the socks in her bag.

When she took them out, the socks seemed a bit dingy from being pressed against grocery receipts and pencils and dirty change for the past few months. She felt guilty about that. The warm round ball nestled in her cupped hands like a chick or a candle. She could already feel the winter mist creeping under the doors and around the windowpanes to get through her shirt and onto her skin. The restaurant was crowded with the breath of many people, though, and peppery vapour burned in her nostrils. She slipped the roll of blue blue socks into the pocket of the blue blue coat. As she turned away from the coat rack, a flicker of too-long hair blown by the wind caught her eye from the doorway. The waiter pointed her towards a table in the far corner, blocked from the draft of the door by a screen, near the heating register. The girl was about to walk towards it, but then the Hindi love song on the stereo changed to something else, a Christmas song. It was "Fairytale of New York" by the Pogues. It was in waltz time. The girl turned away from the warm spot. She went to the only other empty table, which was beside the icy window, but in view of the door, the coat rack and the fiery open kitchen. She sat down and waited to see what would happen next.

Route 99

T HURSDAY WAS SO COLD there weren't even any pigeons out and Ella wound up standing shivering at the bus stop for close to an hour. The seven o'clock bus didn't come and the seven-twenty blew by her. This all made Ella almost but not quite late enough to get fired. Instead she got moved off cleaning rooms to laundry. That meant afternoon shifts, and no tips. It was like getting thirty percent fired, and it smelled like singed hair.

Usually Ella could smell trouble coming, at least from upwind. The skill came from working hotel housekeeping since she graduated high school, getting real familiar with the way bad things smelled – bad food, bad booze, bad hair products. After a couple years, Ella could smell even the bad stuff that didn't leave a stain. A break up conversation smelled like a fart in an elevator, while just an argument smelled more like a fart in a swimming pool, half-dulled by the chlorine. Gossipy people smelled like sour milk and she learned to avoid both. Getting fired smelled like fire, an ashy, nose-drying tinge, and she tried to avoid that, too. But no one could smell a thing that was not there. When the seven o'clock 99 was nowhere there was no smell to warn her ahead of time. So Ella was on laundry, and even then she knew she had to watch it.

So she had to be in for twelve on Friday. Her bus, route 99, took a half hour, except when it didn't come or didn't stop. Then you had to wait, fingers crossed inside your mittens, for twenty minutes for the next one. Ella got to the stop at Jane and Finch at eleven. She was surprised to see Carmen there, smoking and teetering on one of the punk kids' skateboards in front of the Vietnamese restaurant, Pho-Mi 99. The kid was watching her wobble across the icy concrete in her long pink puffer coat.

"At least you'll be well-padded if you fall," Ella yelled.

Ella's voice made Carmen stagger off the board, and when she righted herself and opened her mouth to curse her cigarette fell out. She picked it off the ground, gave Ella the finger and put her still-burning smoke back into her mouth.

"What are you doing here?"

"I got bumped back to half days." Carmen shrugged and her coat bunched at her narrow shoulders.

"Sucks," Ella said.

"My mom wants to know where we're gonna get the rent next month."

Ella didn't know what to say. She and Carmen were bus-friends. Carmen worked at a discount furniture outlet on Arrow Road, right down from the hotel, but though they worked and lived so close together, Ella only ever saw Carmen at the bus stops or on the bus. Depending on what shifts they pulled, they might talk an hour a day, every day for weeks, and then not see each other at all for months.

"Buuussss!" yelled the boarder kid, running across the tarmac, big jeans flapping. Carmen and Ella started off more slowly. There was a bus driver standing at the stop in his burgundy parka. No 99 driver would drive past one of their own, not even Carlson.

Carlson was the driver for the Thursday-to-Monday stretch on route 99. He had a gray beard that brushed his shirt and sometimes caught on the buttons, and he smelled of scorched road salt and acid aftershave. He didn't like a girl who wore a perfectly good skirt and then covered her legs in jeans, the way Ella did. There was a fierce weird wind on Finch that could blow your skin blue in less than twenty minutes. That day she had faded orange-tab Levis under her tongue-pink housekeeping skirt. Lahlay, her boss, hadn't gotten her laundry scrubs yet – those were green.

Walking past Pho-Mi 99, Ella smelled lime and carrots and fish. She and Carmen got to the stop in plenty of time, but the bus stayed away from the curb, as if it wasn't going to stop. At the last second it did, still fully in the road. The waiting driver climbed on but Carlson put up his hand when Ella put her foot on the step. "Nononono," he yelled.

Ella was so startled she took her foot down. Carmen elbowed her in the spine.

"None-ah you fucking skatepunks on my bus," Carlson yelled, and the doors squawked closed. The kid turned fast and slunk off. Carmen turned on Ella instead. "What'd you get down for? You know you're not a skatepunk and so does he!"

Ella looked at the ground. If she lost any more hours, she'd have to move in with her boyfriend again, and she'd wind up being a maid at work and at home. Carmen didn't even have a boyfriend to move in with. "It's his bus," she mumbled.

"No, it's the city's bus."

"It's not *our* bus, it's not our city," Ella said. Suddenly, everything smelled like mouldy towels and soup kitchen bread, the white kind that's mainly sugar. Ella felt like she was going to cry, and then her tears would freeze to her cheeks, and then she'd get frostbite, and then everything would smell of gangrene and then . . .

"How much money you got on you?" Carmen said suddenly.

"$1.76." Ella knew without looking.

"Well, I got some money. At least we can get lunch. Pho-Mi 99 is pretty good, and cheap. And the number's right. Maybe it'll help." She tugged Ella towards the carroty smell and on into the tiny empty restaurant.

Inside there was a waitress perched on the kitchen pass-through with a big stack of napkins in her lap. She was carefully folding them into swans. A row of perfect birds swam next to her on the counter. As soon as the door jangled, though, she set the napkins aside and leapt up. Carmen and Ella were just settling into the first booth when she asked, "Ready to order? What number, please?" She was thin, and trembling, even though the restaurant was warm. She smelled like pepper and ginger and the dusty scent of paper.

Carmen shrugged and her parka made the slidy noise. "I only just got here. Give me a second." She reached for the ties on her hood. The waitress kept her pencil frozen above her pad and her smile frozen on her face. Ella thought she looked young but not young, lines all around her eyes, lines pressed up around her plastic smile. There was no one else in the entire restaurant, unless you counted those napkin swans. "Ready to order? What number, please?"

The frozen ties finally loosened and the hood slid down. Ella realized she hadn't seen Carmen's whole head in months. She was surprised her friend had gotten microbraids, reddish-brown and halfway down her back. Ella's own short, dark hair was damp from her toque and plastered to her ears and forehead.

"Number?" said the waitress.

"Hey, give me a minute here, ok?"

"I don't think she speaks English, Carmen. Just menu numbers."

Carmen whipped her pretty braids around her head. "Fine, fine, give me number 99, then."

The waitress didn't move. "99? Is not a number." She pointed at Carmen's menu. The *Snacks* only went to 20 at the bottom of the first page, Ella could see that even upside down, and when she flipped open the page, she saw that the *Noodle Soups* started at 101.

"Is not a number," said the waitress again.

Carmen was heating up to argue, Ella could see it in the way the braids tossed. "99 is a *number*, I – Oh, there it is. 112, please. '99' Special Egg Noodle Soup and – "

Ella squirmed against her jacket and stayed quiet.

" – two spoons."

The waitress smiled like this was good news, wrote on her pad and then darted back into the kitchen. The paper swans rustled as she passed.

Carmen and Ella were quiet for a couple minutes, staring out at the blank, empty street, at the snarl of skatepunks trying to flip a board up off the snowbanks.

"That bus has gotta show up or I'm out of a job."

Ella opened her mouth, but then the waitress came back, apron flapping, and gently set down a giant vat of steam-shrouded noodles and two china spoons.

"Well, that was quick, at least," Carmen said, and smiled at the waitress.

The waitress looked terrified at the appearance of teeth. "All right?"

"Looks good. Well, looks hot, anyway." The waitress went back to her folded flock and Carmen picked up a spoon. Ella felt guilty, eating Carmen's lunch, but there was enough. And the hot soup felt wonderful sliding down her throat, her chest, her belly. She loved the starch of the noodles and the crisp thready smell of lemongrass. Carmen slurped her noodles and said, "Betcha the next one comes. For real. Eat up."

Ella slurped, too. She was hungry; there hadn't been any cereal left for breakfast. The waitress brought the bill before the last mouthful was gone.

"Well, what do you know?" Carmen said, looking at her watch. "Nine minutes. We can pay *and* have a smoke before the next bus."

Out at the stop, Ella huddled around the cold little flame of her cigarette's cherry, sucking in the muddy dark smell of tar and tobacco and ignoring the skateboarder kids who kept trying to bum smokes. She wanted them to go before the bus came so Carlson would stop, but in the end it didn't matter.

Ella was trying to swat away a kid that was doing flip tricks to impress her when Carmen yelled, "What the fuck?" She turned and looked. It was a bus, a 99, but not a normal one. The route board said, "99 Spec. Steeles Ave."

Ella chomped down hard on her cigarette. Steeles was way north, and the 99 went south from Finch down Jane. This 99 blew right on past and turned left on Jane, heading north.

"It's a special," said Carmen, sounding confident. "It doesn't count. A charter or something. It won't be another twenty minutes for the next one."

Ella shook her head – she could smell something off. Still, at 11:22 another bus did come. It said, "99 Spec. Union Station." Union Station, an hour away and downtown! Then a long lull, while Carmen started to pace and make calls on her cellphone. Then "99 Spec. Ottawa," which headed straight on east across Jane. Ella figured Ottawa was east of Jane and Finch, but they had their own transit. At 11:37, when Ella was well and truly late, she saw "99 Spec. James Bay" turn north on Jane. The cab driver didn't believe their story for a second, but he left the meter off anyway and only charged them ten bucks, as long as Carmen sat up front with him.

ELLA THOUGHT about buses all day while her hands blistered from the bleach in the laundry. Bleach smelled so clean it was poisonous, burning the inside of her nostrils like her hands. She thought about how Pho-Mi 99 had a smell that wasn't just lemongrass and boredom – it smelled like a power, too. The Special was special, that was for sure. Somewhere in all that food, Ella thought, was the right order. But she didn't know where, without a number 99 on the menu, and she didn't have the money to experiment by eating out a lot, or at all, really, and neither did Carmen. She didn't know if she needed Carmen to do it, but she knew Carmen needed her to work it out before she got fired.

Friday Ella didn't see Carmen. Friday the tips of Ella's fingers started to crack from the bleach. On Saturday Lahlay asked Ella to work Sunday, and smelled smouldering, and Ella said yes.

Saturday night Carmen got on Ella's bus. Even though they were two skinny girls in a two-seat, all the layers of coats pushed Carmen's left thigh into the aisle. She said, "I might have to go stay with my uncle for a while, if my mom winds up losing our lease."

"Where's he at?" Ella asked the dirty window.

"North. North and west of us, beyond the TTC. It'd be Mississauga Transit for me. Even worse, I hear."

"How would you get to work?"

Carmen was jittering her knees up and down. "I wouldn't. Well, not at Len's House of Deals, anyway. I couldn't do the commute. I'd have to quit."

They sat quietly for a minute. Then Ella pulled the bell. For all the drama, it wasn't even that long a ride. "What would you do?" She stood up.

Carmen stood, too, and started towards the door. "Anything I could, I guess." The bus lurched hard to a stop, and Carmen staggered, slammed into the door, Ella tumbling against her. She heard a laugh behind her as she stepped down. Over her shoulder she caught the eye of a big man with a big smile and big shaved head. She smiled back before she could stop herself and then the accordion doors creaked shut.

"Nice," Carmen knocked into her side, on purpose this time. "Very nice."

"No," Ella said. "No." She said no because her boyfriend didn't even like her looking. Technically, though, the man certainly had been nice.

OVERNIGHT IT GOT WARMER, and on Sunday warmer still. The ice-blue sky cracked and thawed to a soft gray. It started to snow big soft flakes, like Christmas, not at all like the usual small, sharp flakes of February. Everything smelled like ozone and peppermint when Ella got off the 99 Sunday night. Everything but just one little note, beneath the wet winter smells, a warning tomato-y sniff, even though Pho-Mi 99 was closed.

BY MONDAY MORNING, the world was covered in a thick wet blanket, with more falling. The sky had thawed even more, white as the snow. Everything was white and heavy and wet and smelling of ketchup. Ella felt like a washrag, soaked in ketchup instead of soap. Everything smelled like ketchup. The 99 wouldn't come, she could smell it. She could smell absence now, she realized – ever since she ate that delicious noodle soup. No-bus-ness smelled like ketchup, a packet dropped in the gutter and stepped on by accident.

She waited until four minutes after eleven, four minutes after the 99 should have come and Pho-Mi 99 opened. Then she crossed the snowy parking lot and went into the restaurant.

The doorbell jangled and snow fell off her in clumps. The tired waitress got up from where she had been folding napkins into ducks at an empty table. There wasn't anyone else in the restaurant, maybe not even in the kitchen. It was all snow-muffled silence. The waitress hurried over, a white napkin duck fluttering in her hand. Ella picked up a takeout menu from the counter.

"What number, please?" The waitress reached for her order pad, then realized she still had the duck and tossed it into the air. It flapped once, twice, and turned back towards the table. "Number?" The paper bird alighted with the others and was still.

Ella stared at the bird, but the waitress just said "Number?" again, so Ella returned to the menu. No 99, no 900s, "99 Special" didn't work. Soups and soups and soups. She wanted to get something she could share with Carmen, to pay her back for last time. Carmen would be taking the 11:20 today for the 12:00 shift. The 99 was getting so weird, even sloppy Carmen had started allowing 40 minutes for a 20 minute ride. Poor Carmen. Did she like shrimp cakes? It was only number 9, not 99, but it was small, an appetizer. They'd need two orders each for lunch. "Number 9," she told the waitress. "Four orders."

It only took six minutes to order, pay and get her food. Ella went outside and sat down in a snowdrift at the edge of the road, her backpack under her butt for insulation. The skater kids were lined up in a huddled row by the curb in the snow, sharing a cigarette. They didn't say a word to her, for once. She saw Carmen trudging out of the mall parking lot before she'd even got the Styrofoam open. Snow muffled all smell except the crisp of batter and soy and something sea-salty. There were barely any cars on the street so Carmen crossed against the light. She sat down in the drift. Ella took a cake and put the box in Carmen's lap.

"What's this?" Carmen sounded grouchy and thick through all those flakes.

"Four orders of number nine."

Carmen stared at her.

"Shrimp cakes. Lunch. Eat them."

Carmen picked up one. "It's like a little cookie. Except it smells like the ocean."

Ella was glad Carmen could smell it, too.

"Thank you," Carmen mumbled through a mouthful of batter. Ella took another bite, too, and they chewed together in silence. Ella took the napkins out of the bag and looked carefully at them. They were only folded in the shape of fans and didn't do anything, so she wiped her mouth with one. At 11:19, she saw the blue beacon of bus lights. She got up and put on her backpack. While she was turned around, she heard Carmen yell, "What the fuck?"

She turned back and looked. There were two 99s coming east: one in the bus lane, one in the centre lane. That was impossible, like a sky with two moons. Ella knew from long icy waits and long sad stares at the TTC website that they never ran more than one 99 the same way at the same time. And yet here were two. They were moving awfully fast.

"Are they going to stop?" Ella said to no one.

A tall kid in an enormous black hoodie unfolded from where he was sitting on his board to stagger out towards the curb. "Motherfucker, they're *dragging!*" he said.

They really seemed to be having a bus drag race through the flake-flying storm. Faster and faster, cars pulling off to the side, the two buses rattled along, empty and light, windows shaking, the *whoomp-whoomp* of the poorly fitted back seats echoing. Neither followed the route and turned south. As if in a dry washout instead of an unsnowploughed street, they zoomed straight across Jane in a gust of icy wind, the traffic light blinking from yellow to red just as the lagging one on the inside lane squeaked across the crosswalk. In a moment both were out of sight, and it was just Ella and Carmen and the kids, the snowflakes layering down on their shoulders.

"Four number nines," said Carmen softly.

"No more shrimp cakes," Ella said.

IT TOOK a week for Ella to recover from the four nines, and to put together enough cash for another lunch out. That day, Carmen was wait-ing and the air reeked of Heinz. "Hey, Ella." Carmen slumped over her cigarette as if it were holding her up.

"Let's have lunch," Ella said.

Carmen tugged down her mitten and glove to look at her watch. "It's 11:02. It'll be here."

"It should've been here two minutes ago. It's not coming." Ella shrugged. "I want to go to Pho-Mi 99 again, Carm. I've got money, a little."

"I've got to go to work, Ella." She squinted against her cigarette smoke, glaring. But in three minutes, she said, "I bet they'd give us take-out in less than ten, and we could eat it on the bus."

Ella turned without saying anything and ran towards the restau-rant. She'd been thinking about numbers again, even in the haze of bleach and no days off and her boyfriend wondering how come she was always eating restaurant food when she was too broke to even go to the movies with him. She wanted to tell him about the tinned tomato misery of 99 and the warm scent of fish sauce and lemongrass, but he never listened.

She burst through the jinglebell door. Now she could smell those scents over the bleach on her hands that never went away because it ate under her skin. Underneath all that was the sludgy ketchup smell that wasn't anything but absence. Carmen followed her, coughing a cigarette cough, smelling of sad.

The waitress came out of the kitchen, moving slower than she had other times though she looked as nervous as ever. It took a moment for it to register with Ella that the waitress was on crutches, her left leg was wrapped in a thick plaster cast from toes to somewhere under her shapeless blue uniform skirt. The white of the plaster was blinding, whiter than the snow, than the napkins, than anything in the world. The waitress just smiled and nodded at the girls, though, as if not a thing was wrong.

Ella stared at the menu. There was a new smell in the air, much fainter than all the others – that sweaty smell of a good idea. She couldn't quite pin it down, because now there was a noise in the empty restaurant, some restless rustling coming from the kitchen. She glanced at the waitress who shrugged, shoulders rising awkwardly while her armpits still clenched her crutches. Still, for a moment, she almost smiled.

Ella nodded. "Which do you want, Carm, beef stew in tomato sauce with French bread, or stew duck with?"

"With what?"

"That's all it says, with. You take your chances if you order that. Or else get the beef."

"Number?"

"There's a thousand things on that menu. Why do I only get two choices?"

Ella didn't want to be wrong again, to watch the circus parade of buses headed for Exhibition Stadium, Centre Island, the moon. "Those are the good ones."

Carm shook her head. "Fine. I'll have the beef."

Ella turned towards the waitress's shaking pencil above the little order pad. "101 for me. And number 2 for my friend."

The waitress wrote, nodded and tottered back into the kitchen. When the door swung open the sound was even louder. She was surprised Carmen didn't mention it.

"101 minus 2 . . ." Carmen's breath was hot on her ear.

Ella shrugged. "I can't afford four number 20s and a 19. And 19 is bladder soup, anyway."

"You're crazy."

"I'm going to be homeless in a month unless I stop coming in late. The food tastes good. What have we got to lose?"

"Yeah." A single red braid was poking out from Carmen's hood, like a sword. "And I think she needs the business, too."

"Yeah."

When the waitress handed over the takeout bags, her bleach-blistered fingers matched Ella's, and when they brushed, the smell of bread and tomato and paper mingled to smell like an oven or a hearth, like home. As Ella took the paper sack from the waitress's trembling hand, Carmen looked down pointedly. "What happened to your leg?"

The waitress's hand went to her pocket, and for a second Ella thought she was going to take out her pad and say *Number?* again. But then she looked down, too, as if just noticing her cast. She shrugged, and almost lost her balance, righted herself and said, "Oh, you know how it is . . ." She smiled again, a little smaller than usual, a little less scary.

Outside, the snowbank hadn't been cleared from the sidewalk by the 99 pole, and the thawing and freezing had made it quite firm, like the bench the city had not provided. Carmen flipped open the bottom of her coat and let Ella sit on the flap. It was 11:14. The boarder punks were huddled at the far end of the gas station apron, rolling round and round on six feet of iceless cement.

Ella opened her takeout box and so did Carmen. The Styrofoam creaked like shoes on frozen snow. The duck dish was bony, and a little greasy, but warm and spicy and full of vegetables. The *with* it came with turned out to be vermicelli noodles. Carmen ate with her head bent low over her food, but Ella watched the busless street. It was 11:18. Yesterday had been one of the laundry girls' birthdays, and Lahlay had given them ten minutes to eat the cake someone baked, but she'd yelled when it was twelve instead of ten. Lahlay told them not to laugh so loud. Lahlay smelled as stiff and perfect as nothing at all and she told the guests she'd send up extra towels even when they were short-staffed. Lahlay's parents gave her a new car for her eighteenth birthday and she bragged about not knowing what a bus ticket cost.

Everyone knew what a bus ticket cost.

Carmen was gnawing on her chunk of French bread. "How come there's French bread at a Vietnamese restaurant?"

Ella thought hard about the question, about history class in grade eleven, before leaving school, meeting her boyfriend, the hotel, before lots of things. "The French controlled Vietnam for a long time. I guess they left some of their food behind."

Carmen chewed ardently and swallowed hard. "Was there a war to get them to go? Was that the Vietnam War?"

The duck was warm in her belly, but the snow was hard beneath Carmen's coat and it was 11:21. "No, this was before that, I don't remember when. And then the Vietnam War after – "

There wasn't any smell, there wasn't any sound. No *whoomp* of the back seats grinding against their fittings, no roar of the motor, no sign of the bus to the west where she had been looking. It just appeared before them. The driver pulled to a stop even though they were both still sitting. It was Carlson, but when he looked down at them, he didn't look at their legs, or glare at them, or slam shut the doors. He just smiled, blank, polite, a man doing his job, taking girls to theirs.

Ella and Carmen stood up and started towards the door. Ella was done with her 101 duck, but she didn't feel like throwing away the carton quite yet. She let Carmen get on first and glanced back at Pho-Mi 99 just as the waitress pushed the door open. She struggled to prop it open standing on one leg and finally used her cast to catch it. Ella stepped up and flashed her metropass at Carlson who blinked, nodded, and said thank you. All Ella could think to answer was *you're welcome*. By the time she'd crashed next to Ella in a two-seat and looked out the window, the doors were creaking shut and the waitress was leaning outside on her blond-wood crutches, looking flushed and tired. She seemed to see Ella through the window, though, because she waved. Ella waved back and then, from above the waitress's head, rushed a white storm of paper birds lifting onto the wind, into the air and sky above the parking lot and the bus and the corner of Jane and Finch. Ella stared up, leaning across Carmen's fluffy-coated body, watching their white paper wings disappear into the white of the clouds.

The gears wrenched and squealed, and the bus jolted forward. The noise seemed to alert the boarder punks, who had been contented on their square of cement until the noise. Suddenly they all came pounding across the apron, half a dozen of them in gray toques and bright suede sneakers and low-crotch jeans. Ella didn't know if they wanted to get on or just to celebrate the presence of this miraculous bus, this snowless sky, but as Carlson shifted into first gear they reached the sidewalk shore and drummed their hands against the game show ad on the side of the bus.

Carlson hollered at the closed window, "Get away, you fuckin' punks!" finally sounding a little like his usual self. To Ella, though, the whoops and curses of the kids in those cracky sixteen-year-old voices sounded like trumpets and whistles at a parade.

"I never really understood all that historical stuff, about Vietnam and everything," she told Carmen, settling back in the seat. "It was complicated. I should try to find out."

Fruit Factory

I WAKE UP AND IT'S DARK. When I pull the alarm clock towards me to stop it screaming, my fingers turn green in the glow from the 4:30. I kick off the sheets and stand up before I can think. The sidewalk is right outside our basement window and there aren't any curtains. I look out, but there aren't any feet so I hike my gray T-shirt up and off. My hair statics and crackles. I pick up the black bra from the floor under the window and hook it on. Then I put on a different gray T-shirt. I step into the crumpled figure eight of yesterday's jeans and pull them up over the underwear I've already got on. I look back at the clock as I smooth down my hair with the palm of my hand. 4:34. I have enough time to wash my face and drink a glass of juice today before I get the 4:49 bus to work. This is Monday.

"JOSÉEFRUITSBONJOUR."

"Hi, is Mike there, please?"

"NoI'msorryhe'snot. MayItakeamessage?"

"Travaille-t-il aujourd'hui?"

"Uh . . . ilnestpasici, . . . j'pensequ'non. Voulezvouslaisserunmessage?"

"Oh, no, that's ok. Je peux rappeller."

"Okbon.Mercimadam."

"Bye."

AFTER THE SNACK TRUCK LEAVES, we have a few minutes before the 9 a.m. orders, so Jean and Sami stay out in the gravel lot, chucking yams at the cat. I watch while I eat my cerise gateau doughnut. It is bright pink like no cherry ever was, but it tastes all right. Jean's muscles flex and bulge brown under his bleach-white T-shirt, but all his throws go wild. He never stops smiling, though. Sami keeps trying to get a running start and stumbling over the hems of his fatigues. One time his "Ellison Lube" gimme cap flies off and falls as close to Fat Cat as any of the yams do.

That cat never moves, doesn't even turn to see what's going on. It doesn't have anything to worry about. Neither of them are really awake, and besides, the yams are so rotten that you can't grip them much without sinking your fingers up to the knuckles in goo. The skin gets to be like paper, when they go bad.

Henri is coming at us through the tall grass that pushes up through the gravel at the back of the lot. His tie flaps wrinkled against his chest and smoke from his king size trails behind his head.

"Leave it alone, eh?" Henri says. Everyone calls Fat Cat *it*. No one wants to bother and look to find out if it's a him or a her. Henri looks at us, his lips an O around the cigarette under the perfect line of his butterscotch mustache. "Where the hell's Mike?"

Jean tosses one of the big yams and finally gets close – it crashes in the gravel right behind Fat Cat, all dust and red-orange explosion. The cat runs into a culvert. Jean shrugs. "Mike didn't come today."

"Ah, fuck this shit." But Henri crouches anyway, reaches his hand into the hollow metal, snaps his fingers. Nothing. It has burrowed away, sneaky so we can't follow. The tube is too narrow for Henri but not for a cat, even for a cat named Fat Cat. It is pretty fat, though it's really named after a kind of mango.

"Come back, you caaaaattttttttttt!" Sami yells in a high-pitched cartoon voice.

"Fuck this shit," Henri says again, and gets up. For a second we all just stand there, like we're waiting for a bus or looking at a sunset or something else that you can do together without talking. Then Henri rubs his eyes and presses the skin down like he does, so the red bloody wet part below them shows. He says, "Shouldn't you guys be working? Somebody's gotta do Mike's pallets." He stomps back across the gravel towards the warehouse, but I don't watch him go.

COFFEE TASTES like bitter burning to me and I can't ever force it down. Jean always offers to bring me some and I always explain and he always seems surprised.

"No shit no? Not never?" Jean is leaning over the half door with an elbow and a bleached sleeve and a white-toothed grin all aimed towards me. My cashier booth is small enough that Jean's elbow seems to take up a lot of the space inside. I can smell the sticky-sugar smell of rotten yam off his hands.

"Never. Really." I shrug in my broken chair and it creaks ominously. I stop with my shoulders up and leave them around my ears until I'm sure I'm steady. Then I ease them back down to my usual level.

Jean pushes off the half-door and rocks back on his heels. "Me, I got jess what *you* need."

"*Jean!* Leave'er alone, eh? Et viens ici and get this shit up from the floor. The sugar cane guy's gonna be here this hour." Henri's voice floats in from the loading bay. I can't see him from where I sit, but Jean rocks even farther back to talk to him, hands gripping the top of the door.

"Minute, minute. I'm coming. You!" He flops back towards me, hitting hard against the door with his stomach. "You, I'm gonna fix you up ok. You gotta not be so tired, because you gots to smile at all of us all day and be nice, ok? Ok."

Jean is so handsome he almost doesn't matter, like a poster for a movie I'll never see. Except for the three pink scars striping along the skin under his jawbone. I can see them through the shadow beard he wears. When he turns away from me, I can see the outline of his knife in his back pocket, too. He uses it to cut plastic wrap, and boxes sometimes, but it's not the one Henri gave him. He already had one. By the time he walks away, it's already 2:39 – only an hour before it will be time to get the bus for home.

DAYS ARE LIKE DAYS ARE LIKE DAYS. When you wake up at four-thirty in the morning, it's a lot like not waking up at all. Tuesday is like Monday, except it is raining. I wake up and it's dark. I get up and get dressed and get wet and get the bus. I get to work and the phone rings at six on the nose. Someone who knows when we open.

"JoséeFruitsbonjour!"

"Um, hello, may I please speak with Mike?"

"I'msorry,Mike'snothere.CanItakeamessage?"

"Pourquoi pas?"

"Wh – pardon, madam?"

"Pourquoi est-il pas là? Is he sick?"

"I'm sorry, I don't know, ma'am. Would you like me to ask someone for you?"

"Oh, non. C'est ok."

"Peut-être il serait mieux appeller chez lui?"

"Yeah, I tried but I'll . . . yeah."

"Good-bye, ma'am."

THIS IS WHAT MIKE IS LIKE: he's too skinny. He wears shirts with numbers on them, hockey or baseball, and when the wind blows against him you can see his ribs through his skin and shirt. The one he wears most is number 12. He's about twenty or so, just like me. He has short hair, brown I think, but he always wears a baseball cap so I haven't seen it much. The cap has a bison on it. He smiles a lot, and even when he's not smiling he looks like he is because his teeth are too big for his mouth.

He's only been working here a couple months. Mike's anglo like me, too, the only other one, but I don't hear the accent much because working on the floor isn't like being cashier: he doesn't have to talk if he doesn't want to. Usually he doesn't. He's not too good at the work – his arms aren't strong and sometimes he can't carry the big bundles of sugar cane, or the biggest boxes of yams. When Henri yells at him he never says anything back, but once I saw him kick Fat Cat after Henri walked away.

Mike laughs at all the dirty jokes, but never tells any. Mike eats peanut butter on white bread in the mornings. He keeps the sandwiches in his pocket, so they smush and the bread goes see-through and wet. Once he gave me half, but once he called me a bitch because I couldn't find his paycheque right away. Mike isn't very interesting, or even that nice, but I liked him well enough.

SOMETHING IS DIFFERENT: on Tuesday night there is a crisis in our laundry room. One of the driers has shorted out, a loose cord hissing and sparking into the big gray washtub. When it happens, my back is turned and I'm stuffing underwear into the washer. I just hear the snap of static, feel the heat in the air and in my hair. I turn just as the big Greek guy in the blue Adidas track suit ducks under the folding table. "C'mon, c'mon," he yells, trying to wave me under the table without getting up himself. I stand still with the faded red panties in my left hand, watching yellow and blue sparks until the super comes running in in her bathrobe and flips the fuse. Then I have to pull my dirty clothes out of the machine in the dark. It's dark at our place, too. He's home, banging on the television set, so I tell him about the cord and the fuse. Then there's nothing to do in the dark, so I just go to bed.

Wednesday, in the absence of anything else to wear that doesn't have cat food or engine oil or yam on it, I have to wear a short floral baby-doll dress from high school.

"Whoo, yeah," Jean yells from the forklift as I walk past at 6:04. "Why don't you dress like that every day, chère?"

I walk fast into my office booth and shut the door, but it's only a half-door and everyone who cares to can still see me. They can't see my ass, though, when I bend over to check Fat Cat's food dish. The bottom half of the door guards me, but I hear applause anyway. Fat Cat's dish is full to overflowing, but I pour more kibble in just in case. I don't even look that good, in the dress or ever. I'm just the only girl here.

SAMI'S GOING TO GET FIRED SOON. No doubt about that. When he wraps the pallets of fruit boxes in plastic, big ribbons of it trail around the bottom and sometimes he doesn't cover the boxes all the way up to the top. He says it's because he's too short, but he's not that short. Sami's got a beard that points across the room, except for the patches where it's not there at all. Sami's got eyes that run with tears in the mornings. He says it's hay fever but it's all year long. Sami's got one plaid shirt that he wears every day and a tremor in his hands.

Some days he doesn't show up, but then he does and he says how his apartment got broke into and he had to go down to the police station and his girl, she was so upset and he had to stay with her, plus the cops, they wanted him to be a witness. Some days he comes even though he isn't on the schedule and then Henri tells him to go on home. Sami gets mad about wasting the bus fare, and about how he's already started working on the limes and got four boxes sorted, and don't that count for nothing? Sometimes Henri says, "Fuck this shit" and makes Sami punch out, and sometimes he drags on his cigarette and says, "Fine, do your eight. We're short anyway," but everyone knows that Sami's going to get fired.

EVERY HOUR TODAY:
"JoséeFruitsbonjour!"
"Hi, can I speak to Mike?"
"I'm sorry, Mike's not here. Can I take a message?"
"Non, merci."
<click>
"JoséeFruitsbonjour!"
"Est-ce que Mike est là?"
"Non, pas encore. Puis-je prendre un message?"
<click>
"JoséeFruitsbonjour!"
"Is Mike there?"
"No, I'm – "

WHEN I WALK ACROSS THE FLOOR with my purse, the new price lists, my cerise gateau doughnut, I am four minutes late from break again and there is soca music playing. It's really muffled, like the speaker is turned towards the wall or covered with a coat. This is something that I like. Like ice-cream truck music with a beat, like a concert in a park three blocks away, it sounds soft and swingy. It glides through my head and my headache and the boozy-bleach smell of unripe mangoes. I let it glide me almost to my office at the edge of the warehouse floor, but then Sami is there in front of me, his teeth cigarette yellow and his voice cigarette strange and loud, getting Jean to turn and look at us, at me.

"You like this, yes? You like the soca?"

"The music is good. I like it." I nod. I reach my hand out for the doorknob to my office but he steps in between.

"You're a soca fan!" Sami is dancing dizzily from foot to foot in his steel-toed boots. "To really love soca, you gotta dance to it, ok? Come, you can dance with me." He lurches towards me but holds out his hands like a gentleman in an old movie. I hold on to my doughnut.

"I can't dance." High school dances flash across my mind, jerking stiff-legged across the floor, waiting for the tug on my waist that means we're going out the fire-door, to the parking lot. Same damn dress, flipping in the wind around my thighs then, hanging heavy from my shoulders now.

"I seen you move across the floor when this music is on. I know you got a rhythm in you." He looks at my breasts, or where they would be if the dress fit properly. I'm skinnier now than I was in high school.

"I don't want to dance." My nails are digging through napkin and I can feel them catching crumbs. Pink bits crumble onto the floor. "I have to get started working."

"Ah, now, one dance won't take no time." Sami's eyes have flecks of sleep in the corners and even when he looks me in the face he doesn't quite focus. His smile is so big he could eat my doughnut in one bite. He steps closer. I hear Henri bark from behind us.

"Fat Cat! Eh, Fat Cat! Viens-ici, viens-ici. Si tu manges pas ton Miao Chow, tu n'serais pas un Fat Cat encore!" Henri is standing on the lip of the loading bay shaking a bag of kibble so we can hear the rattling food inside. When he starts to turn, Sami tugs my sleeve and says, "No say, heh?" He skitters away from my elbow and disappears into a row of boxes of alligator avocados.

"You know where Fat Cat is?" Henri swings the sack of Miao Chow at me. "He don't eat out of his bowl today."

I give up on my doughnut, all crumbs now. I toss it into the trash by the door and take the sack from Henri. I wonder, if I asked, if I could have some fruit. I've never seen anyone here eat any. Except for the lime crates, most of the boxes don't even get opened. I don't want to remind him about Fat Cat, but Henri's face clenches around the king size, waiting. "He's been gone since Monday. When he ran in the culvert."

"Oh, fuck that. He no has come back? Shit." Henri turns towards the boxes of big green avocados and then turns back to me, pointing down the row. "And him, Sami, he bother you?"

All I want is to put the cat food on the shelf, my bag in the drawer, the files on the desk. "No, Sami's not bothering me. No one's bothering me."

"He's not supposed to have this shit on. I'll tell him to turn it off." Henri is still muttering as he walks away, "Where'd he get this tape player? And why this pallet is not wrapped? He said he do it before he left last night."

In a few minutes, the soca goes off and I don't see Sami for the rest of the day.

I WAKE UP AND IT'S DARK AND IT'S THURSDAY. The alarm clock screams until I click it off. Uncurl from fetal position and roll off the futon, the T-shirt up over my head and standing to stretch a moment in panties and street-lamp glare from the basement window. I should buy a curtain someday. The floor seems to lean. I am lagging, searching for any two socks in the laundry basket, an elastic for my hair. Staggering around, trying to be quiet, trying to see in the dark, my arm hooks a ten-dollar lamp off the bureau and it smashes to the floor. He moans like creaking hinges and twists away from the sound in the bed. In the gray dawn I can just see slices of china on the tile, his arm flung across the mattress going still again as he falls back asleep. If I hadn't wasted time on the elastic, socks, stretching, I might have had time to do something, but without the lamp to turn on, I can't see the little pieces anyway. I leave the shards to stab at nothing and go get a piece of paper from the recycling, but all I have time to write is *Sorry.*

"JOSÉEFRUITSBONJOUR!"
"Um, hey."
"Hello."

"Um, est-ce que Mike est là?"

"Chais pas . . . Je l'ai pas encore vu ce matin. Je peux demander . . ."

"Yeah, could you ask . . . Henri or someone."

"Henri . . . Certainly, ma'am."

As I push my stool away from the switchboard, I can feel my stomach trembling. I haven't eaten since yesterday. Mike hasn't been to work in four days. Henri is sorting a box of limes, the usual cigarette burning in the corner of his mouth. The limes are under-ripe, neon-green like tennis balls.

"What." Not even a question, just letting me know that he knows I am here and that he's not going to look up.

"Is Mike here today?"

He looks around like he's in a children's story. "Do you see Mike?"

"Is he coming in later?"

"I dunno."

It is hard to stop. "Is he coming back ever?"

"He hasn't been in since Saturday." He closes the lime box and throws it onto the pallet with the others, finally looks at me. "Me, that's all I know." He takes the cigarette out of his mouth, puts it back in. He doesn't seem to exhale any smoke.

I start walking away.

"Who wants to know?"

Without stopping. "Um, I think it's his girlfriend."

"His girlfriend?" His laugh sounds like a book slamming onto a table. "Tell her to call him at his home!"

I turn for a second. "I think there's a problem here, Henri." When I get back to the phone, she has hung up.

IMAGINE THAT YOU ARE A LIME. You are hanging on a tree in Mexico, not yet ripe. You are worth a penny. If you fall, no one will stoop to find you. They might even step on you. If they pick you, they'll chuck you into the field if you're too ripe, not ripe enough, discoloured. Same at the first warehouse. Same at the second. You'll travel in a truck, you'll travel in a plane, you'll travel in a better truck. You'll reach the new land, but if you have a spot, if you are pale, if you bounce out of your box and under a truck, you are nothing. If you don't, you are twisted and bled onto a plate of salmon. You are now worth twenty dollars. What I want to know is, how did you get so special? Why are you so valuable?

JEAN HAS BROUGHT ME SOMETHING IN A VERY SMALL TIN CAN. It is red and the writing is silver and the writing is not English or French. I don't want it, but Jean's small teeth shine at me in the sunrise. We are standing outside the loading bay. It is just after eight.

"Go, you drink that and you be feeling much more well, not so tired always."

"What is it?" The tiny can fits in the palm of my hand. I roll it with my fingers, looking for some word I recognize, even though it's still too dark to really read.

"It's for energy. We drink 'em at the clubs, *you* know. To dance."

"Oh." I don't know.

"So . . ."

I shrug and pull the tab on the top. It hisses like a pop can. I take a sip and it catches in my throat. It feels thick and bubbly and the taste is way too sweet, with medicine underneath, so strong the roof of my mouth burns. I start to gag, stop, swallow.

"*So . . . ?*"

I am about to say it's fine, I'll drink it, I'll drink it later. Then Henri appears at the mouth of the loading dock, his big boots just above our heads. He's shuffling dollars in his hands and looking out at the stripy sky. Then he looks down at us, at me, and waves the dollars. "Monsieur Marc, he bought ten cases of the 14s. I gave him the little discount."

I nod and reach my hand above my head. He gives the twenties over and I clutch them in the wind. Henri says, "Get on, then. There's more to come in," so I can toast my little can at Jean and hurry in without talking, or drinking anymore.

MONEY IS ALWAYS GRAY WITH SOMETHING I CAN'T IDENTIFY. Counting bills all afternoon makes a ridge of grime all along the side of my index finger and turns the pads of my palms gray, too. I am counting twenties. The money is old and wrinkled, muddy-smelling, the old queen green and wrinkled, the paper creased, with torn-off corners. When the stacks get bigger than $200, they puff up like accordions and tip into each other. The first time I counted was $2,040, the second time it was $1,980, the third time $2,020. Every time Jean walks past my window, I have to take a sip from the tiny can. Sometimes, Jean is the only person who talks to me all day. I finish the can. By the time I've finished counting, I can feel the thick liquid pressing through me. My eyelashes are touching my eyebrows.

"JOSÉEFRUITSBONJOUR!"

"Bonjour. Je voudrais parler avec Mike, s'il vous plait."

"SorryMikesnot – Jeveuxdire – Mikeestpasiciaujourdhui."

"It's ok."

"Quoi?OrImeanpardon?"

"It's ok, I speak English."

"Oh. I know. Mike's not here."

"I know."

<click>

I WAKE UP AND IT'S LIGHT. This is wrong for Friday. Sun comes through the window without curtains and wakes me. I am alone and it's light, but I'm still tired, deep dizzy tired, like a hangover, like sunstroke. This can't be good. I roll towards the edge of the bed and the clock. 9:17. I have overslept by close to five hours. If I didn't have to pee so bad, I don't know if I'd be up even now. Standing up makes everything whirl. When I get back from the bathroom I look closer at the clock. The sliding button on the white plastic clock is stuck in between ALARM ON and ALARM OFF. I push it all the way off. I look over by the door, where the shards of the broken lamp have been swept up, where his sneakers are missing. I wonder if he thought about waking me. I look at the gray sheets, crumpled in the sunshine. If Henri fires me, I will go back to bed and sleep until noon, and then go to the employment centre.

I pick up the phone and then put it down when I realize I don't know the number. I never call, just answer. I find the yellow pages under the bureau and listen to thirteen rings before the click and Henri's voice.

"Ouiallo." It could be anyone, anywhere, but I know it's Henri.

"It's me. I'm sorry I didn't come in."

A pause. Voices in the background. "What happened?"

"The alarm didn't go off."

"Oh. Are you going to come back?"

I look at the bed, the yellow light on the gray sheets. "Yes. Yes, I'll come now, if you want."

"If I want? Yes, I want you to be here three hour ago."

"I'm sorry."

"I'll do your work until you come here. Where is the key to the cashbox? Where is Fat Cat?"

I start pulling up my jeans from the floor, pressing the phone between my ear and shoulder. "The key is hanging from a hook hidden far under the desk."

"Wait." Muttering, stumbling. "Yes, I have that."

"Fat Cat's run away still. I'll be there in an hour." But it is less than that, since there are more buses during the day than before dawn.

WHEN I FINALLY GET THERE, Henri is talking on his cell and the cashier-office phone, both at once. He shoves the office phone at me and keeps yelling in fastfast joual at the cell – something about mangoes rotting because they got held up at customs. While I'm taking an order for fifty cases of limes, *ripe this time,* he empties his pockets onto my desk: order slips, a roll of twenties, the cash key, a crumpled cigarette packet. He leaves it all there and turns, still yelling, and goes off towards his own office. The only words I can understand are the curses.

When I get off the phone, Jean comes over from out of nowhere. I tell him "Hello" and start unrolling the cash.

"Hey, you. I was worried about you. You always here. When you don't come, I thought, now it's like it was with Mike."

I look at him. He's smiling, swigging out of another of those little cans. He doesn't seem to mind how it tastes. "What's with Mike?"

"*That* guy. Don't get me started about *that* guy. He's a guy got problems, ok. But is you I want to know. What is wrong with *you?* Are you sick, you?"

I shake my head, slowly. My brain feels like it is sloshing around in there. I don't want to tell Jean about how sick I feel, or ask what's in the little can. I don't want to talk about being tired, or ask him if he would have woken me up if he'd been sleeping beside me and my alarm didn't go off for almost five hours. I don't want to know about Mike's problems. I want to know where Fat Cat is.

Henri's silver cellphone comes flying past and bounces off an orange and white carton of yams. When it hits the floor, the flippy part snaps off. Henri yells without coming out of his office, "*Jean!* Mike is quit and Sami is not here, too. You got to do all these orders for tomorrow. You got to find me some more better guys, heh ok? Jesus. This shit."

Jean smiles at me and shrugs. He tips his head a bit, and leaves the can on my desk when he goes to the forklift. The can isn't empty and it smells like the morning after a party. I take a sip. It stings my throat, but I have another six hours to stay awake.

MY HEAD IS POUNDING. A truck misses the loading bay by three inches and slams into the brick wall behind my office. The bare bulb flickers once and is gone. This has happened before. I can hear my pen roll across the desk and off. I can hear Henri yelling at the truck driver. I stop. Everything stops.

When he comes in, a moment later, I can see only silhouette led by the cherry of his cigarette. "Fucking shit." The outline of his head moves back and forth. He goes up on tiptoe and clutches the bulb with shadowy hands. I can hear the hiss of its still-burning heat on his fingers. Then it's light again, but there's not much to see, really. "Fucking high technology," he says. I nod and stoop for my pen, he nods and reaches for the door. Then the phone rings, and he slouches against the wall, to wait and see who it is. It's usually for him, anyway.

"JoséeFruitsbonjour!"

"Yeah, hi. I called before, about – "

"Mike."

"Yes, Mike."

"He hasn't been here since Saturday, I don't know if he's coming back. No one seems to."

"Oh . . ."

". . . Ma'am."

". . . Désolée . . . Je'n veux pas . . ."

"C'est ok, madam."

"Mon nom est Karen. Karen. Please. Tell him that I called. If . . . If."

"Yes, ma'am. I'll write that down. Any number?"

"He has – No."

"Ok."

"Merci beaucoup."

"Madam . . ."

"Oui?"

"I'm . . . sure – I mean, things will be – "

<click>

I hate myself. Why should I say anything to her? It's not my business. Still, I keep my eyes on the table, running through ideas, options, theories, but the thing about nothing is that it's nothing.

Henri seems to be about to leave but then he doesn't. Instead he says, "Has the cat come back yet?"

"I haven't seen it."

"Shit." He takes one last drag and jams the butt into an empty Coke can behind me.

"That's two, lost," I tell him. The world is purple spots behind my eyes.

He looks at me and says, "Nobody is lost. They go away." But he looks awful, too. He gets up earlier than I do.

I WAKE UP AND IT'S DARK. I wake up and it's dark. I wake up and it's dark. Saturdays are the hardest. Tomorrow I can spend unconscious, face down, ignoring the world. Today I kick out of the sheets, wavering onto my feet. I'm alone this morning, but the bed still smells like salt and pine, like him. My stomach is sliding. The floor is sliding and I have to catch myself against the corner of the bureau. Tomorrow I can spend unconscious. Tomorrow I can spend unconscious. Today I don't have time to wash my face.

TODAY THERE IS A STRANGE CAR IN THE PARKING LOT, an old blue Civic with rust on the doors. I don't have time to think about whose it is, but then I see a skinny girl coming out the warehouse's side door. The door props open behind her and I can hear Sami yelling in the background. The girl catches me staring and smiles, even though her face is tear-streaky.

"Hi," I say since she's looking at me.

"Bonjour." She nods a bit and then goes to unlock the car and I go in towards the yelling and shut the door.

I head past the forklift and onto the floor. Across the warehouse, half behind the new pallet of Fat Cat number 9 mangoes, Henri is firing Sami. Sami isn't yelling anymore but he dodges and dances, his gimme cap appearing and disappearing above the edge of the boxes. When I get halfway across towards the loading bay, I can see that Henri is barely moving at all. He and Sami look like they are parts of two different conversations. Henri taps the half-wrapped pallet with his index finger, then his chest, then he points at Sami. Sami bounces back and keeps bouncing, like a boxer. His arms jerk out at angles from his sides and then jerk back in again. All that moves on Henri is the ribbon of white smoke that comes up from the tip of his cigarette. Finally, finally, Sami turns to go. When he tries to catch my eye, I am caught.

"Well, you not gonna see Sami around here no more. I guess . . . I don't know what I'm gonna do now." Sami's not bouncing his body anymore, but his eyes are everywhere.

I have nothing to say. I don't think anyone really expects me to say anything anyway. I twist to look at Henri half behind me. He's leaning his left arm against the top of the pallet and he's got his cigarette out of his mouth, in between two fingers on his right hand. The rest of the fingers are massaging his forehead. I look back at Sami.

His eyes freeze on me, just for a moment. "What am I gonna do now?"

Walking across the floor is all I can think to do. When I reach the lip of the loading dock, I look out into the murky gray, and jump, land awkward in the gravel and keep walking. The sun is just rising, candy pink over the dusty gray grass. I go on towards the road. The rusty Civic is gone from the lot. As I pass the culvert, I look inside and Fat Cat's flat gray face glares out at me, eyes wide and waiting. I go on towards the road.

Linh Lai

S HE'S WATCHING ANOTHER MOVIE about a man who can fly sideways, kick his enemy's skull and then land gracefully on the other side of the now-dead body. Her father comes into her room and tells her to pause it, even though the volume isn't too loud, so she knows there's something important. There is: he's decided she should finish high school in Canada so that she can learn English and be a successful person. She can live with her uncle Steve in Toronto.

Steve emails her and says that an excellent Canadian name is Jinny, which is what he used to register her at the high school near his house. She doesn't know what's wrong with her Vietnamese name, but a month later at Pearson airport, when Uncle Steve says, "Welcome, Jinny," she answers with her new Canadian word, "Hello." The airport has very tall escalators that she imagines would be good for chase scenes, even for jumping over the sides.

The first week of school, she can't talk to anyone, so she just smiles and listens and notices that all the white Jinnys have a different sound in their names from the *ihh* in hers. She finds the proof pinned up in the art room: a beautiful black horse signed *Jenny N.* in pink paint. She wonders if she ought to tell people to call her that, too. She wonders if she ought to tell her uncle. She doesn't do either. After school, she walks around until she finds a video store, and then she feels a bit better. When the boy at the counter asks her a question, she hands him her student id, and he makes her out a rental card. When he asks her another question, she just smiles until he smiles back, and then she rents four Chinese action movies, just like at home. Her Chinese is way better than her English. When she calls her friends at home, they've seen the same ones. When she calls her parents at home, she doesn't cry very much.

The third week of school, her uncle makes her a resumé on his computer and tells her to find a part-time job. She takes her resumé to Pho-Mi 99 because she can walk there and because it has neon Vietnamese characters in the window. They say *Beautiful Mrs. Duck Soup*, and *duck* is spelled wrong, but it's something. Clutching the resumé, in the distressed jeans and high-heeled boots that her aunt gave her for school, she cuts through the kids skateboarding around the gas station outside the restaurant. The boys are skinny and slouchy but their boards are fast and flying. She wishes she could stay and watch, but her uncle said apply for jobs today.

She knows she has to speak English to be a waitress, and she does now, some words. Maybe enough words for a restaurant where everything is Vietnamese except the customers. The door jingles when she opens it. There are no customers, no people at all. The room is full of paper table-cloths, and bright-patterned carpets that look like wallpaper. There is a bamboo bar with a golden cat waving on it, next to a jar of charity mints. The air is steamy warm, and it smells like fish sauce and cilantro. She waits, in her stiff tight jeans and heavy shoes and finally calls, "Than tu?" It feels funny to say a home word in Canada, but there it is, *Than tu,* in a poster right above the coffee maker.

A man comes in from the back who is not Vietnamese – he is all white, skin and hair and clothes, although the clothes have some stains of other colours. His speaks English very loudly. "Ah, *something something,* an Asian girl!" The man throws his arms around. He is very tall. "You come about the job? I've been waiting for one of you."

She shifts from heel to heel. "Yes. The job." She hands him her resumé.

He reads and then, as if he hadn't, says to her, "You go to high school?"

She nods.

Loud and slow: "In Canada?"

She nods.

"And you're Vietnamese?"

She looks around.

"Yes, you."

"I'm Vietnamese."

"Oy, my lucky day. I'm Koenberg," says Koenberg, sticking out the hand that isn't holding the resumé. It's dry and warm when she shakes it. He points at her. "Jinny – Jinny Lai?"

". . . Yes."

Koenberg goes to the bar and gets a tray stacked with empty glasses. "Jinny, carry this across the room. Don't fall down."

She weighs the tray on her palms, then hefts it above her head as she has seen real waitresses do. She walks across the room, her shoulders loose and even, her steps small and sure. She doesn't fall down. As she walks, she watches skaters jumping and sliding outside. One of them can hop his board up onto the newspaper box. She wonders if she could do that. Once, at the beach back home, she jumped right up on a lifeguard tower, just because someone said she couldn't, and that was without a skateboard.

As she walks back to the bar, she hears Koenberg say some things: *Vietnam it up* and *too much like Jenny.* She understands those words, but not why he said them. Koenberg is spinning the dial on a label maker. She sets down her tray while he puts his label on a clip-card. He shows her: *Xing.* "Whaddaya think?"

It's not a Vietnamese name, it's not a Canadian name. She doesn't know how to pronounce it. It's a no-name. She nods.

"No one will even know how to pronounce it," Koenberg crows. He gives her the name tag. He also gives her a black apron, a menu ("Learn this!"), a smile. It's starting to seem like he has given her the job. "Come back Tuesday. You know Tuesday?"

"Yes."

"Three-thirty, you come on Tuesday."

She nods, but still he looks doubtful. He points at her watch – "Three-thirty." Then he windmills his arms, right straight sticking out, left pointing down at the floor between his feet. "Like this."

"Three-thirty. Tuesday. Yes."

THAT GIVES HER two days to clear her schedule, which means homework and DVDs. A week after she found the video store, her uncle saw her watching *Master Killer* and said, "Chinese! You should watch Canadian movies and learn to speak! Chinese! You waste your time!" He gave her a stack of new Canadian DVDs, silly things, *Love Actually, My Best Friend's Wedding,* something with dogs in it. So now she rents the English dubs of Chinese films, where the actors lips never move at the right time. Mainly the talking doesn't matter; she just likes to see the killers roll unhurt from moving cars, ninjas leaping over each other's heads, people who can fly just a little.

On Monday night, she is so nervous she can't sleep. She watched and returned all of her DVDs, and she can't stand her uncle's "Great Canadian Movies," but on TV is something called *The Matrix.* It turns out to be like an action movie where everyone is Canadian, and it's not that good, but a few of the stunts are ok. A man runs up a wall. Her feet twitch like they know what to do, like her mouth twitches when she hears a song she knows the words to, like her hand twitches when she sees a guy whose hand she used to hold. That doesn't happen in Toronto, of course.

She thinks it's probably possible to run up a wall, if you are fit and light. She is. She turns off the TV and goes to the far side of her room. The wall has only one picture on it, *NYSNC, from before her cousin moved out. She runs past the bed, the TV, the bookshelf, puts her bare feet on the wall and keeps running. She runs up, so easy she gets brave and tries her right foot on the ceiling. She falls hard on her back; that part wasn't in the movie.

She lies there a moment, getting her breath back, waiting. She made quite a thud, falling, but no one comes. After a while, she goes back to bed. Her back hurts, but not that much. She thinks she knows what she did wrong: not leaning her body forward along the ceiling, towards the light fixture. She could do that. When her back stops hurting, she will. Finally, she falls asleep, thinking of the how easy it would be to swing from the high vaulted ceiling of her school hallway, and not at all about how her mother used to rub her back when it hurt.

TUESDAY AFTERNOON, she walks back across the gas station tarmac. Boys and a few girls are skating again, yelling, "Awight" and "*Niiicce*" and "Rough, next time!" The skaters don't see her, but she sees them, recognizes the ones that go to her school. She's seen them sliding their boards down the south stairs, jumping onto and over benches in the smoking quad. Now they hop the curb towards the gas pumps and swirl around her as if she were a lamppost. As they pass, she smells smoke on the wind.

The first part of waitressing is easy: she shreds things, wraps things, dices and fries and smiles politely while Koenberg talks and talks. Just when she's starting to unclench her sore shoulders, he takes away her cleaver and says, "Dinner hour!"

She feels like she has to confess. "Mr. Koenberg." He turns away from the stove – this is the first time she has spoken today. "Mr. Koenberg, my English is . . . not so good."

"What??" His eyes open wide as windows. "I know, girl, I know." Then some things she doesn't understand, except "just the best Pho there is." He sounds excited, waving his cleaver, but she can't follow. Finally he just points the blade towards the swinging door, and she goes out to face the customers.

It's ok. People mainly want food, not talk. When they ask questions it's awful, staring blank into other blank faces, but if people point at the menu or just say numbers she's fine. If someone asks her a question with the number in it, she says what she memorized off the menu. They have menus right in front of them, but people seem to like to hear it from her.

What they really like is Koenberg's food. Pho-Mi 99 is a cloud of lemongrass, tomato, starchy batter and hot oil. It's funny to see Pho at dinner instead of breakfast, but nice to see it at all – at her uncle's house, they have Canadian foods always. Long before dinnertime is over, her belly is tight and hollow, and her feet pulse hot in her heavy shoes. When finally the restaurant is silent, she puts the last dirty plates into a plastic tub and carries it into the kitchen.

"Oh ho, my little Jinny!" yells Koenberg, running with his hands out towards her. She starts to pull back but he just takes the tub from her, hands it to the dishwashing boy. Koenberg's talking very fast but doesn't seem to be telling her to do anything, so she sits down on a chair by the swinging doors. She lets her feet flop sideways, her shoulders sway back. "Very good today, eh, Jinny? You did a great job."

"Thank you."

"You want to eat? Pho? Banh bao? I could make anything, whatever you want."

"Yes."

After a moment he understands that she'll take what she can get. He makes the summer rolls carefully, slicing in extra egg, asking if she likes cilantro. She doesn't know that word, but she knows the word *like* and she knows what is in his hand, so she nods. The rolls are fat and damp and glossy white on their white plate and she smiles at them and then at Koenberg. He goes back to the dishes while she eats, but she knows he's watching her. She picks up a roll and digs her teeth through the rice wrapper, snapping the stems of the herbs. She thinks of her mother's perfect black-and-silver kitchen.

"Very good."

"I know," he says. "I have a gift." She doesn't understand, but she knows what he means. She puts her empty plate by the sink.

"Oy, this one, she keeps her thoughts to herself. Tomorrow? Three-thirty?"

"Three-thirty."

AT HOME HER UNCLE finds her looking in his Canadian Dictionary, which always makes him happy. "That's good, that's a good way to learn," he tells her. "What are you looking up?"

She points on the page, to *oy: exclamation of disgust, exasperation or dismay. Oy, that movie was dull!* Her uncle says, "Good! A new Canadian word! Oy, I am sad today!" He pats her on the shoulder.

She goes upstairs and puts on a movie. She has forgotten the name and the rental box is blank. The actors prowl through Beijing and talk out the sides of their mouths words that must have made sense before they became English, about pride, honour and not stopping for supper. Once, during a battle with a hundred ninjas, a fighter jumps into the air and kicks out his leg whirling, knocking half a dozen black-suited bodies astray. The disk cuts out before the credits, but she saw the best bit. She feels her feet twitch again, and runs to the middle of the room, leaps up, kicks out, whirling around and around, four times before landing. All her cousin's china dolphins and unicorns are still standing, but if she'd been surrounded by ninjas, she would've knocked them all down. If her friends had been there, they would've cheered.

AT THE RESTAURANT she gets better, or at least she learns more words. She learns to tell people where the bathroom is. She learns to point to her favourite meals on the menu, the special duck usually, unless the person is a very skinny woman, in which case seafood soup. Her uncle tells her to say soup, not Pho, but when Koenberg hears her say, "The beef ball soup is very good," to a table of businessmen near the kitchen, pots and pans crash until she goes back.

"This is a Vietnamese restaurant, use Vietnamese words!" He waves his arms above his head. "Well, not most of them. But the ones on the menu. Ok?"

"Ok." Remembering what words to use is the hardest part of her job.

When it's slow, Koenberg experiments with new brands of glass noodles and knives. She practises her spring roll wrapper folds and breaks up sugar cane for the shrimp paste and tries to surf the vacuum cleaner across the silly dining-room rugs. And she folds paper cranes out of napkins. Customers squawk happily over the white birds, even though all they do with them is crumple them up and wipe their fingers on them. "Mishegas," said Koenberg, whatever that means. "I'm so lucky to have a Vietnamese girl to do that."

She lets him think the birds are a home thing, instead of something her Canadian math teacher taught her, one day when she couldn't read anything on the blackboard and he felt sorry for her.

She likes whatever work she can do in the dining room, because from there she can look out the window at the kids who skate endlessly in their bright suede sneakers. They can flip their boards while jumping up and stand on the thin edge. They can make their boards spin in a circle under their flying feet. They jump up and down and up and down from the curb. They can really move fast when the convenience store clerk is chasing them, gliding down the sidewalk, one foot steady on the board and one windmilling off the sidewalk for speed. Her feet twitch.

SHE GOES TO WORK, she goes to school, she watches the skaters, she watches movies. She gets her cousin's old computer working so she can IM her friends and download movies again. Her parents won't get IM no matter how much she says it's easy. She talks careful English to her aunt and uncle, does homework and practises jumping from treetop to treetop in the dark backyard. She got that idea from a complicated Canadian-Japanese movie that she likes because the women jump and fly as well as the men. It's getting too cold to do everything barefoot though, and her boots are far too stiff and heavy to jump properly. With her first pay cheque, she goes looking for low soft sneakers like the boarders have. She finds purple ones with a gold word on the side. Her uncle smiles at her Canadian shoes, and asks what the word means. She's ready, already looked it up. "Big Canadian cat," she tells him. He smiles some more.

One of the boys smiles, too, when he sees her walking through the gas station in her purple Pumas. She thought they'd be comfortable to work in, but she also thought those board boys might not think she was a lamppost if they saw her in shoes like theirs. She would have to make friends with them before they would let her borrow a board. Maybe not even then. On the website where she looked up the shoes, she saw boards, too, and now she knows she will not be buying one with her second paycheque. So when the one with the gray toque smiles at her shoes, she smiles back.

Koenberg smiles less. "Those are not Vietnamese," he says to her feet.

She takes off her coat and walks towards the kitchen, and Koenberg follows. "This always happens. It's for the best, really. They always – " and then a long word she doesn't know, something starting with *A* that doesn't sound very good. He doesn't talk to her much that shift, which shouldn't matter, because she almost never actually understands what he's saying. Still she's kind of lonely without him talking big words every time she comes into the kitchen to pick up an order.

When she leaves at the end of the night, the street lights have blown again – that happens sometimes. As she walks across the dark pavement, she notices tiny orange flames moving around the bus stop. The smokers yell, "Hey," and she doesn't know why so she just stops moving. One of the glowing cigarettes leaves the rest and moves fast across the paving. The speed and scraping noise mean the lighted cigarette is on a board. The light flies past her, then up where she knows the bike rack is, quivering a moment before dropping down with a crash of wheels. Suddenly car headlights flash on the toqued boy. "Thanks," he says as the car passes and he fades back into dark, except for the orange shadow of his face.

"Ok." She should've said, *It's ok,* that's another way for *You're welcome,* but just *ok* means *yes.*

The flame starts to move away.

Yesterday, on a Canadian skateboard website, she learned a new thing to say. She says to the dark and the dot, "Nice trick," and doesn't know if she's said it right or if he heard her, but it doesn't matter because it's true.

AT LUNCH HOUR, she sits alone on the grass across from the south stairs. She eats whatever her aunt packs for her. Even if Koenberg makes her pork buns or special summer rolls, her aunt makes her cheese and ham sandwiches on bagels or hot dog buns. Not even baguette, even though some Canadians are French, too.

She sits on the grass and watches the skaters smoking, jumping, yelling, spinning, bumping down the steps or sometimes gliding smooth down the rails. Only the best do that, the ones with the spines like wire. The toque boy can. He sometimes notices her now, even smiles. He bounces hard when he tips off that high railing, and people applaud. Mainly it's girls who clap, sitting on the grass, or wandering around, sharing cigarettes, laughing, fiddling with their hair. A few of the really good boarders are girls, but she isn't too interested in them, because it is the boys who share. One kind of girl are good skaters and have their own boards. The other kind flirt and clap and never do anything interesting, except one thing, and that's what she wants: Sometimes a boy will let a girl stand on his board. Usually the girl just laughs and puts her hands on his shoulders while he pulls her around, or else she tries on her own and tips right off. The girls who get to try can't skate at all, no muscles in their arms or legs, although they have the right shoes. They couldn't carry seven bowls of Pho at once, either.

She is so sure she'd be different, she would almost clap for a good trick. But that would make everyone look at her, and she isn't sure that it would make anyone lend her a board. One day, though, the parking lot boy comes over without her clapping or anything. His words sound fuzzy, but she recognizes *Pho-Mi 99*, so she says, "Yes."

He says something else that she misses. Some Canadians are easier to understand than others. She wishes he would open his mouth wider. She shrugs and smiles. He says it again, slower but not clearer, and points to the board.

Is he offering? "I like your skateboard, yes," she tries.

"I practise a lot, that's how I got good. These stairs are better than the Pho-Mi lot, but the *something long and angry-sounding* after school."

She shrugs. She thinks this is a good start, maybe they will become friends. How long before she can ask to borrow the board? The buzzer goes but no one moves much. The boy takes a step away, but then one back. "I'm Jimmy."

For a second she thinks he is teasing her, but then she realizes that it sounds a little different. "I'm Jinny."

"Ji*mmmmy*." Laughing, but not mean laughing.

While she is wondering if she should laugh, too, or say it again, he asks her something. She knows it's a question because it goes up at the end. "Yes."

He smiles and shakes his long hair off his face. That must've been the right answer.

WHEN SHE GETS OFF the bus that afternoon, Jimmy jumps off the bench and comes over to say something she doesn't get. She is squirming wordless until she looks over at the restaurant and sees Koenberg waving his arms like a crazy clock in the window and it makes her laugh. Jimmy laughs too, a seal bark and cigarette cough. "You have to go."

"I have to go."

Inside she ties on her apron while Koenberg rants. "You talk to those *something something* boys who *long something*. Bad for business, Jinny."

"Sorry," she says, because she has to say something.

"Don't get *something* bad *something*, Jinny."

She starts stacking glasses. "I work hard."

Koenberg whips his arms back like he is going to hug an elephant. "I know that. It wasn't an *something*. Listen, I am Koenberg, best chef of Vietnamese *something* in Toronto." He keeps talking after that, but she misses more than she catches. It all ends with *see?* so she knows she is supposed to answer.

She starts hanging the wineglasses above the bar. She has to admit that she doesn't understand, and she hates that. She wishes the restaurant weren't empty. "I don't know."

Koenberg sighs. "Come here." He runs into the kitchen, bashing the door back against the wall. She follows, carrying the bar tray. Koenberg whirls in the centre of the kitchen, like he might lift off, kicking, but he's just pointing at food. "My gift." She knows what he means: Pho clear as glass, creamy white congee lumpy with egg and mushrooms, bi cuon rolled perfectly tight. Her banh bao waiting for her in a steam tray, round and warm. He picks up the plate, thrusts it at her chest, waits while she takes a bite. Flour petals, spiced pork, bite of the onions. "That's my gift, Jinny. What is your gift?"

The doorbells jingle-jingle, so she doesn't have to tell Koenberg that she doesn't know the word *gift* in this way, or if she does, he probably wouldn't like what hers is. She goes and serves spring rolls and fried shrimps to a group of blond secretaries.

When she gets off work, Jimmy is spinning around and around, board tipped up, under the street lamp. His friends are all trying the same thing, up and down the sidewalk. Jimmy stops and waves when she comes out, but no one else looks away from their feet. "Hey!" He tucks his board under his arm and comes running slowly towards her. She feels happy, but wonders what Koenberg would think. Mainly, she just wishes she had a board of her own.

"Hello, Jimmy."

"Hey, you remembered."

"I remember you."

"Well, well, you never told me your name. Is it . . ." he looks at her chest and it takes her a moment to remember that her name tag is there. ". . . Xing?" He pronounces the *X* as a *Z*, as good as anything the customers have come up with.

It doesn't seem worth it to correct him when it isn't even her name, so she just smiles and curves her body forward to match his. They smile and smile until she can't stand waiting anymore and points at the board.

"Will you let me ride?" She has been practising those words in her head all evening.

He looks at the long purple board that matches her shoes, the skull and soda pop stickers on the bottom. When he pulls it in front of his body, the wheels rattle. "You want to ride?" His eyebrows wrinkle.

"I can do it. Puma shoes." She kicks her foot out at him, accidentally taps his green Puma with her purple one, but he doesn't seem to mind.

"Well, I could help you. Sure."

She lets her bag slide off her shoulder and clonk to the ground. She'll be sorry if her container of bun bo hue has opened and spilled. Still this will be worth it. She reaches out for the board.

Jimmy lets her have it, but he looks nervous. She bends from the waist to put it on the ground even though she has seen the boys drop them a thousand times. It seems wrong to drop something that isn't hers.

"Ok, ok, now put your left foot at the . . ." his voice disappears down the front of his sweatshirt, but she knows what to do. She puts her left foot in the middle of the board and her right foot towards back, where there is a little rise that she hadn't noticed from a distance. She stands still a moment, Jimmy's hands framing her waist, her hands above his, not touching, for balance. She's a little wobblier than she expected, above the wheels.

A bus arrives at the Jane stop and the dark windows reflect Koenberg coming around the corner of the restaurant with a garbage bag in his hand. She puts her right foot on the ground and pushes.

She feels each bit of gravel under the wheels, the cool fall wind and car exhaust on her skin. Jimmy jogs alongside her. She bends her knees and feels her weight steady as she flies forward, a wonderful wordless feeling of *on on on*. She can jump up on the newspaper box, easy. She leans backwards, slides her left foot forward, bends her knees. She jumps and the board jumps, too.

Up!

She's only there for a moment, the bin is small, before she leans forward and tips off, no loss of speed. Jimmy's long low whistle comes from behind her; he's stopped following. She picks up speed, heading for the gas pump, which is almost as tall as she is. She can feel the twitch and strength in her thighs – she can do it.

The smell of gas in the dark. She tips back, her weight steady, and jumps higher than she ever has, but the angle is wrong, and the top of the pump is rounded, just slightly but she didn't expect that, and the wheels don't hook on. She's up for a moment and then it's just like the ceiling – too far and she falls back, feet higher than her head for a moment until her spine hits the blacktop. Then the board comes down too, and the edge bangs hard off her left shin, and that's what really hurts, so bad she closes her eyes for a minute to make the world silent. When she opens them again all she sees is the ash-white glare of the lamppost, and then Jimmy's face, and Koenberg's too, blocking the light.

"Zing! Zing! Are you ok?"

"Jinny, can you hear me, Jinny?"

She has no idea who they are talking to.

The House on Elsbeth

W E GOT THE HOUSE on Elsbeth for the summer because, one sleety day in April, Leah's stepfather backhanded her hard on the jaw. Ted's blow snapped her mouth shut mid-argument and made her bite straight through her tongue. Then he was sorry. Leah forgave him but she remembered Ted's bony wrist slamming her bony face. She remembered it so hard that Lane and Tracy felt like they remembered, too. When we moved into that hot tight house, all three of us felt the story leaching out of the walls: the arc of his hand stopping at her narrow jaw, a drop of blood continuing the arc across the room to spatter on the bone-white fridge. That's not a picture you can blink away, even if you never actually saw it.

Ted wanted her to blink away. In the floaty white chaos of the ER, he told Leah maybe they'd get on better with more space between them. He'd give her one of his nicer properties – semi-detached – for half rent . . . if she could find friends to share it. A little dig, but nothing Leah couldn't handle. Nothing the three of us couldn't handle.

Of course we would live together, though we had never spoken outside of anthro tutorial, and then only to borrow old notes or compliment a new tattoo. Barely conversation, but contact: always the urge to stand too close, to brush arms, shoulders, bellies, without a word to say. So of course we'd live together, to get as close as possible for all the hours in the day. We made us feel better.

THERE WERE PROBLEMS with the house on Elsbeth, though maybe we were waiting for problems, or drew them like lemmings to the sea. Maybe we made mountains out of molehills. A punch in the face is a bad thing to have happen to you, but it's not so great to hear through drywall from the other half of the semi-house, either. Through a wall, we couldn't precisely identify the thud of flesh on flesh, but when that thud interrupted *I didn't, you said, you never, I hate*, when it was followed by the stagger-back of shoes and the crash of body into furniture, and then a wail, we knew what it was.

The first thud came a week after we'd moved in, during dessert. Lane

69

dropped his spoon and pictured the small woman with ragged red hair who lived next door. He imagined any blow, even from her spindly bearded husband, would toss her back quite far. Lane imagined himself – tall, with tennis muscles – being tossed back. Less far, but still. He'd imagined this before. In front of the bathroom mirror, Lane and Tracy had both, separately, tried whipping their heads around, arching against the bathtub, wondering about angles and impact. Even Leah wasn't sure about the choreography; it's hard to remember what you weren't expecting.

There was a wail through the wall, short and sharp. Leah stopped picking the cherries out of her fruit cup and looked up at the wall, staring hard, as if she could melt it. Tracy looked too. Leah was thinking, not about falling back but falling down; about how it is to fall down and look up at someone bigger, someone who has just been proven stronger. A blow knocks you down, but it's the looking up afterwards that gets you.

Tracy thought, Getting hit in the face is not the worst thing there is. It's not a killing blow. You can heal, recover dignity, get up from the floor.

Leah just nodded. She could speak easily by then, in May, but she didn't like the sloppy-drunk way she sounded. Still, it had been a speedy recovery. And the neighbours recovered even faster after that first blow – just a few minutes of sobs led to tender murmurs we couldn't make out. After even those quieted, we heard footsteps moving deeper into the house.

As the heels echoed away, Tracy picked up the spoon, covered with fluff and hair, and set it on the table. No one was eating; no one looked away from the bone-white wall.

When we felt sad, sometimes we played games. Leah sighed and said, "Pear," and Lane closed his eyes and stuck his fingers into his fruitcup tin and picked out a translucent cube of pear. As he put the fruit in his mouth, he held out the cup above Tracy's head. Leah said, "Cherry," and Tracy shut her eyes and took a cherry, pink with cheap dye. She reached across the table to place it carefully on Leah's stitches.

Leah chewed and swallowed, licked at the juice. "Delicious." It sounded like a lie in her slurry voice, thick with healing.

SOMETIMES WE SAW the neighbours by the garbage cans, in the groceteria. They were little flabby people in slacks with elastic waists, but they took in their mail, mowed their lawn, carried their sacks of empties to the Beer Store. They seemed functional.

On our side of the wall, things moved slowly, and the tins and bottles piled up. The summer rolled on, June anyway, and we couldn't get much done in that dark, hot little house. The wood panelling absorbed the heat and breathed it out at us.

Lane had the most energy. He had a summer class, and that Tuesday morning, the morning in question, he shot like a spitball down the stairs, shower-damp through his shirt, white-blond hair slicked translucent to his skull. Some of his freshness dissolved in the living room. It was only footsteps through the wall, but they were hard on the heels, hard on the ear.

We had slept on the floor downstairs, where it was cooler. Tracy and Leah were still there, sprawled like starfish. It was really too hot to touch but somehow bare legs always tangled on the thin gray rug. Leah's pale, blue-threaded waitress legs hooked Tracy's tanned landscaper's muscles. The image sapped Lane's desire for micro-economics, even though his own legs – not so pale, but not so tan – had been in the twist just twenty minutes before. When we closed our eyes, we could still feel each other.

When we closed our eyes, the chatter and clatter next door seemed to get just a little louder, a little too loud.

That morning, Leah was zebra-faced with last night's makeup and Tracy was eating dry Reese's Peanut-Butter Cereal, puff by puff, without raising her head from her pillow. The heat had nearly totalled us.

There was a slam from the wall, wood against metal.

Lane sighed and stood still. "I gotta go to class."

Leah nodded, dark hair sliding into her mouth. She spit it out. "It may be too hot to go to class, Lane. It may be too hot to go on at all." Her voice was still slow, but no longer slurred: tidy drunk.

Tracy was just thinking, *Rain rain rain.*

"Maybe we should be doing more outdoor stuff, barbecues and frisbee." Lane was thinking about how it would feel to flunk a summer course, one he'd paid for, and he didn't want to think about that. He didn't like the salt-chocolate taste of Tracy's cereal. "I don't think we have enough summer fun. At least it'd be a distraction."

Rain. He sat down on the couch and Tracy squirmed up to lean on him. *Rain.* Her skull felt heavy against his thigh. She nibbled on another peanut-butter ball, and finally said aloud, "They're earlier than yesterday." She was thinking about how she had to go to work and she didn't know if she could face the bus, or wearing clothes.

We listened for a long time, eating, stroking hair and rubbing feet, silent. The voices on the other side of the wall didn't separate into a man and a woman. A single snarl of anger, braiding alto and tenor until the blow fell again, again again.

We squirmed at the cartoon *bonk* of a head on wall. It sounded like a dropped shoe. But it wasn't. Tracy stopped chewing. We imagined we could hear recrimination, apology, the smack of freezer door. Then we imagined the hissing sting of ice on a hot bruise. Lane and Tracy looked hard at Leah's dirty face, watching for any pain that could be comforted.

Leah slipped off the couch and walked across the room. She stopped when her nose bent against the wall. The other side was fading into tears and mutters. She thought, *Rain.* She thought, *Tomorrow my stepdad's coming to pick up the rent.*

It was hard to believe that it was the end of June already, or that it hadn't always been June. Tracy slid her head off Lane's thigh. Freed, Lane stood and went to touch Leah's shoulder, bend his nose against the wall, too. "Does he own that place, too?" We all knew he was going to ask, but actually mentioning the neighbours aloud was startling.

"Not relevant. But yes. Tonight, we should do something fun," Leah said firmly. "Before the rain."

"Rain?" asked Lane.

"It'll rain tonight," said Leah.

"Rain," said Tracy.

YOU'RE FUCKIN' SHIRTS can't get dry the humidity you don't listen never listen fuck fuck fuck

Lane and Tracy were in the backyard after work. The radio said it was too hot and smoggy to be outside, but that was assuming you had some indoor place to go that was air-conditioned and didn't smell like old beer and dust. Lane had managed to get the coals lit, though the burns on his hand itched and tingled. Tracy had found a Frisbee, black and gold, but she'd left it by the back door. Tracy was starfish sprawling again, on the dead grass on the other side of the yard, counting the singed hairs on the back of Lane's hand. She hadn't showered after work and Lane felt the slick sweat on her nose and neck. He picked up a glass from the ground and went to kneel beside her.

"You should drink. It's 38 out here, the radio said."

"We're 38 degrees, too. People are. Neat." Tracy kept her hands resting it at the vee of her ribs, hands folded as if over a funeral bouquet. Lane drank instead, the cold water slithering her throat, Adam's apple bobbing. She kept her eyes closed. They could both see the sun shining through blood vessels in her eyelids.

I've never lying your mother my mother my ass you take the recycling your mother I hate

Tracy wished for Leah.

"Working. Or on her way home from work . . . " Lane squinted at the sky. "Yeah, she'll be home . . . in a minute."

Clouds were starting to gather around the vague intention of a sunset. Snap and crackle on the radio. Leah came in from the street gate in her black uniform, each leg outlined in sweat on her skirt.

"What's up?" Lane stood and watched her walk towards him, the rub of her damp skirt against the hair on his thighs.

"One of the sous-chefs ditched and they put me in the kitchen. Fuckers. I cut my hand dicing onions and got burnt off the toaster." She came closer and shoved her hands towards Lane's face. Her fingers were long, skinny and pale. Each knuckle was cross-hatched with tiny cuts or crusted with a larger scrape. Across the veiny back of the left, a long cut bled a mirror heart line through Barbie-coloured Band-Aids.

"Ok?" He pointed at the cut.

She flopped onto the grass next to Tracy. "Cuise wanted me to get looked at, but I didn't have cab fare and bleeding on the TTC in this heat . . . you know?"

Lane reached down and pressed his burns against Leah's. "You want a drink?"

"Sit with me a minute first. Tracy's asleep."

"No." Tracy opened her eyes. "Hello, Leah."

Lane sat down, draping himself over Leah's sticky back.

Tracy sat up. "Hey, the sky is purple." She dropped her head into Leah's lap.

"Ah, the puppy pile." Leah patted Tracy's head with her less-injured hand.

Clashing voices from the other side of the house, again. Again and again and again. The air was heavy with rage and the possibility of rain.

"I hate it," Lane said after a minute. Thunder rumbled, not too far off.

Just once your part I mean jesus you expect nine to five the weekends really jesus

We were quiet for a moment. The neighbours were not quiet.

Fucking fucking fuck

"What time is Ted coming tomorrow, Leah?"

"Early." A slammed door. Then more voices. "But we've got it under control, right? So it doesn't matter."

Never see it comin' just like bitch and this weather one time in the now that I'm making

"Next door?"

Leah stared at the fence. "We not gonna mention it, are we?"

Hurting me hurting dinner on the table what bastard responsibility bacon totally hate

"Ask him to ask them . . . "

"Ask them what? Please stop what? . . . everything?"

The fence was painted pudding-brown. At the base was a moat of dirt, which the heat had bleached blond and shattered like glass.

It wasn't clear who said it. Maybe we all said it: "Please stop hitting her?"

He hit her. We were too far to hear the blow, and there was no cry. In the sudden silence, though, it seemed obvious.

The sweat had dried off Leah and her clothes hung free. She was still staring at the fence. Lane curved over Leah, chest on spine, heart on heartbeat.

The clouds were building. The air smelled like grilled chicken, brown sugar and bourbon, dead grass, sweat and botanical products radiating off our bodies. We were listening through the steamy air to a murmur that, deep in the house, was building again. The woman's voice was not young, gravelly, enraged. The man's was higher, more hysterical. We were losing more words now, but they seemed all one syllable, *bang* like hammer strokes, shattering. *Bangbangbang,* the woman's voice, *I want, you did, this house, I hate, stop.* Then the man's voice. Then both, again. Then silence, then the crash of china and another crash of voices.

Lane got up and went to poke a fork into a scorched chicken breast and flip it. A small flame blazed, then died.

"I don't feel too good," Tracy said to the sky. She was looking past Leah's profile above her.

Leah reached down to clutch Tracy's hand. She looked down at their twined fingers, all the cuts and dirty bruises and rings between them. Shriek of children, happier neighbours elsewhere. She yawned, her hands entwined with Tracy's, mouth uncovered.

Tracy breathed. "Hey, your tongue's healed. You don't even have a scar."

A shout that sounded like a parting shot, and then the bang-back of a screen door, the stomp of shoes on grass. The last cloud finally floated over the platinum sun and winked it out. A rustle, someone in the next garden, *him*.

Leah clamped her teeth tight and hard.

Tracy pulled her fingers free.

The thunder rumbled again, closer, louder.

Lane poked at a chicken burger, burnt on one side, raw on the other. He hated the pink of the raw.

Tracy was trying to dig in under the grass. She didn't like the feel of the dry dirt. She wanted it to be mud.

"It doesn't matter," Leah said, wanting one punch not to matter. Ted was coming by in the morning, and she wanted to like him again. "I get hit in the face once, we get Montreal rent in Toronto." He'd probably want a cup of coffee, minutes together, minutes and minutes in the hot ugly kitchen, and she couldn't like him again. "What happened to me is not what's . . . there." Silence from the next yard. Leah thought of her stepfather's pinched face when he'd been working too hard, the strain lines and the smile lines around his eyes. "For her . . . "

Lane tried to put a chicken breast onto a bun, dropped it in the grass, picked it up and burned his fingers with an audible hiss, dropped it again, finally got it with the spatula.

"I'll eat that one," he said. Burn blisters were forming on his index finger, but he just set the plate down and reached for the next one, concentrating on not dropping anything else. He looked over when Tracy said, "Can I touch?"

She was kneeling beside Leah; she tapped her on the right corner of her mouth. Leah shrugged and put her tongue out again: lizard-long and ham-pink, cracked like dry soil, spit bubbles and pasty tastebuds. Tracy stared, Lane stared, even Leah was looking, her dark eyes crossed.

It was late afternoon and our yard was nighttime dark and we could hear the neighbour's hoe smacking soil. Tracy rubbed her index finger on her shirt but it still looked dirty gray. Leah didn't flinch when she touched her. Under the rough pad of Tracy's finger, Leah's tongue felt silky wet, trembling faintly. A tongue is all muscle. Lane set down the plate and came close, watching the pale of Tracy's fingernail stroke. He could feel the shiver of tongue in the wind against his body, but still he knelt on Leah's other side and raised his right index finger, blistered and meat-greasy. He waited for Leah's affirmative blink before putting the bubble of blister next to Tracy's finger. Hers was cooler, but both brushed gently where tooth had slammed at the blow, where the scar should have been. But there was no scar.

Then the rain hit our backs.

We should have gone in but we were so wet so fast it didn't matter, and anyway, it was the first cool in a long time. So we ate in the rain and the echo of thunder, the roar of curses from the angry man in the next yard. The buns melted to sponge, Tracy's hair went slick on her shoulders, and Leah's makeup made black rivers on her cheeks. Lane ate his burger and then half of Tracy's and then he picked up the Frisbee. Its plastic lightning bolts were far thicker than the true stuff in the sky, shel-lacked glossy and still. Real lightning rents the world.

We fanned into a triangle to play, flawless throws and catches despite the pounding-down water, despite Lane's burnt finger, Leah's cut hand, Tracy's rasping breath. The small clonk of a thumb hooking the edge of the Frisbee soothed, despite the weight of sodden clothes clinging, the weight of everything in that house or near it.

The air was full of lightning, spiderthreads of white heat. We should have gone in, but so should the neighbour, who was rattling already-rusted lawn chairs into his shed, crashing and cursing. We could almost hear him over the crash of rain and thunder.

A distraction. Leah lofted the Frisbee up, slicing rain, over Tracy's idle hand, over the fence. At that moment, a crack of thunder, an arc of light flickering into the corn, hot and sharp. A hiss of fire, then a heavy body falling, then nothing.

The walls were silent, the fence was silent. We bowed our heads a moment before we went to the fence. Only Lane was strong enough to haul himself up, but what he saw we all could imagine – the open palm, the scattered chairs, the slack bleeding mouth.

Then we went around front and across the neighbours' driveway. Leah knocked on the door to the other half of our house. Dripping and not invited in, we told the woman what we'd seen, and we took her to the garden to show her our Frisbee beside his scorched palm. After the silence had passed, we pressed our wet bodies against each other's, and then hers, as she wept.

The Words

Colleen

COLLEEN SHUFFLED THE GOD PAMPHLETS in her lap while Mr. Andrews chalked square yellow letters on the board. Boring. The white paper one was cheaply printed: the yellows did not line up with the reds or blues, so Jesus was all halo, no body. Inside was just a boring list of Sunday school and Bible-study classes. The glossier one had pictures of candles and sheet music, a paragraph about the joy of faith, a couple things that sounded like cheers. Even better, no church address where her father could go and ask questions. Not that he would.

"Ok, people, *focused* attention . . ." Mr. Andrews dropped the chalk into his sleeve. In her notebook Colleen wrote, *Bible study group. Leader: Drew.* Then she crossed out *group* and wrote *cell,* like terrorists. Scarier.

Mr. Andrews was saying, "I hope you'll really get *involved* with this project, come to see poetry not as words on the page, but reality interpreted in words."

Colleen wrote: *The leader will interpret the reality of God's words.*

"Well, that's the hour. Thanks, guys."

Colleen stayed in her seat, waiting for Andrews to skedaddle out. She stared at her blue-ink, red-underline title: *Mindfuck.* Date in the upper right-hand corner.

She flicked through the Bible she'd got out of the library. She was worried, a little, about accidentally brainwashing herself. Not *very* worried, but she'd watched talk shows. She knew about Mormon harems and Catholic perverts, kids going naked on compounds in Arizona, parents selling their houses to pay for deprogrammers.

Her mother would have had something to say about that. But her mother's car had gone spinning off black ice seven months ago, and Joe was always at work or partying when anything good was on TV.

Joe

"NO, I WANT THE GIG, but I can't rehearse tomorrow. I've – I've got something else." He dragged deep, held it in. *Something else* was recruiting focus groups of people who bought more than a litre of cough medicine a year, but that didn't sound how he wanted to sound. He exhaled into the exhaust fan. "I know the set, I could jump in after the opener."

Joe was on the kitchen phone, watching the window for Colleen on the basement steps. He'd have time to pinch the joint and shove it in a pocket before she got to the bottom and opened the door. Ever since her silent rage at the tinfoiled ball of hash beside the bathroom sink, he was trying, but the exhaust fan wasn't that strong. When she lived across the country and they were together only two weeks a year, she'd been a little more forgiving. The turnips boiled over as he hung up, and he slammed the phone down. Joe knew seven recipes; tonight was root vegetable casserole.

He was pretty sure the drugs were part of that silent rage, but not all. She didn't say what made her unhappy, or even that she was. But no one moved that fast, turned that sharply, with any joy. There was so much shit, it was hard to guess: dead mother, strange father, new school and apartment, plus nobody liked root vegetable casserole, it was just all he knew how to do. That was a problem with a lot of what he did.

Other girls her age talked more, he thought. Marcy had . . . probably. He'd only been with her three weeks and he hadn't been sober all the time then, either. But it seemed that Marcy had bitched about homework, cried about dead birds, yelled when he stepped on her toes. Colleen never said a word.

Then again, neither did he. There was a cushion missing from the back of the couch where he slept. In the night, his right foot slipped through the gap and the ripped upholstery to the cold springs, the jagged edge of the broken one. He didn't have the money for a new couch, nor the time to find a new cushion the right size. He just tried to keep his feet still at night, thought about sleeping in shoes, bandaged his right foot in the morning. Maybe they weren't the sort who talked about troubles, Joe and Colleen.

But Joe's last relationship, and several others, had ended with *normal people talk things over*. But Colleen had left "The Lessons of Deuteronomy" mixed in with his dead mail and sheet music. But he didn't *mind* talking, really. So he scraped the serving spoon through the casserole, sat down across from her and asked, "So, you've been thinking about religion?" Then he took a bite. The rice was mushy.

"Yep." Colleen was picking out all the carrot medallions and lining them up around the rim of her plate.

"That's cool. I went to church when I was your age. Sometimes." A long pause, for chewing. He hadn't cooked the turnips enough tonight. "You like Deuteronomy?"

"Yep." Colleen was eating everything except for the necklace of carrots, even the tough turnips. "You know about that one?"

"Not really, much. But I care about whatever you care about. Tell me."

Colleen chewed hard, blankfaced. Then she stood and left the room. He listened to the kitchen door's creaking swing, put some salt on the rice, took a sip of water. He had no idea if she'd gone to get ketchup, to vomit, to Paris, reacting to something he'd said or the voices in her head. When she swung back in and snapped some pamphlets down on the table, he was relieved to see her again, relieved that the church stuff was pretty low-level. He was relieved to put down his fork to read. Nothing about hell, or door-to-dooring, not much even about God. Kids could go to YouthZone and learn Christian alt rock on Tuesdays. He wondered about that sound; probably lots of acoustic guitar, hand slaps against the wood. He wondered if he had the cash for pizza.

"This sounds cool." He set the papers down and picked up the knife again. "Fine."

She shrugged and dug the tines of her fork into the twelve o'clock carrot. "I'm trying for more than *fine*."

"Trying?"

"To know God." She brought the carrot to her mouth and bit it in half. "To understand the universe." Her rage was radiant and he couldn't guess why. He couldn't guess anything about her, not even whether she liked carrots most or least.

Colleen

THE BAY JEWELLERY WAS EXPENSIVE, and Claire's at the mall was just embarrassing. Besides, she wanted something over-the-top, a printed shopping bag that would make even live-and-let-live Joe squirm. She wanted Family Christian Bookshop.

It was so far east there were no sidewalks. Every asshole driver who saw her had to honk – to tell her she was in the way, that she was hot, that she wasn't, who knew? There was an even better-sounding store across town, but she couldn't have walked that far, not even for Loaves and Fishes.

Family Christian Bookshop was pretty good – sky-blue carpeting and glass-fronted cases with wet streaks of Windex. Everything – T-shirts, aprons, stuffed dogs – was printed with Bible verses, or numbers and dots that maybe meant verse numbers. Clocks and bike helmets with prayers, T-shirts about chastity. Two mud-haired toddlers running around, jangly guitar music on the speakers. It sounded a little like tunes she heard through her bedroom wall when her father rehearsed. Other than that, pretty good.

When she asked the walleyed clerk where to find the "talismans of faith," she sort of got told off. "I don't think *talisman* is the right word to use. A talisman is supposed to bring you, like, luck and power. Talismans do stuff. A cross represents something, but it doesn't *do* anything. You should read – "

Afterwards, she went down a new path in the slanting sunlight, trying to cut home through the ravine. She had her library Bible in her bag, thunking heavy against her thigh.

As she walked, she dangled the silver in front of her face like a hypnotist, poked at the cross with her fingertip. Her fingertip was bigger. The thing was actually from the baby jewellery section. It wasn't likely Joe would notice more than a glint at her throat. She trickled the chain back into the bag, and uncrumpled the receipt.

FAMILY CHRISTIAN BOOKSHOP
Silver cross/chain – $4.95.

She would leave that somewhere prominent, maybe.

Four-ninety-five could've bought what she'd meant to buy, a rhinestone WWJD, but with the one eye watching her, the too-familiar guitar, those kids with their clean soft faces, Colleen couldn't think.

The receipt wasn't going to be much good soon, she was rolling it ragged, fretting the edges. Soon it would look like garbage and Friday 6 a.m., when Joe ran around throwing things into grocery sacks, it would be gone. She carefully tucked the receipt back into her pocket.

Colleen wasn't sure where she was – the path seemed to have zagged away from the underpass, and she couldn't hear traffic anymore. She still didn't know this stupid town very well. She tipped her head down against the laser sun, now almost parallel with her face. The clerk's weird gaze had felt like a laser, too, an X-ray of her brain to see she wasn't one of them, a different sort entirely, a liar, not very nice.

Marcy had always said her father was a nice person, just not ready to be a dad when Colleen was born. And when he'd finally turned up, when she was four and she'd visited him those summers he wasn't tree-planting, she didn't think he'd gotten any readier, though he *was* nice. He was always trying to give her stuff she didn't want or like: a hat made of straw, candles stuck in wine bottles, once a puppy that got sick. Nice didn't mean anything. Nice was just how you looked at it. If red was blue, it wouldn't make a difference, really, in what you saw. Seeing your father as God on a cotton-ball cloud or a guy in Toronto who never called you – just a perspective thing. You didn't get to have dinner with either of them.

Except now she did, when they both were home. She was hungry, and the sun was giving her a headache. It was possible that someone – a teacher, not Joe – had said not to go to the ravine, or maybe just not alone. She wanted spaghetti, the best of Joe's suppers.

Different ways of looking – he tried so hard to be nice to Colleen, but he'd ditched her mom when she was pregnant. Not so nice, not so . . . Christian. He said, "I care about what you care about, Collie."

Colleen shut her eyes. "I've been born for a long time. You only now care." She was talking to no one. By the pink slant of the sun, she knew it was nearly night.

Marcy had been right. Joe wasn't ready for anything, not even trash day. He'd met Colleen at the bus station the first day with a milkshake, tried to hug her and got milkshake all down her back. Her father was a very nice person, but that didn't mean much. It was just a way of seeing the world.

She heard the *shush* of the highway at last.

Joe

"COLLIE, HEY, LEAVE YOUR SHOES ON. I dropped a glass. I – "

"Colleen." She stood on her right foot, her left foot braced against the wall, the laces on the green suede sneaker half undone.

"Colleen, please leave your shoes on." Joe was crouching by the piano, a wet paper towel shredding in his fingers. He had liked that glass. "And why'dja miss dinner?"

"What do you have against my name?"

Joe sighed, put the gray wet lump on the parquet. "The N just slips away when I'm talking fast. You missed ratatouille." He swabbed at the floor, wet mixing with the shards. This didn't work too well, but he couldn't find the dustpan.

Colleen thwacked her unlaced shoe onto the floor. "You don't like my name."

"I like your name. It's yours, it's you." He pressed down on the paper towels, wringing a puddle onto the parquet. "Listen, I'm playing tonight, I've got to get going."

"It's because my mother gave it to me."

Joe pitched onto his knees. He had meant to reach for the glass glints near the wall, but she startled him and he toppled too fast, hard. "Why would you say that?"

"Because you didn't like *her* either." Colleen stepped on the heel of her untied shoe to get it off; then the other with her bare toes. She didn't have socks on. "Right?"

"Colleen, where are you getting this?" Joe looked at the sharp spots of light, at Colleen's naked feet, at her pinched mouth. "I never said a word against your mother."

"Yeah, you've never said a word."

His knees popped as he rocked back on his heels. "What do you want me to say?"

Her eyes glinted like glass. "Drew says to honour our mother and father –"

"Drew?" Joe wasn't really listening, fretting the paper to mush, pricking his fingers. He tried to remember the exact definition in *1001 Beautiful Babie Names* at Chapters.

"Drew says to honour is to know. She gave me my name."

"I'll honour it, I'll remember." He wanted to say that he would honour Marcy's memory, too, but that would sound too much like a lie. His memory of Marcy was thin as a summer dress, Baby Duck wine, vending machine condoms. "Who is Drew?"

Colleen tossed her hair down her left shoulder, smiling with only the left corner of her mouth. "Don't worry, he's someone *nice*." She started towards her bedroom.

"Just, I want you to . . . be careful." Once she had crossed the floor unflinching, slammed her door, he relaxed, until he saw the smudged blood on the wood.

They were the same blood type. He had a whole box of words and letters to clarify who he was dealing with. Late at night, when he didn't know what the fuck to do, he went page by page: birth weight, grades in kindergarten, eye test, blood type. No baptismal certificate, he was nearly positive. But it didn't matter, he couldn't imagine her from the documentation, could barely imagine her when she was in front of him. Maybe imagination was the problem.

He hadn't been able to imagine why independent Marcy was trailing him along the library shelves, the autoshop hallway, the soccer field. He hadn't noticed her puffy face, her refusal of a smoke. She was a party girl-friend and he wanted them to be party broken up. So he told her his band, no name yet, just three guys and a drum kit, was going to Montreal in his uncle's old van. They had a gig, sort of.

She'd nodded, sniffled, said, *Call me when you get back. We need to talk.* But it had been so much easier to forget about flunking trig tests, fighting with his dad, returning the van, calling Marcy. So he didn't go back, not for a long time. Even when she got his number, even when he sent her money, even when he was visiting and sitting with Marcy and four-year-old Colleen in the sweltering ball-room at McDonald's, they'd never really talked. He'd always been sorry, and he'd never imagined. He didn't think that made him any less of a douchebag, really.

Colleen

LITTLE KNOWN FACT: Colleen hated falling asleep when her father wasn't home. Of course he didn't tuck her in, or necessarily even notice that she was going to bed to say goodnight, but she liked him there at night. His breath, rustling pages, voice.

Colleen listened to her father. In one sense, he knew: she obeyed, mainly. The other sense of *listen* – that she heard his voice – she was happy to keep to herself.

Good nights, she lay awake after homework and teeth-brushing and laying out school clothes, and listened to what Joe was rehearsing in the living room. Through thin walls, his voice was light but not soft, smooth as a muddy path. He took hours to perfect a song, a verse, a bar.

When she was only visiting, when she didn't have time to get used to things, his tenor would get into her head and vibrate there. Now she didn't mind. Through the plywood and drywall, she couldn't make out the words, but the sound was edgier than anything he ever said, and stuck in her head in a way their conversations never did. Sometimes, she heard something wistful, a dreamy minor key. Those times, she could treat his voice as a lullaby, or at least it lulled her, and she fell asleep more or less peaceful, more than she might have been otherwise.

The nights he wasn't home, falling asleep took hours.

Joe

PEOPLE USED THE WORDS *holy fool* if you were thirty-two and still messing around with your guitar. If you wore stretched-out T-shirts with band names on them and played for free at parties while the only perk at your real job was a headset phone. If you couldn't afford cable or brand-name cheese, but you thought you were a musician. Joe accepted that, mainly. When he was on break from querying strangers about laxatives, and someone said, "How's the music?" he said, "Ah, you know how it is," which meant anything, so was safe. He'd looked up *holy fool* on Wikipedia and knew it didn't seem to mean what everyone seemed to think, sort of heroic, really. Probably Colleen knew what a holy fool was, or at least would've understood the Wikipedia page. She knew a lot, his daughter.

The bands he was in always broke up, or something less, something less violent than *breaking*, maybe *fell apart*. But there was always a friend's band that needed a second guitar, a wedding, a fundraiser, something in a bar with no cover – always a stage somewhere where he was welcome. Not his melodies, not his count-ins, but all right. If the lights were bright enough, he couldn't see the audience. He could pretend to be just fooling around in the living room, the same chords again and again, until they were perfect. If that was all, it was enough.

But there was more, after: beer and hugs and kisses. Of course there were reasons to go home: the 8-to-4 shift tomorrow, the shoes he'd spilled soup on, the cheap silver cross that he had found tangled in the shower drain, and what could he say to her? He kept listening to the chords in his head, kept drinking and feeling good and liked and talented. He didn't go home until drunk verged on hungover, and when he crash-landed on the couch, he left his feet on the floor.

The clatter of pans woke him, too early, in time for work. Colleen was at the stove when he swung through the kitchen door. She kept her back to him, pretending she hadn't heard the creak. His head felt inflated and rubbery, aching as if slammed against the floor. Finally, to her flagpole spine, he said, "There's this movie."

She turned, what he'd wanted, but then she winced. Joe could imagine his face ridged with pillow creases, too-long red hair standing sideways, bruisy bags under his eyes. The room spun. He wanted to sit, but felt the advantage of height.

"I was thinking you'd like it."

She shook her head fast and her braid almost flipped into the eggs. She looked tired, too. He knew it was exhausting to sleep unhappy. "I have things to study, I haven't time for entertainment." She reached to spatula the eggs onto plates.

He collapsed heavily into a kitchen chair, skidding it loud across the floor. He'd heard about the movie at work, or the bar, or something. He mainly remembered. "It's about – um, it's, like, the life of this saint, this woman in . . . like, the 1500s. I think."

"So, it's a choice between thoughtful Bible study with my cell, and two hours of Hollywood faux-spirituality?" She thrust a plate at his chest, two lonely eyes of eggs.

He set down the plate of black-edged whites. "But you can have both, can't you?"

"Drew says . . ."

He waited out the pause, staring at the gritty floor: bits of onion peel, a gray spider web, a flake of stale cereal.

"Drew says to avoid distractions."

"Drew is – *This* is . . ." He abandoned that comment, slouched lower and cut a yolk to watch it bleed yellow across white and black. "I don't know who Drew is."

"I'm learning from him about the . . . powers in my life." She was scraping up burnt shards of egg.

Joe had to be at work in forty-eight minutes. He couldn't do more than eat his breakfast and hold his head steady. He wondered if she felt happy about what she said. She didn't look happy. She picked up her plate, char and little else. Moving towards the hall, she paused and rested her oily fingers on the bone of his narrow shoulder. The touch was so sharp and fast that it was almost a pinch, but it seemed to zero in on the tense spot there, and her gaze was softer than her grip.

All she said was, "I will honour your request as a dutiful daughter. I will check the listings for an early show." She took her plate to her room. It was something.

Colleen

BY THE TIME THEY HIT the Mariah-Carey Muzak at the movie theatre, it had occurred to Colleen that she was being stupid, stupid in a very tiring way. The cuts on her feet hurt and before she lost it, the fake silver off the little cross had itched a crucifix rash into her throat. Joe was confused by the parking meter for five minutes before they could go inside. She was too tired to think of another plan.

They walked across the lobby, and Colleen thought: *Do I do it now? Toss myself to the carpet before the snack-girl smiles at him. What will he think? The thing about tongues is how does anyone know it's tongues? What if he thought I was having a seizure? Well, so, fine: hospitalized for glory, holy in a paper dress.*

How long can I writhe on the floor? How long could God speak through a girl? I don't know if I can lie any more. Lies are sins, too. My mother would hate this. How did I fuck this up? Why's he buying popcorn? We'll never eat it. If I don't fall now he'll get close enough to see the lie in my face. What do tongues say? Did Marcy ever believe in God? She didn't teach me enough words. What words did she love? Did she love my father, let him leave her? Why didn't she say something?

I wish I had a script. The words of God should be perfect. I don't want to shriek and thrash. I want to say beautiful things, just this once.

Her father walked fast, spilling popcorn, looking worried. Colleen spun away as he approached. "I'm going to the bathroom."

The bathroom was cold and smelled of cinnamon disinfectant. Colleen stood in the third stall. Her feet hurt and her throat hurt and she was so tired. This would be the last scene of this performance, and even now she needed a script. Colleen felt very young. Just a few years older, Marcy had had the world in her belly.

I want to say, I want to say . . .

Colleen pressed her forehead against the metal door. She could hear the perfect words in her mind, like the classroom words she was supposed to look up but never did – they were perfect as they were: *lambent, id, fulcrum, mercury, palatial.* Colleen fumbled in her purse for a pencil, couldn't find any paper. She was imagining how she wanted to sound. Smooth, elegant – like a melody. She did not want to mutter, twisting face down on the popcorn-scented carpet. She raised the pencil to the wall and began to write all the good words she knew, or sort of knew – *aerial, liar, Perspex, munitions, Galapagos, countess, illustrious, wire*. Stopped, thought for a moment, wrote more over the toilet paper – *taint, Toledo, dwarf, darn, coffee* – the feminine product disposal – *clavicles, lackadaisical, tree, direction* – the slide lock – *arboretum*. She wrote, *milk, calico, fury, endive, halo, zip, emery, lithe*. Crouching, around the hem of the door she wrote, *tinsel, bruise, munificent, remunerate, suicide, Maybelline, fortunate, dial*. She wrote until her brain spun, the pencil smudged, and shoes hammered heavy across the tile floor. She saw them stop under her wall of words, but she kept writing – *cascade, gelato, mirth, plebiscite, ennui, night* – until a thick, tired voice said, "You wanna come on out of there, ok? I wanna have a word with you about what it means to deface property, ok? Now."

Crouching surrounded by her script, Colleen surrendered to whatever surveillance cameras or omniscient God told security when kids wrote on the walls. She surrendered that scripting tongues wouldn't work. She stopped writing.

Without standing, without putting away her pencil, she reached up to slide the bolt, tipped sideways to open the door. Colleen looked up at a thick young woman in a blue security uniform, sky-blue blouse half untucked from navy slacks. She had nothing but a walkie-talkie on her belt.

When the woman didn't lunge for her, Colleen asked, "How did you know?"

The guard shrugged, tugging more shirt from her waistband. "Sometimes I just get a bolt, you know? A bolt from God."

"These are His words." Colleen jerked a thumb at the wall. The words went all the way up, from hinge to bolt. *Calliope, sugar, tandem, gloss, mistral, concubine, zeal*. Colleen didn't know how long she'd been writing.

"God writes on the bathroom walls? Huh. Could you stand up, please? Grafitti's a call-the-parents one." Colleen didn't want to stand. She put her cheek down on her knee. She could feel the pricks on her soles, painful, for such shallow cuts.

The guard was not small, so it surprised Colleen when she crouched to meet her gaze. Her eyes were very light brown, like beer or shadows on sand. Her light eyes travelled over the walls, over the beautiful words. "Congruent," she said softly. "Mica, Marlboro, toreador. Cardiac." On *cardiac,* she leaned closer, looked harder. Then she licked a finger, and smudged it through the *r*, the *d*, up into the *x* of *excelsior.*

"Pencil?"

Colleen shrugged. She was getting a cramp in her left thigh.

"Well. Well." She stared at the dirty wet floor. "Still vandalism," she gazed up ". . . but who hath heard such a thing? Who hath seen such things? . . . We gotta go call your mom and dad."

Colleen propped her chin up on her right knee, watched a pair of red boots stride by, then pink sneakers, plain black loafers. "My mom's dead," she said, "but my dad's out by the popcorn stand."

Joe

NOBODY LOVES A LONE MAN staring at a ladies' room door. Joe stood well back, but he was too scared to move out of view. The snack bar clock said twenty-four minutes. Could she have collapsed? Escaped through a window? Ascended radiant and immaterial into heaven? Other parents twitched their daughters closer, seeing him staring ravenous at the little lady symbol, clutching an untouched jumbo popcorn.

Joe knew God in the grace of his daughter striding across a crowded lobby. A miracle of a daughter, a sin by some standards, but a win somehow, anyway. A provisional victory: a woman in blue followed her.

When Colleen stood in front of him he had nothing to say. All questions, accusations, pleas dissolved before her sword-straight body. Her gaze was barely on him. She was looking at the point you punch for, that spot on the back of the skull.

"Who is Drew?" he asked finally.

"Drew is my study advisor." She was motionless. So was the woman behind her.

"I . . . Collie – you and . . . Drew study the Bible?"

"The world. The world is confusing and complex, and Drew – "

"Yes."

"What?"

"Yes, the world is complex and confusing. I was just agreeing with you."

"Oh. Ok." She shifted her weight, then again. "Wait. No. It is only confusing if we let extraneous matters distract us."

The guard cleared her throat. When they turned, she said slowly, "They that forsake the law praise the wicked: but such as keep the law contend with them. So I'm afraid you'll have to come with me. I've got to write this up."

She started towards the guest services desk without checking to see if they followed. Joe did. After a few paces, he looked back, eyebrows raised. Colleen caught up, light on her sore feet, and they went on together to the long blue desk.

"What did you do?"

"I wrote on the bathroom wall."

"What did you write?"

She slumped, almost leaning into his shoulder. Almost. "The words of God."

"Yeah, ok." Joe felt the burn of fear returning to his belly. He wished he had anything Colleen needed: strength, insight, advice, wit, anything but the stupid crinkling sack of popcorn still bundled in his arms like an infant. He couldn't even think of an appropriate question to keep her talking instead of staring at Ticketholder Privileges. The guard rummaged for a form. He whispered, "What words does God use?"

Colleen finally met his eyes, green to green. "The best words."

Joe inclined his head.

"I – I didn't know what words God would use. I don't know God. I just tried to guess, words that, words that sound good."

There was a crash of thunder through the theatre wall and Joe realized that the movie had started. It didn't matter; the posters in the lobby all looked holy-war bloody, and here, now, while the guard peered at her papers, there was a moment's peace.

Joe thought about God and had no answers, and his daughter was praying with a man who wasn't real to a God he doubted she believed in. Colleen didn't seem to believe in anything at all. Stop. He didn't know what she believed. Stop. He had never asked her. She was sad and Joe wanted her to have what made her happy, even if it was false gods or complicated mindfucks or imaginary friends. Stop. He had to ask her to know what she wanted. She probably wouldn't say, but that would be an admission, too

He asked her, "Did you write your name?"

Wall of Sound

J AMESY TURTLED INTO HIS HOODIE, the white earbud wire dangling from throat to pocket. He walked with big jerky steps, jostled people instead of excuse-me'd, jaywalked so cars screech-stopped. This was his way of being inconspicuous, blending in.

As he walked, Jamesy listened for birds. The nub of the white wire dangled in his empty pocket; he'd found the earbuds on a bench at the bus station. Without music to play, they did nothing at all: you could hear right through them, mainly arguments and traffic and the blind people's *beep*-beep signal. There weren't many birds in this neighbourhood – not enough trees. Just the twittering sparrows, cardinals sharper and higher, stupid moaning pigeons. His head ached a little, but nothing he couldn't handle.

His grandparents didn't have a driveway, just a walk. The daffodils were shrivelled onion husks, the asters tall and weedy. He'd have to mow again soon. He wouldn't mind, the vibration of the push bar, the gasoline and grass smell, the feeling he was helping. He wound the earbuds into his pocket.

The bell was still broken, and they never heard knocking. He could hear Ronnie Spector singing through the door, so sad, so loud. His grandmother had a surprisingly powerful stereo. He tried the knob. If they were home, it was open.

In the cool indoor dark, his grandparents were hunched at the dining table over the *Metro* Suduko, jousting pencils, muttering, "Six, there, no, *there*," in each other's ears to be heard around Ronnie's pleading. He was nearly onto the worn living-room shag before Emma turned. "Oh, *Jamesy*! Oh, and we haven't a thing in, just date squares, and the plums, and . . . Jim, put the kettle on. Yellow plums, Jamesy, very sweet, you like those. G'on, Jim, and turn down the stereo on your way."

Jim stood slowly, smiled slowly, shook Jamesy's hand in that grave, job-interview way he'd had since Jamesy turned fourteen, too old to hug. His granddad's pinstripe shirt was crumpled and looked misbuttoned, though it wasn't. He said, "She made you a new mixed tape, Jamesy. Good one, be sure she don't forget to give it."

To the old folks, his name was Jamesy, even though he was taller than they were, even though he smelled like a man, sweat and ash. Jim was his grandfather's name, and Jamie had been his own dad. Even though the man was long dead and even longer gone, Jamie was not an available name. And no one was called James; if someone loved you, they couldn't call you that.

Jim snapped the tape player's STOP and moved into the kitchen, muttering about caffeine in the afternoon. The sudden silence made Jamesy's headache pulse in his ears.

"It's barely past lunchtime, you don't need to sleep," Emma yelled, then said more quietly, "Lunch, Jamesy, did your mother make you something? I could make you a sandwich, easy peasy. Bologna? Cheese?" She pressed herself up on the chair back and shuffled across the carpet in her red embroidered slippers. Jamesy backed away without meaning to. He smelled, he knew he did – the city had finally got wise and turned off their water. He hadn't been able to find another place to shower yesterday or today, and he couldn't face not coming. She didn't follow his retreat, and Jamesy was relieved and sad both. If he mowed, it wouldn't be strange to ask to use the shower. He'd hug her goodbye.

"I'll get you a sandwich." Emma nodded, sharp and quick into her neck. She did not move very fast – arthritis, cataracts, cheap slippers – but still somehow she was through the kitchen door before he could stop her. He didn't stop her. He was hungry.

He wandered down the dark hallway to the wood-slat back porch. He'd never sit in front, that was like being on TV. Beyond the porch was the patch of lawn, then the razor-straight garden rows, the weathered shed. The tomato cages were dark with green leaves, decorated like Christmas trees with red and green and orange balls of fruit. The dill had flowered. Even in the yard, the birds were just occasional squeaks.

His grandfather came out and over to the vinyl cushioned swing. He sat slowly, bracing the seat with his palms until he was firmly on it. "Tea's coming, Jamesy. You're all right?" He patted the cushion. His nails were thick, opaque.

Jamesy sat down. His jeans weren't dirty, he'd had them under his mattress all week since the Laundromat, so he could sit on the furniture today. It didn't matter, they were outdoors, but it did matter, anyway. "I'm ok, Grandpa." He looked at his own ragged nails. They tore easily, like paper. Hart had told him it was because he didn't drink milk. But who drank milk? "How are you?"

"The lettuce's gone to seed, the dill, too, so I'm gonna quit weedin' them. Thistles getting in, anyhow."

"I'll do it for ya, Grandpa." Jamesy unbraced his feet to let the swing swing.

"Nah, s'all right. Mala said she'd do it, too, but s'not worth it."

"Who's Mala?"

Jim pointed at the property-line hedge. "Neighbour girl. Your age, real nice, helped out a time or two here. Pretty, very pretty."

Jamesy did not know the girl with the funny name. The hedge was short, but the neighbours didn't garden much, so there was rarely a head to be seen. Jamesy remembered from grade nine French that her name meant bad, evil.

Music came on inside. Jim propped his feet on a low porch rail and gazed out with a wide-stretched smile. "We did a good job this year, think?"

Jamesy stretched his own mouth. "I'll come out again in a couple weeks and we can turn it over then."

His grandfather glanced at him. "Not until then?"

"Well, sooner, too, of course." He hadn't planned that, but he could. Better than this Mala, whoever she was, evil, coming in and picking all the tomatoes.

A tray tapped his shoulder: skin-pink bologna on rye, pickles cut in half, soap-smelling mugs of Earl Grey. His grandmother, behind them, glaring. Jamesy took the tray so Emma had her hands free for balance as she shuffled to face them. "The boy is not the hired gardener. He's got school to worry about now. How's your year shaping up, Jamesy? Like your teachers?"

He set the food on the table and picked up the plate with the extra pickle, the thickest sandwich – his, he knew. He should've waited for her to sit, but didn't: teeth through soft bread, tomato, the slight resistance of quadruple layered meat. The sun slanted August in his eyes. No, not August, September.

"'Sall right." He chewed some more, trying to picture a skinny hallway with orange lockers, a heavy book with a rainbow prism on the front. "Physics looks hard."

A slap on the shoulder. "Physics! Smart boy, takes after me."

Jamesy had a bite of pickle, another bite of sandwich. He couldn't help eating too fast. He said, "Sure," with a mouthful of food.

"I could've gone to the university, you know. But you will."

"Of course you will." Emma was fidgeting with her pickle. "And if your mother can't . . . there's always scholarships, and we could help – "

Jamesy hated being helped. "I could mow behind the shed. Gettin' long now."

"Aw, you don't gotta . . ." Jim batted the air. "Sit for a minute."

"It won't take me long." Jamesy stood, still chewing open-mouthed. "I'll just run over the back up to the alley, take a shower, good as new." He back-stepped towards the stairs, jamming the last of the sandwich into his mouth.

"There's a new can a gas that's gotta be put in."

"I got it." Down the first step, chewing.

"Let him be. He's strong enough to lift that can on his own, now." Emma grinned. Her teeth were pale, ghost teeth, almost see-through.

He went past the caged tomatoes grappling with their bars, the seedy dill, and tangled cucumber vines. The grass was over the sides of Jamesy's sneakers. Time to mow.

The shed smelled of dry dirt and gasoline, and was a shock of windowless dark after the sunshine. *Birds.* Jamesy stared at the mower, the sack of fertilizer, and the wood-slat six-quart baskets. Birdsong surrounded him. A steady rhythmic *cheepcheepcheep* drowned out the rustling plants and distant traffic. *Birdsbirdsbirds,* shrill and deafening. Jamesy went deaf and still, waiting it out, the way he usually did.

Sometimes Jamesy would just be struck silent, surrounded by the ringing song of imaginary birds. He couldn't have said a word over the sound, could scarcely think. It was ok, he was used to it, it never lasted too long. The condition was something he might have inherited from his grandfather, Jamesy seemed to remember someone saying. Who knew, though, what others heard inside their own skulls? Who would know that Jamesy heard birds that weren't there? He never told Jim, or anybody. Jamesy knew the old man loved him too well, would've been distressed over the genetic dead weight he'd given him. So he kept his silence when he needed to, let people think he was sulky, or deep, or who knew what others believed.

The noise stopped fast that time, in only a few minutes, before Jim could come looking for him. Jamesy found the gas can and got on with mowing the lawn a smooth, even green. His grandparents watched and sipped their tea.

THE SHOWER WAS HOT AND STRONG. Yard sweat and city dirt sluiced gray down the drain. It felt good to be clean. He made sure he was polished pink before he wrapped himself in one of Emma's towels. The fuzz was almost gone, but they were deadly bleached. Jamesy thought about his blood pure as water, his head clear and focused.

Towel-skirted, he palmed a patch of the mirror clear and looked hard at the bruise around the rim of his left eye. Jim would never wear his glasses unless he was reading, and Emma was due for cataract surgery in October. After that, though, he'd be able to come less – a bright-eyed Emma would spot bruises in a second. He poked below his eye. It didn't hurt, just looked like the gray dirt that had washed down the drain.

He yanked his fingers through his wet blond hair and prowled out, still in his towel. When he'd come in from the lawn, Emma had yelled, "Oh, Jamesy, look at your clothes, filthy – toss 'em in the washer. No, no, it's no waste of hydro, we've got almost a full load ready. You'd think you'd learn to bring a clean shirt, every time you come here you get put to work. You haven't got a date later, have you?"

He'd only shrugged, only waiting for the itchless fabric, pine-scented and drier-warm on his skin, no girl in the universe as nice as that.

From the hall, he could hear the Mickey-Mouse squeak of the sped-up dubbing, and over it, her voice: "It'll be a bit, Jamesy. Guess you'll have to stay for dinner. Shucks darn." He couldn't tell what the sped-up music was. He went into the living room. Emma was hovering over the tape player on the sideboard.

"I'm making you another mixed tape – " she hit STOP " – to listen to while you study. It's all girl groups this time, Phil Spector wall-of-sound tunes, to block out distractions. That apartment of your mother's, it must get noisy with the traffic." She flipped the tape out, slid another one in.

"I haven't got a tape player, Grandma, I keep on telling you."

"Now, surely Rosalie would give you a little pocket money for one, they can't be much at Radio Shack."

He put his hand on her back, felt the gouge of bra into her soft flesh. "Radio Shack changed its name to The Source."

Jim yelled from the kitchen, "Mala has one."

"Jim, don't shout her name near the door, she'll hear." The chipmunk voices whirled again, click, pause, whirl. To Jamesy, she added, "Nice girl. Pruned our rose bushes for us one day, we didn't even ask her."

Jim came in and eased onto the couch.

Jamesy clutched his towel. "I woulda done it."

"You're busy. She didn't mind."

"Your grandmother made Mala a big-band tape. Mala said, too, that no one has tape players anymore, but then she found one."

Emma flicked open the player and handed him the tape. The plastic was warm in his hand. "She's got one of those ones you wear around your waist."

Jim smiled as wide as if he'd invented the thing. "Imagine that. Now she can listen to her tape while she gardens."

"Imagine that," Jamesy said. The room was suddenly silent as the drier shut off.

ON THE WAY BACK to the bus stop, Jamesy swung the sack of egg-shaped yellow plums, listened to the rattle of his new useless tapes in his pocket. He cut across a convenience store parking lot even though skaters were jumping off the newspaper boxes and the benches. He'd had a board once, nothing fancy, but he could do a few tricks. Well, he'd been learning. When he'd sold it, he'd found out his mom had bought it at Zellers, and he'd only got twenty bucks for it, and that only because the pawnshop guy thought he'd looked "so sad" when he'd realized the board was basically a piece of shit.

These guys tricked so fast and easy. He'd never been able to flick off the curb like that. Jamesy didn't want to watch. But he didn't want to go back to the squat, either, and watch Samir and Hart flipping plastic spoons at a silk top hat they'd found in the garbage. They'd eat all his plums in twenty minutes, chuck the pits in the hat, too.

Up and crash down. That blond boarder was impossible to injure, like a robot or an angel. His friends were yelling at him, hard and mocking, but Jamesy's ears were all birds. He realized that it had been like that for a while, that he wasn't hearing traffic or voices or the scrape of boards. His mind was inventing it all from inside. He did that sometimes. The blond guy left his board by a bench while he went back to the sidewalk.

The southbound bus was across the street, stopped at the light. Plenty of time for Jamesy to jog to the bench and scoop up the board. He jogged back just as the bus pulled up. The board felt as light and loose under his arm as if it were truly his. It was. The change for the bus jingled.

THE SQUAT had been a house before a defective popcorn maker burnt out half of it. Now, only a couple rooms had walls, and it was being torn down in two weeks, or two months, or something. No one really knew. Jamesy stuck the skateboard in the brambles that had once been hedges and went in where the door had been.

Hart and Samir were playing cards on the couch, sitting sideways to face each other. He walked heavily across the roofless hall so they would hear him and not be startled. Hart hated to be startled.

"Hey," Jamesy said.

Samir was facing the window. They were both all silhouette. "Where you been?"

"Grandparents."

Hart looked up sharply. Jamesy handed him the bag. Hart smiled wide, and popped in a plum.

Jamesy leaned on the back of the couch, testing his weight on it. The fabric was thin velvet, a light, twenty-dollar green. "What're'ya playing?"

Samir laughed through his nose, threw down the six of spades. "C'mon, you don't expect us to *tell* you."

Jamesy put his full weight on the back of the couch and tipped his body sideways until he was lying across it. "Don't actually care."

Hart turned so that they were face-to-face, breathing on each other. "Don't lie there, Jay. You'll break the back."

Jamesy was worried about Hart's tone, but he was tired from the mowing, the big meal, the sunshine. The couch, even the hard narrow spine of it, was comfortable.

Samir tossed out something diamonds. It fluttered onto the cushions, face down.

"I mean it – it's *deli*cate. Get off."

Samir laughed from down by Jamesy's toes. "'Cause this is classy furniture, goes with the end tables, beds, hutch – *Hutch*!" Jamesy looked at him. "'S a funny word. It is."

Jamesy closed his eyes.

Hart poked his thigh. "Don't sleep. Why are you sleeping?"

"It was hot today." Jamesy shrugged, which made him wobble a bit. He wasn't quite asleep when Hart grabbed his hip, and flipped him face down onto the floor. His palm crunched flat on a bug. A chemical smell coated his tongue. "Sleep in your own bed," Hart yelled above him.

Jamesy crawled over to his mattress. His palms and stomach were gritty. The shower had lasted him two hours. He pulled the cracked tape cases from his hip pocket, shoved them beside his mattress, and shut his eyes. He wasn't going to fight with Hart. He wasn't badly hurt, and he wasn't much scared of the knife Hart kept in his sock. It was just a little pocket knife out of one of those grabby-claw arcade games. But it was hard to tell what Hart would do, or why.

Maybe an hour later, Hart yelled, "Drag, Jay?" That was Hart's way of apologizing. Jamesy didn't need to open his eyes; he could smell the sweet-sweat smoke. He wanted a drag, only one, only weed. But no, he was clean now, inside, anyway.

He kept his eyes closed and breathed in wisps of smoke. He could hear the slap of cards, the whisper of cars. No birds. He slept, hot and shifting, until first light.

THEY DID SQUEEGEE STUFF on the Gardiner on-ramp at morning rush. It didn't work too well, but they made a few bucks, usually from scared out-of-towners. No one else really believed in squeegee kids anymore, it was so long since squeegeeing was cool. Jamesy remembered watching a music video in his mother's basement when he was in grade two. He thought the kids in the video looked happy enough, that he could do that. He did do that, but his head ached in the sun and his hands blistered from the blue cleanser and they barely made enough for breakfast.

When the cars thinned out, they went to Burger King and had Big Omelet Sandwiches. The cheese had squished through Hart's. "Fuckers. My way, my ass."

Samir snorted coffee. "Complain. Demand a new one, and if they don't give you one, *escalate* it to the manager." Samir had worked after school in a bookstore, back when he went to school.

"Eh, it's ok." Hart slipped his knife out of his sock and flicked it open to cut his sandwich.

Jamesy made like he was gagging. "Oh, nice. Very sanitary."

"What else dider G-ma give you? No holding out, eh, cash, cookies, what?"

"You saw me when I came in. Nothing."

"The hell? No cash? They're old people, what else they gonna spend it on?"

Samir laughed, he laughed at whatever Hart said, but he was actually watching the blond cashier lining up cleaning supplies on the counter. Jamesy remembered when he'd been a busboy: you weren't supposed to put poison cleansers on a food service surface.

"They're retired, on government money. Not much better than welfare, yo." Even Jamesy thought the *yo* sounded feeble.

"Old people got it good. But what I don't know is if they're holding out on you, or you on us? Which?" He set the cheese-streaked blade on the table.

"Nobody's holding anything. My gram's making mixed tapes again."

Samir actually turned his eyes from the girl even though she was leaning forward to wipe the countertop. "Like, hip hop?"

"No, like, actually cassettes, yo." He couldn't stop now with the *yo*. Hart was going to call him on it soon. Jamesy pulled one out of his pocket, rattled the spinners.

Hart took it. Grease prints appeared on the case. He flicked it over in his palm. "How you supposed to play this?"

Jamesy shrugged. He was having trouble finishing his Big Omelet, though it wasn't that big. "Dunno. She won't believe me that no one has a player anymore."

"Player, heh," Samir said. "Doan hate thuh playa, hate thuh game."

"Gotta find a player, gotta find one so we can listen to the *mixed tape*," said Hart. He flicked it hard against the table.

Jamesy wiped the fingerprints off on his shirt before putting it away.

HE MEANT TO GO BACK to his grandparents' on Thursday, as near as he could judge to "right after school," before Mala would be home, or anywhere near the garden. He meant to go help till soil, pick tomatoes, whatever he could think of.

But things came up. On Friday morning he woke up dizzy and forgetful, sore all along his ribs. He hauled himself up, went outside and puked in the hedge. Not much, just a Big Omelet and a couple plums, but a bad combination. He was careful to aim away from the rain-soaked skateboard. The alley spun, his head dipped and twisted, the taste of the plums was acid on his tongue. He wondered what he'd done, what he'd taken, who he'd gone with. He didn't wonder too hard though; Hart had ideas about what was good for people, and when Jamesy was feeling bad Hart could sound pretty convincing.

The last time Jamesy'd tried being in school, living with his mom, being a serious kid, they'd made him go to a social worker. Mrs. Kyte, shiny hair and a big engagement ring, mainly worked with anorexic girls. She said he was her "change of pace." He told her that his mother made him feel like he had no air in his lungs, that he was already dead, just like his dad. She said he had a tendency to be a bit melodramatic, to think things were worse than they were.

Jamesy had been mad about that, thrown his chair at the wall, said she didn't understand, banged the door back and run out. But after, he realized maybe he *didn't* know when things were so bad and when they weren't. Maybe lots of things that felt bad were really fine. And though he never saw Mrs. Kyte again, never went back to school again actually, he thought of her sometimes. Not very often, but sometimes.

It was hard to prove what was bad and what was fine. Life was just life. The board was safe under the glossy-leafed bushes, though the axels had started rusting. He pulled out his earbuds, plugged in, and set off stumbling. He nearly fell twice, then tried sliding his shoulder along the wall for support. By the time he realized that the brick would tear his shirt, it nearly had. The clean sun was warm on his dirty skin, though. Jamesy swallowed the vomit-sweet spit, breathed deeply, coughed, kept walking slow and shaky to BK.

Samir was drinking orange soda with his French toast sticks. Carly Simon was singing on the Muzak. Jamesy got the biggest coffee, a croissant, ketchup in a cup lid.

"Gag," Samir said when Jamesy set down the tray.

"Yeah yeah yeah." They sat in silence for a moment.

"You ok?"

"Sure."

"Last night – "

"Leave it."

"You have bruises."

Jamesy stopped chewing, a warm lump of greasy dough on his tongue. He tried to say *Where?* but it sounded like dough. He swallowed. "Where?"

Samir waved towards Jamesy's throat, as if he were afraid to touch him, as if he were electric, or biohazard.

"I was gonna go see the grandparents. Think they'll notice?"

Samir shrugged. Jamesy went to the washroom. A kid was being held up to the urinal by his father. The kid stared at Jamesy while Jamesy stared into the mirror at his throat. The bruises were big blue spots near the hollow of his throat. He couldn't remember last night's guy. He tugged out his collar and saw dark purple and yellow on his ribs.

He couldn't remember. He didn't care. He would find a shirt with a higher collar. He would wash his face. Nothing mattered: the bruises, the kid staring, the pain all over him. He could still go to Jim and Emma's. He felt well enough, now that he'd had coffee, food. How old was he when he could stand at a urinal for himself? Before that, who had held him? The water splashed burning ice on his cheeks, tricking down behind his ears. It was ok, ok ok ok ok.

"Dammit, Tyler, pay attention." The man dumped the kid onto the floor and stared disgustedly at his own wet shoe. Jamesy wiped his face on his T-shirt and went back to his table. Samir had eaten his croissant, all but the edge with ketchup on it. Samir said something that was probably an apology, but Jamesy didn't hear it, or the Muzak, or the manager when they were asked to leave because of Samir's shouting.

IT WAS EASY ENOUGH to keep his grandparents from worrying. He just said his mom didn't like them, so they couldn't call the house or visit. That wasn't even a lie, technically – his mother really didn't like them, since long before the divorce. He just left out that she didn't like Jamesy, either.

Their house was quiet when he got there, the door shut. He was wearing Hart's My Chemical Romance T-shirt, the only thing any of them had with the neck high and unstretched. Jamesy coiled the earbud wire into his pocket and went around back to work while he waited. Hart wouldn't like him sweating in his shirt, but Hart could fuck off. The grass was still nice and even. He didn't want to touch the garden without Jim. It was really time to turn things over, but there were still fat mint-coloured tomatoes in the cages. Maybe they'd ripen before the frost.

Jamesy's stomach clenched in on itself. He hadn't had anything to eat since the half croissant. He looked carefully until he saw a blushing fist-sized tomato hanging just outside of its cage. It wasn't very red, but it popped easily off its stem, and tasted of sun. He went into the shed chewing, and found the clippers. The hedges were getting scraggly.

When he came out, the sunlight made him blink blue dots. He was walking towards the wall, swinging the clippers in one hand, biting the tomato like an apple, juice running down his chin, when a head popped up over the hedge. A girl with a tight dark ponytail. He'd never seen her before, but his brain said, "Mala."

"Oh, hello, I thought I heard someone." Her voice was loud. The way she'd pulled her hair so sharply back made her pale forehead look huge.

Jamesy was chewing, so he couldn't really answer, only grunt.

"Are you the grandson, the famous Jamesy?"

He wished she'd called him James.

"They talk about you all the time, Jim and Emma. They're the greatest."

Jamesy thought she didn't probably need him for this conversation, that he could go and she would talk on. Still, she paused and he swallowed, so he tried, "That's nice."

She ignored him. "It's lovely what they've put into the garden. Great vegetables."

Did she spend all her time staring over the hedge? "Yes."

"Of course, it's a lot of work and they're getting on a little bit, but what are neighbours for?"

For staying in their own fucking yards.

"Hey, you got one of those homegrown tomatoes right there, eh? They're good enough to just eat straight, eh?"

Jamesy wished he was not carrying the tomato. Not because he felt silly, or because it was dripping stinging juice into his hangnails, but because the urge to throw it at her enormous forehead was so strong he was scared he would.

She opened her mouth to say something more, but instead came the high twittering of birds. Jamesy knew the sound came from his own broken ears, but standing there, staring at Mala's lips, it was more interesting to think that she was singing to him.

It was a while before she stopped talking and seemed to wait for Jamesy to respond. With someone else, he might have tried to say something he could not hear, something general and slippery. But he wanted Mala to go away and not bother him anymore, so he was content to watch her mouth not moving *birds*, then moving *birds*, then more, fast and angry, while the birds sang and sang. Finally she spun and ran off.

By the time Emma came out on the back steps and yelled, "Oh, my, Jamesy, what a surprise," the hedges were straight as bookshelves. "I made you another tape, the Ronettes, Jamesy, and we bought a new kind of freezer fries, with spicy batter. C'mon inside, Jamesy, and I'll turn the oven on."

Or something to that effect. She was speaking to him, warm and kind, smiling. He could make out a few notes of her voice through the fading sparrows. He felt better. He'd seen Mala slam away behind her own screen door twenty minutes ago and the hedges were perfect and Emma and Jim were there and nothing hurt. He could go and sit with them. His hearing was clear, well, clearing. He could. He went in.

"I hope you are staying for dinner, Jamesy, you'll really like Mala."

"Mala?" He could hear his own words better than Emma's. "I saw her in the yard."

"Your granddad and I invited her to dinner, to thank her for all the yardwork."

Jim shifted in his chair, reached across the table for the orange juice pitcher and poured a glass, gaze on the wall. He wasn't hearing a thing, Jamesy could see it.

"Mala's a pretty one, isn't she?" Emma was lining up condiment bottles.

"No."

She stared, batted absently at her gray cloud hair. She was so beautiful, he hated to disappoint her.

"Well, um, I only saw her for a sec."

Emma went back to tumbling frozen fries onto a cookie sheet. "You'll see she's a charmer. Jim, pop over and ask her to bring that little tape player, to show Jamesy." She waved him away without noticing that Jim didn't move, or glance at her. To Jamesy, she added, "These *Walk*man things, so fantastic. You'll love having one."

Jamesy sat down, suddenly boneless tired. The tomato acid burned in the back of his throat. "Sounds cool, Grandma, but I haven't got the cash."

"Maybe we could help . . . Jim, aren't you going?" She stared at her husband. Jamesy imagined sparrows swarming inside Jim's skull. Emma caught Jamesy's staring and stopped her own. "I put a couple Ronettes songs on the new mix. *Fan*tastic. 'Be My Baby.'" She opened the fridge humming and rummaged behind the door, bits of onion skin flitting down below it in the yellow light.

Jamesy was relieved she'd stopped on the help. "Fantastic."

"Oh." Mala appeared at the back door, unescorted, uninvited. "Hello."

Jim smiled. "Hello, Mala." Jamesy wondered if he'd heard his own voice.

"Good to see you." Mala spoke to Jim but she watched Jamesy as if he might swallow her whole. Her hair was slick to her skull like chocolate sauce. The hems of her cut-offs were neatly folded. To Emma, she said, "You know how I love the Ronettes."

Jamesy's mind spun like a nightmare, trying to remember music that was always in this house, as memorable as air. Emma was taking pinches of meat from three hamburgers on a platter to make a fourth. Mala was the dinner guest, he was the intruder.

Jamesy could remember a name, at least. "Phil Spector was the real genius."

Mala's smile stayed exactly the same, just became less real, as if her lips were propped over a mold. "Well, Spector helped them, but – "

"Well, then you know what I'm talking about." He didn't know what he was talking about. He didn't know why she would wear an elastic rainbow belt with an enormous beige plastic Walkman weighing it down from her waist to the top of her thigh. He didn't know why she was sucking up to his grandparents.

"Why don't you light the grill up, Jamesy?" Jim was hearing this – he must have been to interrupt. That was something. He handed Jamesy the long metal fire starter.

Emma thrust out the platter of four tiny burgers "And Mala can take the meat."

Jamesy had to run round Mala to open the screen door. They went onto the lawn. Nice mowing, nice hedges, Jamesy thought, but Mala didn't mention the yard, or the starlings in the trees.

"What school do you go to?" Mala clanked the platter onto the wooden slatted edge of the barbeque.

School felt like long ago. Blue cigarette smoke in the parking lot. He'd been a bear in *The Winter's Tale, A Winter's Tale*, whatever. No lines, no friends. "Westview."

"Yeah? I heard it's tough there."

"Yeah." He flicked the lighter, no light. Flick, no, flick, no.

"I go to Northern. It's far away, but really good. Lots of electives."

"Yeah." A thin blue smear finally spread out over the coals. He was sweating. He hated Westview. The bear suit was hot like he was hot now. He hated talking to teachers like he hated talking to Mala, he hated eating lunch alone in the caf. Mala probably spent lunch listening to the Wall of Sound on her Walkman. He hated Mala.

"I get a lot of homework done on the bus."

"Yeah." He didn't actually know anything about barbequing. He wondered if you had to warm up a grill like an oven. He wouldn't look at her, no matter what she said. He looked at the pink swirls of ground beef pressed flat by Emma's palms.

Mala was prowling around the barbeque. The plastic Walkman jogged with each left step and hit the metal clasp of her belt. *Tick* step *tick* step. "What sub – " *tick* " – jects do – " *tick* " – you like?"

Jamesy couldn't remember if he'd washed his hands after putting down the hedge clippers. He didn't think so. He tried picking up a burger with the shiny spatula, but was distracted by the clicks. The blade slid into the heart of the burger. "Music."

"Yeah? Really?" She took a step closer as he finally got the first patty onto the grill and smacked the loose pieces flat. It hissed a little, like a TV commercial for beef. The Walkman was tugging so hard on Mala's belt that the little hairs beneath her belly button were exposed, the red-pink line where the waistband had sat before. All that good music stored inside her stupid machine and she wasn't even listening to it, or the birds or anything. "I'm into music, too. I play viola and clarinet. I'm better at viola, not a natural reed player."

He flipped the next two burgers properly, proudly.

"Sometimes I play for your grandparents. They seem to like it."

An orange flame shot up when he put on the last burger. "I'll eat that one," he said, smiling at her as hard he could bear.

JAMESY ROLLED OFF HIS MATTRESS. Hart was watching, flicking the tiny blade of his knife openshutopen. Hart's eyes were red-veined from the chlorine at the pool. They'd discovered they could shower for three dollars at the community pool. Duck in, duck out, ten minutes, easy peasy. Only, Hart had started wanting to actually swim, lap after pointless lap, his Q-tip arms spinning in the blue water. Swimming wrecked Hart, he'd collapse on the couch at the squat, but still want to swim the next day.

Now Hart chucked a shoe at Jamesy, a brown loafer that he'd found in the locker room. Jamesy didn't know if he'd found it single, or if it had had a mate that Hart hadn't wanted to steal. It was hard to tell why Hart did anything.

It hit Jamesy just above his hip, one of the few soft places left on his body.

"What are you going to do?" Hart demanded. "Not squeegeeing?"

Jamesy looked at the shattered window. The sun was bright and tilted, probably about ten. They had overslept the rush hour, and anyway, Samir was still curled asleep, a river of glistening drool on his chin. No one was squeegeeing today, clearly.

"I wasn't – "

Hart threw something else at him, Jamesy didn't quite see it, maybe a balled up sock. It skimmed past his knee, across his mattress, and scattered the pile of cassettes by the wall. There had been maybe 10 Jenga'd there. Samir squirmed.

"What?"

Jamesy picked through the tapes, checking if any had chipped. They seemed ok.

"Why keep those?" Hart asked. "You haven't got anything to play them on."

"My grandmother gave them to me. She made them for me."

"You *haven't got anything to play them on.*"

Samir was flopping on his mattress like a hooked fish, but Jamesy stared at Hart. Hart had his uses. "This girl I know has one . . . ."

Hart smiled, his lips tight over his teeth. "A girl?"

"A girl." Jamesy put the last tape in the pile. He had nine, now that he'd counted. He'd never heard any of them, ever. "A bitch, really."

"Ah." Hart's smile dropped away as he flicked himself over the arm of the couch. "Wanna go see her?"

Jamesy nudged the corners of his nine tapes into alignment. "Yep."

Hart kicked Samir to get him up. Hard.

HER SCHOOL was way nicer than Westview. Carved stone, benches, and some sort of weird sculpture thing. They'd had to take the subway, then walk from the station. Hart was pissy, chewing open-mouthed on his McGriddle. "This it?"

Jamesy shrugged. He had four hash browns in his paper sack and he was trying to make them last, trying not to get ketchup on himself.

Hart flopped his hair around, disgusted. The sunlight made his freckles stand out like stones in a pool, hard and dark. "I thought you knew this chick."

"I know her, doesn't mean I got a fuckin' sonar on her."

"There's a field in back." Samir pointed. "I was here once, for badminton."

Hart gave him a shove. Samir laughed. "It was grade *nine*, the fuck did I know?"

The sun was past noon. Behind the school it was lunchtime: kids in the bleachers and on the grass, eating, yelling, playing Frisbee. Jamesy wondered which kids were cool. He didn't really know how it worked — even when he was in school, he was never in school. Jamesy guessed Mala wouldn't eat outside, probably had no friends to eat with. She'd probably eat in the library trying not to get mustard on the books.

Maybe she was all right, maybe she'd stop gardening, disappear. Maybe he didn't hate her. His mother wore cutoffs, sometimes. Sometimes when he was little his mother would make oatmeal from oats in a pot on the stove. It was better for you if you didn't do it in the microwave and she'd put the bowl down in front of him and kiss his hair.

He thought about that for a long time, until the sun tilted and there was less noise on the field, then less still, and dark blue shadows from the trees. Samir and Hart were sprawled on the grass, smoking. The hem of Hart's jeans was rucked up and Jamesy could see the outline of the round knife-case in his grayed sweat sock. They'd been there all day, it seemed. Then he spotted Mala walking across. She was wearing normal blue jeans, the clip of the Walkman hooked onto the fabric, big black earphones over her hair. Hart and Samir were smoking and staring at prettier girls. Mala moved towards the empty part of the field behind the bleachers, where no one could really see. Hart and Samir wouldn't have noticed her if they hadn't noticed Jamesy staring. Hart nodded, waiting. "That her?"

Now that there were fewer kids outside, Jamesy could hear birds in the trees. Or not in the trees. He wasn't sure – it sounded like the screech and squawk of crows, but more ordered, like a drumbeat. Anyway he didn't see any crows weighing down the top branches of the trees. He looked and listened for a long moment, until Hart started to fidget. Then he nodded, said, "You can cut the cord if you have to. I got my own earbuds."

At least, he thought he said that. He felt his lips move, but he couldn't hear the words. Hart and Samir stood. Mala kept walking, her small dark head lowered.

Kids These Days

JAKE WAS LICKING FROOT LOOP SILT from the bottom of his bunny bowl and Marley was dissolving a paper napkin in her mouth. It was the first snow day of the year, all of us still wearing flannel midmorning – Jake in SpongeBob, the baby in a rosebud-pink sleeper, me red-plaid boxers. Raeanne was eating strange cereal in another house in a nicer neighbourhood, but I could perfectly imagine the clingy white cotton of her PJs.

Jake let his bowl thunk to his placemat, knocking over the salt. "What do we do now, Daddy?"

"Now we . . ." I could see the computer looming through the living room door, files heaped beside it. I had promised Rae, across town and cellphone towers, that I would call a new ophthalmologist for Marley, do some research on the internet. Marley faced me, munching her napkin, seeing nothing. It was easier to go back to bed with only the baby present. "Now, you play quietly while I get some work done."

"What umma gonna play?" He was licking his palm.

"Um, maybe you could play in the snow. It is a snow day. Go outside?"

"By my*self*? In the *front*? By the *road*?"

Who had taught him this outraged alarm for his own safety?

A hiccup cough from Marley. Jake flopped onto the floor while I turned to her. There was a froth of paper pulp on her cheeks, probably more down her throat. More coughing – pink blotches of panic on her cheeks. I picked her up as her eyes went watery, her mouth wide. Could the paper choke her before it dissolved completely?

Jake kicked up at the underside of the tabletop. "Whadda we gonna do? <kick> Do? <kick> Do? <kick> And when's Mommy coming back?"

Wail. There we go. At least she wasn't choking. I clutched her heaving body closer and let her shriek in my ear. "You'll visit her on the weekend, right? You know that." And then one of Jake's kicks jarred the bunny bowl into the air, to shatter on floor.

Marley's sobs caught in her throat. Jake sat up fast and scared. "I'm *sorry.*"

"Fine. It's fine. We're going to go visit a friend of mine. Put your clothes on."

THE MARCH through the snow was dismal. The buggy's thin wheels wobbled over every lump of snow, salt, ice, and Jake whined unintelligibly through his scarf. But it was worth it when Pho-Mi 99's glass door jingled open and my glasses steamed. I could smell fish sauce and cilantro, hear Koenberg's rusty mutter.

Even at 10 a.m. there were customers – Pho is breakfast in Vietnam, Koenberg always insisted, though he compromised to include Westerns and bacon, too.

The customers were unhappy ones, snow-day'd teenagers standing awkward while Koenberg stared over the hostess podium at them. He was tossing and catching a fat red tomato, waiting for a bad comedian to take the stage.

Jake, somewhere in his hood, squalled "Da-ad." I put a palm on his head and tried to shove down his hood, but the tie caught his chin.

The old man yanked a menu out of the taller kid's hand. "I remember you – three months ago, you ran out while the girl was behind the bar, forgot to pay for the spring rolls, two cokes. And your friend – " dark greasy ringlets below gray toque " – the beef ball soup." Koenberg had a mug-shot memory, at least for the dine'n'dash set.

"I don't know what you're *talking* about," said the little one, leaning against the hostess podium. He seemed to be trying to get into Koenberg's face, but he was a head too short. "We just wanna get some omelettes."

"Yeah," was all the bigger kid managed.

Koenberg rounded the podium, careful not to brush their giant basketball jackets. "I don't know *why* you'd wanna come back, food not worth paying for can't be worth eating, either." He swung open the glass door with a merry jingle. "Pho-Mi 99 is closed to you. Shall I phone the officers or will you eat elsewhere?"

The little one looked around, eager for an audience, but Marley was asleep, Jake couldn't see past his hood, and I was Koenberg's biggest fan. I polished my glasses.

"Ah, fuck this." The little guy headed out and his companion followed, knocking against the podium, sending the menus sliding.

Koenberg tidied up without even a sigh. "Eh, Theo." He saluted, then looked down at Jake. "This one's new. How's the girl?" He came over to the buggy with the tomato, which he waved over her head like an incantation. "Gotta get her used to vegetables, else she'll be a picky eater."

I kicked out the brake from the buggy wheel. "I told you, man, she's too young to eat anything, and she can't see. She's blind."

PHO-MI 99 HAD NEVER HAD A REVIEW, or a full house, or light bulb of less than 100 watts, but truly, it was something. Beyond the purple "Persian" rugs and the Mix 99.9 ambience, there was the clearest, richest pho this side of Dien Bien, weightless glass noodles, rose-cream red tea. Of course, a lot of the diners were kids who didn't appreciate anything, who thought congee was a funny word, fished the petals out of the red tea, dine'n'dashed. I, on the other hand, was working from home while my wife was living in a sublet and regretting my failure to love her with any certainty. Her words. So I had plenty of time to eat Vietnamese food and talk about it, or anything, with anyone who wanted to talk to me. And Koenberg liked an audience.

We wheeled Marley into the steamy warmth of the kitchen and I unwound Jake's scarf, jacket, sweater. As fast as he was free, he twisted out of my grasp and squawked, "It smells like noodles. Are we going to eat?"

"Who you got, Theo?" called Koenberg.

"Are you cooking? Can we eat that?" Jake went straight for the slick floor underneath the kid-sized pot.

Koenberg didn't crouch to Jake's eyeline, just bent a little, one hand extended. "I'm Koenberg. What do you eat?"

Jake thought a second before putting his paw into Koenberg's. He was big for his age, but Koenberg's hand spanned up to his elbow. "What do you got?"

"Ah, just like mine – hungry, no judgment. Kids don't change much. Sit there, boyo, 'fore I knock something on you. I'll get you some dumplings."

"We're not eating, Jake, we're just here to visit. You've got kids, Koenberg?"

"You go to a restaurant and don't eat? What's the matter with you? Sit down, try the new brand of wrapper – don't seem great to me. And I got *kid*, one, that I know of."

I hesitated, hovered, sat. Jake jumped, apparently for joy. I was happy, too – I knew those dumplings, at least with the old wrappers. "Really, you're a dad? You did this, too?" At that moment, *this*, parenting-wise, amounted to kicking Marley's buggy occasionally to make it wobble, but she wasn't complaining.

"Another Jakey, even, just like yours. Well, bigger, now. Anyway, that – " he pointed at my wet sneaker jammed in the pram wheel " – I've never done."

"I want a dumpling." Jake didn't know what a dumpling was, I was quite sure.

Koenberg lined up the bowls with one hand, already ladling from giant pot with the other. "Teenagers go through a phase when they think thievery is rebellion . . . hell-*air*-ee-ish." He flicked something green into the bowls. "They just don't wanna pay. They're not rebelling against nothing."

"Your boy was a hoodlum? Is?" It was hard to tie bloodshot Koenberg in his soy-spattered apron to a wife and kid, a house. He looked as though he slept beside the stove.

"Eh, mild one. Not mucha me in 'im – can't slice a shallot without blood. Got his own gifts, I guess, whatever they are."

"Is a dumpling sweet?" Jake was trying to climb onto the bar stool by belly flopping onto the seat. His skull tapped the counter. I tugged him upright, watching Marley kick at her invisible dreams. It was hard to keep an eye on both kids, the boiling pot, all of Koenberg's knives. The kitchen had never looked so dangerous before.

"Could be sweet, usually isn't." Koenberg slid over bowls of soup and dumplings, wraps so thin I could see the dark spiderweb of herbs inside. "I hear in the Midwest they do a thing with apples that I want no part of." Koenberg waved his arms. "Eat."

We ate: delicate dough overstuffed with pork and sprouts and cilantro, perfect.

"These are fine, Koenberg. Nice thin wraps."

"Bup," said Marley. I scooped her out of her buggy and gazed into her blue eyes.

Koenberg glanced at the baby. "What's the kid want?"

"She's a baby – who knows what she wants?" She was waving her arms upupup. "The moon? The ceiling fan?" "She couldn't see the fan to reach for it, though I believed she knew it was there.

A dumpling flopped off Jake's spoon and splashed into the soup.

"Gwan, fingers never killed anyone."

Jake grabbed a dumpling like a bear catching a fish.

"You let your Jake do that?"

Koenberg shrugged. "He wants to eat with his hands, he's too big to stop. I hope he don't do it on a date. I want him to move out of the house at some point."

"Admirable wish."

"Not to hear Lorelai tell it. She thinks he'd perish without her to cook and clean." Koenberg was staring out the tiny window above the sink. Nothing was moving out there except falling snow, a Finch bus and insufficiently dressed skatepunks. The world looked paused, frozen. If I made the doctor's appointment, then I could call Rae again and try to "really talk" but I wanted to wait until the skies cleared. In the thick weather, good news felt impossible.

Jake was singing the school-bus song, a sign he was getting full.

"You can take the Transformers out if you want."

"'Kay." He dove for the bag under the pram.

"Careful!" No real danger, but I felt limp with the snow and steam, unable to cope with almost anything. "Your wife cooks, too?"

"Not *too*. She cooks how she cooks, and I do how I do it."

"She doesn't cook Vietnamese?"

"No, she does not. But also I cook to *cook*. You burn down the restaurant, outlaw the production of the Pho, I'll get a little speakeasy going out behind the gas station within the week. It's not like the cooking you do when people gotta keep up their strength and it's suppertime."

Jake muttered over his square-headed monsters. I loved it when he talked to inanimate objects – it was so *kid*.

"Listen, today's not gonna be high volume even if God himself tells people to eat Vietnamese. You wanna move in the new chairs? I gotta watch the shop."

"Sure, Koenberg. You got new chairs?"

"Police auction. Van's in the alley." I plopped Marls back in her pram and she bleated, but contentedly. Jake slammed an Autobot against the tile and a limb popped off. He didn't cry, though – robots could re-attach bits, or do without them. When Cassandra the tiger lost a leg in the car door, it was a different story – he knew mammals don't grow new legs. Smart kid. Koenberg handed me his keys.

I put on my coat, fidgeted with the buggy. "Koenberg, watch the babies?"

"Hey! I'm not a baby!"

"Watching, watching. White van." He handed me a fistful of

keys, went back towards the chopping block. Jake glared as I went out.

It was more truck than van, gray under the snow-white snow, which was still coming down like an avalanche. The rollup door reluctantly rolled to reveal a half-dozen cream leather bar stools. Very disco – I wasn't sure how they'd go with the plastic chopsticks, chili sauce, purple rugs. I hauled one up the steps, perching it in the slush while I opened the door.

Inside, my glasses steamed away the dirty kitchen. All I could hear was Mix 99.9 storm warnings, the rat-tat-tat of the French knife, and Koenberg's voice saying, "Of course, some people would stick chives in a recipe that called for *shallots*, but those people buy knives at Ikea. Great, Theo. Jakey, get the rag from under the bar and wipe the chair before he puts it down." Jake took off running through the swinging door. "You, Theo, put it behind the bar, where no one'll slip."

"Yes, sir." I pushed through the dining room door and Jake flew at me, rag presumably in hand. I was only making out light and dark through my steamed lenses. "Wait until I get behind the bar, ok?"

"Mr. Ko'berg *said*. And it's *drip*ping."

"Jake, just – " The front door chimed and a big somebody came in, blotting out most of the window light. A smaller body followed, in a puffer coat so voluminous it could've been either gender. "Some weather, eh? I'll get someone to get your order."

They didn't answer. My glasses had cleared, finally; they both wore ski masks, the big guy with a Leafs logo low on the forehead, almost between the eyes. The mouth was on his chin. Creepy.

Jake suddenly dug his fingers into my upper thigh, which startled me enough that I dropped the chair, which in turn startled puffer coat enough that his hand flailed to his chest, spasmlike.

Leafs grabbed the hand. "Easy . . ."

"I'll just get someone . . ."

Leafs smiled through his mask. "Ok then." Puffer jammed his elbow into his companion's oblique muscles. They were waiting for me to go, but Jake was now on the floor, carefully polishing the chair even as the slush dripped into the rug. The radio was talking about a very inexpensive vacation package.

"Koenberg." I wanted him to come out without me having to leave Jakey with the creeps. I wanted Marley, too, but I couldn't think how to get her. "Hey, Koen*berg!*"

Puffer didn't like shouting – his hand flew back to his zipper and pulled out a gun.

"Shit."

Jake looked up at me admonishingly. I tried to grab for his hand, missed.

Puffer waved his weapon, and said, wool-muffled, "Empty the register."

"Um . . ." was my only stalling technique. Koenberg still did not appear as I stepped behind the bar. "This isn't my place, I don't know . . ."

"Do it." Even through the mask, I could see Puffer's scowl. The other one was fidgeting; the silent muscle. The register looked as complex as an electron microscope.

A little too pleadingly, "I'll send the kid in the back, ok?"

"I'm not a kid!" Jake polished harder.

"Jake, you're six, you're a kid. Go in the back."

"No, don't go anywhere. There's a phone in the back, right? Stay still, *kid*."

Jake froze, clutching his rag, glaring at me.

"Can he come behind the bar with me, then?"

"Theo, who are you *talking* to?"

Koenberg. Good. Knowing the old man, he might have a gun of his own. "Jakey, here, now." Finally, he scurried over. His head didn't clear the bartop, which made me feel a little better. I wondered if Marley was awake, if she'd sensed the strange shifting in the air. I wondered if Rae, snowbound too, straightbacked and pajama-clad at a foggy window, had sensed it.

Enter Koenberg. No gun – tomato. Damn.

"Oh, fer fuck's sake, what's *this*?"

"We're robbing your restaurant, dude." I remembered them suddenly, the dashers. If Koenberg did, too, he didn't betray it, examining his lipstick red tomato, the picture of cool. "Come. *On*," said Puffer, but it wasn't clear to whom.

His partner answered: "Shut it. Be cool."

Jake was climbing the bar shelves like a ladder, trying to see over. His boot kicked a glass ashtray: smash.

"What the fuck?" yelled Puffer.

"Oh, that's right, bust up the place," yelled Koenberg.

"Ehhhhhaaahhh!" yelled Marley. It was so good to hear her voice.

The gun wavered crazily. "That a siren? Fuckin' silent alarm!"

"It's not a *siren*," said Leafs, but Puffer was already out the door. Marley segued into full-blown sobs, heart-rending even from the kitchen. The big guy bolted after his partner, muttering, "Fuckin' moron."

"What *hap*pened?" Jake wailed. The door jingled shut.

"Hell if I know." Koenberg set his tomato down on table four.

I sprinted towards Marley, dragging Jake by the paw. I wanted all children on my person right then.

Marley was red with fury and steam, but fine. I clutched her close, tears soaking my shirt.

Koenberg came in. "Well, no losses, except the ashtray. And there's a law against smoking now, anyhow. We're closed, locked up. I'm done." He slumped onto the old stool. I'd never seen him sit before.

The kitchen still smelled like lemon steam and crushed cilantro. It felt good to be warm and quiet for a moment. "You gonna call the cops, Koenberg?"

He slouched forward, a tent without poles. "Dunno. Gimme a sec."

Just a second with just the bubble of soup and the burble of Avril Lavigne before Jake said, "Can we go home and watch 'The Price is Right'? I think it's on soon."

I lugged Marley over to the wall phone. She was damp, but quieting to a whimper. "We'll go in a sec. You want me to call the cops, Koenberg?"

"Eh?"

"Koenberg. 9-1-1?" I had the greasy receiver off the wall, ready.

Koenberg waved at the receiver in my hand. "Let's just pretend this was a non-event, ok?" he said sadly. "Jakey's already saying I'm too old to be running this place."

"I don't think you're old."

"Other Jake, kid. My boy. Save me the embarrassment of telling him, if no cops."

"No embarrassment for you – they ran from a tomato and a baby, after all." Marley's warm melon head rested in the hollow of my chest. "I should call my wife."

"You got a wife?" Koenberg straightened a little. "You never say."

"I don't, so much. Have a wife. But, what little she's on the books for, I think it's near-death experiences. Really. Right?"

"Eh." Koenberg wobbled his head, an undecided nod. "Maybe. Sure. If you want. You won't catch me callin' Lorelai right now, no. But I can see as you'd want to."

There was a *thunk* from outside. Koenberg and I looked at the door at the same moment. "Did you leave the van open?" he asked hoarsely.

"Shit. I thought I was going right back."

We sat in grim silence for a moment. Finally Koenberg said, "Maybe kids *are* newer models these days. *This* sort of bullshit I've never seen."

Koenberg sighed and went over to the big silver fridge. He opened it and picked through a pan until he had a fistful of hearts, livers, necks. Then he went and opened the fire door with his clean hand. I could see blowing snow, clear blue icicles on the railing.

His voice boomed: "Outta the truck. I can see you. It's a barstool, right? I don't think you can sell it anywhere. I wouldn't envy you trying to haul it through a blizzard."

Jake was trying to reassemble his broken Go-Bot. This was new maturity; usually he'd just wait for Rae to do it.

"Yeah, yeah, you got a gun. Me, I got a restaurant to run." He heaved back his gelatinous handful and whipped it overhand out the door. I was too far to hear the splat, if there was one. Then nothing; Koenberg slouched against the door frame, wiping his bloody hand on his apron. Marley and I went over beside him and the three of us stared out. The alleyway was bridal white, the open white van like an igloo. I was expecting red and maroon splattered around, but there was nothing – the offal must've only hit the kids, or gotten buried in the snow. Standing half in the storm, half in the kitchen made my glasses steam again, clouding the snowy alley into a bright white haze, shadows and shapes all white as heaven. I knew this could be, must be, the world as Marley saw it.

Tech Support

i. Tech

CLINT STAYED UNDER URSULA'S DESK, staring at the green glow of the power bar light. After a while her yelling and spike-heeled stomp on the carpet ceased, as if she was thinking things over. Clint didn't need to see to know her hands were fisted on hips, legs planted wide. He thought he could feel her glare on his spine while he hunched over the CPU, fiddling, not really working. Finally she hammered off down the hall.

The screws on the old adapter were bent and wouldn't turn smoothly. It didn't help that he was coming at it from an odd angle, jammed under the desk, and that his fingers were slick with sweat. He heard rustling above him, but kept on with the screws – Ursula wasn't capable of making so little noise and no one else was out for his blood. When he'd finally gotten the broken plug off, it only took a few seconds to put on the new one. The shiny puffin emblem caught the light that filtered down between the desk and the wall.

When he pulled back to sit in front of the desk, Anna was sitting on the floor next to him. Her ankles were tucked under her thighs, a mug in each fist. She held out the left one, pale beige, the way he liked it. "This one's yours."

He took the scalding ceramic in his hand without thinking, and had to set it down on the carpet to grab the handle. He sniffed. "You make this?"

"Had to. Luddock's hungover."

She took a sip and smiled forcefully, like an advertisement, so he did, too. The coffee was thin and opaque and nutty – good, for office coffee.

"'S great," Clint said. "I guess Ursula misses out on this."

"What was that all about?"

Sitting on the floor across from her, Clint could quite clearly see Anna's panties. They were navy. He tried to concentrate on her face. "What?"

"Ursula. I heard her come storming out of here."

"Ursula storms to the bathroom. You're working up here today?"

"Just an hour or so. A couple new monitors in Creative. But what happened . . . ?"

"Oh. I. I wasn't . . . She thinks I work too slow. She wanted you, I believe."

"Ah. This was the monitor adapter?"

"Yep." He opened his damp palm to reveal the dented plug and warped screws.

"Well, that's ruined. What'd she do, kick it?" Anna grinned into her mug.

. Clint didn't smile. "Looks like." He pitched the thing over his left shoulder as he stood up and was pleased to hear it ping into the wastebasket. Then he collapsed into Ursula's ergonomic desk chair and started checking screen settings. "Fucking Ursula."

Anna pulled her cup away from her lips. "Don't let her get to you, Clint."

Clint kept his eyes on the screen – the resolution was off and he wanted to reset it and reboot before Ursula stormed back. "She said I'm a worthless tech tool."

"She's got Dallas next week," Anna said quickly. "She's pressed." Anna gazed at his coffee cup. "Don't you want this?"

"It's too strong to drink fast." He reached down and hooked the mug handle with his left hand, still mouse-clicking with his right. "Luddock's got to get it together."

"Buck up," Anna said softly, face still pointing towards the floor.

Ursula's computer wallpaper was a Rothko painting, bright rectangles dotted with icons. It was hard to tell how the screen read on it. "This look all right to you?"

"It looks like a sunset." She stood up then, pressed her hand down her thighs, smoothing her skirt.

He hit RESTART and stood up, too. He wanted to be taller than her again. "You think we should have an intervention for Luddock?"

She slouched onto her left hip. "Yeah."

"You coming?" He extended his arm and she twined hers around it. They went everywhere like this, from cubes to assignment to lunch to elevator. Anna was just an arm-linker. People made assumptions, but Anna didn't notice and Clint didn't mind. He'd learned to take what he could get.

LUDDOCK WAS SITTING cross-legged on Clint's desk. "Whatja fuck up?"

"I didn't. What did you get into last night?" Clint put his mug down, rolled his chair back, sat. A rubber chicken was lying on his filing cabinet. He hadn't put it there.

A raised-eyebrow leer. Luddock started unfolding his stick-figure legs. His left loafer tapped Clint on the sternum. "Sorry. I heard Ursula shrieking at you."

"No big thing. She's just – "

"Madly in hate with you, I know. Could be a cover for lust."

"She doesn't even know my name. She has no specific emotions related to me. She just likes to yell."

"Yeah, yeah. If she makes a move, I say screw the corporate ladder . . ." Luddock went into his own cube but kept talking, the sound undisturbed by the fabric wall ". . . and go for it. Worth any Tech job, hellion like that."

"I'm glad you costed it. Listen, what time are we meeting the cab tomorrow?"

"Six, as discussed." The squawk of the springs in Luddock's pre-ergonomic chair.

"So early? We're gonna be sitting around with social committee."

"You're too new – you've never seen this place get non-denominationally down to celebrate the birth of Christ. The open bar gets less open every year. This time it's only the cocktail hour, not after dinner. Cheap bastards."

"It's to keep people from driving drunk."

"You buy me a car, then we'll worry about that. Trust me, the free dinner does not pay for dry-cleaning, let alone the cab."

"And . . . Trinity?" Clint couldn't really say the name without blinking a couple times, it seemed so likely that Luddock had made her up.

"She's driving from work. She's worried about traffic making her late."

"It's cool if you don't have a date, you know. I haven't got a date, Anna hasn't – half the department's stag."

"She'll *be* there, she might just be late." Luddock just went back to clicking and Clint rolled back to his station too, and there was silence and they both got three-quarters of an hour of work done before Luddock said, "Anna's not bringing someone?"

"You knew that. She said it before the Oracle meeting on Thursday."

"Yeah. But, I thought she was, like, kidding."

Clint stared hard at the cloth wall that separated his desk from Luddock's. "Yeah, weird." Anna and Urusla. Weird. Clint wondered, if he told Luddock, would he be crude about it, or would he have something wise to say. Luddock was often unexpectedly wise, and often not. And Clint didn't know if he could even tell the story, if it even was a story.

There was the click of three or four keystrokes, another chair creak, then, "She's not . . . she's going with *us,* right? She's not going *with you,* right?"

Clint sent pages to print before setting his forehead on the mouse pad. "Yeah."

"Ah." Resettling of weight. "*A priori* it didn't seem likely, but I thought I'd ask."

Already a week ago, just a glimpse. Still the memory unfurled inside his eyelids like an epic: in the parking garage, in the stairwell just above Parkade C, he saw Anna's hip pressed awkwardly against the railing and Ursula's fingers against Anna's jaw. Just a moment, before Ursula raised her eyes to his face, and made him skitter up the stairs.

"I'm gonna go bug her while she's on helpdesk. Wanna come, Clinty?"

Clint knew that Anna was probably waiting for him to come ask about the rubber chicken, so he didn't. He put it into the drawer with the other toys that had turned up in Tech: water guns, Beanie Babies, Kinder Surprises, Nerf balls. He wondered if he would get any more if he stopped asking about them.

"Nah, I'm gonna work on the Firefox presentation."

The rumble of chair wheels stopped. "No one cares about Firefox, Clinty."

"They care about pop-ups. I can just do a quick PowerPoint – "

"Clint, Clint, Clint. No. One. *Cares. No one* is going to switch, because it's too much effort. It's too much effort to listen to the presentation."

Clint opened his notes on consumer-protection features. "It's going to save aggravation in the long run . . ." A rubber band shot over the partition. "Luddock, you know I'm right."

"You're right, you're right. I'll get you a notarized letter to that effect if you don't disrupt the meeting trying to make things slightly more efficient for, like, four people – "

A Pearl eraser tapped Clint on the neck and half a dozen paperclips rained onto his hair. One fell into his mouth and he had to blow it out before he could speak. "Hey – "

" – and *piss off* everyone else in the meeting to the point where they're jerks to *all* of Tech for the next *month*, 'cause they can't remember – " a tissue box knocked Clint's jar of pens onto the floor " – which of those fuckheads made that *useless* presentation."

Clint let pens roll onto the floor and started writing about tabbed browsing.

"Clint, are you listening to me? Clint, if you make that presentation, so help me god, I will wrestle you to the floor before you get past the first pixilated fade. Clint?"

Clint gazed at the air above his screen, thinking about pixilated fades and the futility of PowerPoint. Something cracked hard across the bridge of his nose. *"Jesus!"*

"Clint? Just close the file, ok? Close it and work on something that matters."

"You threw a calculator at me, Luddock?" All kinds of extra *B*s were inserting themselves into his speech – *Yoob threwb ab* . . . His screen had gone static. So had the walls and air.

"I've got a desk set, kid. I've been here longer than you. I can take you *down*."

A blotch of sunset red appeared on the beige desk. "I'm down." *Ib dowb.*

"What?"

"Calculators are hard, Luddock. I'm wounded."

"Ah, shut the fuck – "

Clint stood up. His hands were shaking and his upper lip was hot, but it seemed vital that Luddock not know the extent of the damage. "Back in a sec, bud." He went towards the bathroom the way that didn't pass Luddock's cube.

The hallway lights buzzed, which they had never done before. The office was really a bit too nice for that sort of thing, so Clint thought maybe he'd sustained a brain injury through his nose. He wanted to put his hot face against the cold bathroom mirror.

Ursula was a parody of her own name: tall and skinny as a flag-pole, unbrushed curls the colour of halogen light. She wore a brilliant green suit that day, no makeup. Her face went bond-paper white when she saw Clint. She even stopped striding. Her forward momentum had been such that her shoulders lurched forward after her feet stopped.

"Jesus, Clint. What the fuck is this?"

Clint could feel his blood pounding in his nose like another heart. He wondered if she could see it. "You know my name?"

Ursula's enormous raspberry lips were working in and out very fast. "I know your name. And I'm gonna get you some ice. I'm really not that much of a bitch, you know. That much." Clint could hear her heels *pock*ing towards the kitchen. The hall spun like a windmill blade. He staggered into the men's room.

The mirror held no good news. A Yosemite-Sam moustache of blood. The stuff was a fake-looking red in the white-tile room, like slasher-movie ketchup. When he tried to swipe his sleeve across his face he got blood in his eye. Tears mixed with the blood. Clint's stomach was starting to buck and weave. He hung over the sink and watched his blood dilute in the tap drip. Tipping his head forward seemed to make the blood flow faster. It was too thin, too, Clint thought. Too thin and too much, couldn't be right. He tried to remember what he used to do about nosebleeds in elementary school, besides cry.

The door swung open and Ursula burst in, frost-crusted Lean Cuisine box in her hand, her hair standing up like an electric shock, stunning as usual. In the summer, one of the interns had had such a crush on her he'd had to quit.

Ursula's heels made the same hammering sound in the men's room they did anywhere else. Clint wondered why he was surprised. She pressed the chicken primavera box across the hard bone of Clint's nose.

"Tip back. And press the ice. Well, there wasn't any ice."

Facing the ceiling, Clint tasted blood sliding down the back of his throat, like a salty penny. He tried to clear his throat and gagged, spraying red onto the picture of chicken. When he got his breath, Clint said, "Thanks for letting me bleed on your lunch."

"It isn't mine. I just found it in the freezer." Ursula seemed deflated by this admission, sagging back against the sink, getting blood and damp on her skirt.

"Thank you for stealing someone else's lunch for me."

Ursula's laugh was like a seal bark, echoing off porcelain toilets.

Clint smiled, then winced, then stopped.

"It hurts?"

Icicles had started to stab back into Clint's sinuses, but he shook his head. A blood drop hit Ursula's left breast. She looked down at it and her pink nostrils flared. "Stop moving."

Clint stopped breathing.

"You need to give it time to clot."

Clint started to nod and then stopped. There was a tiny curve across Ursula's hips where her skirt bunched like the knot on a bow tie, a fan of wrinkles. Under the fluorescent bathroom bulbs her white face looked funeral beautiful.

"You need to stay out of people's way, Clint. You piss people off." Ursula was running the blade of her right stiletto up and down over her left calf, shredding her stocking. She didn't seem to notice.

His chin and neck were going crunchy with dried blood. When he tipped his jaw to see her, Clint could feel it flake over his jugular. "I didn't tell anyone. I mean, I didn't yet and I won't. So . . ." He was thinking about how warm Anna was, if you brushed her shoulder, and how Ursula looked hypothermic.

"What?" The heel *pock*ed back down onto the tile. "Is that a threat?"

"No. How could it be?"

Her hands were long and full of ocean-blue veins that pulsed as she gripped the countertop. She'd put one of those icicle hands along Anna's cinnamon skin, brushing her hair back, caressing her face. It was impossible he could've seen mouths and eyes in the exhaust-fume gloom, but his mind extrapolated, filled in gaps. A narrow hand stilling Anna's chattering mouth. Ursula leaning over, Anna's head tilting to the side. Or tilt*ed* by Ursula's firm hand. Anna, anyway, under Ursula's slim shadow.

"I just wanted to tell you I won't tell, so you can stop trying to scare me so I won't. Because I *already* won't." Clint could see himself in the mirror, head back under the white box. The veins in his throat were as blue as those in Ursula's hands. "And I'm already scared. But that has nothing to do with it."

Ursula brushed her corkscrews in no particular direction. "What do you mean?"

Clint had lost thread and risked straightening his neck to see her face. He hadn't stopped shaking, but he was getting used to it.

She was looking down sorrowfully at the scraps of her nylons. She bent to tug at the fabric. Clint heard the threads snapping. When she straightened up, she looked hard at Clint's swollen nose. "Do you mean, you being scared of me has nothing to do with whether you'll gossip about me and Anna?"

Breathing through his mouth made his teeth dry. Clint had to swallow even just to say, "Yeah."

Ursula raised her skinny eyebrows towards her hairline. "Lucky Anna. I guess." Then she leaned back on the counter, reaching a hand underneath her skirt. Clint could see her hand moving like a green ghost. "Your nose . . . is it broken?"

"No."

With the pantyhose around her knees, Ursula was stepping out of her shoes, concentrating mainly on them and not on Clint. "Your voice sounds nasal. It could be broken. I'll take you to the hospital if you want."

"No."

"No, it's not broken, or no, you don't want me to take you?" Bare-legged, she slid back into her shoes and straightened, carefully centering herself back onto her spikes. "Wait, don't answer that. Don't ever ask me for anything. That is the only thing I'd do for you." Ursula peered at him, her eyes enormous and gleaming blue as her veins. "You don't know shit, you know that, right? I could paint walls with what you don't know."

Clint could smell her spearmint chewing gum over the urinals and chlorine cleanser and Alfredo sauce. He was startled to realize his nose was functioning again, that it would be okay. He could see his face in the mirror over Ursula's shoulder, the rivers of caked blood on his neck and collar and smeared up to his left eye. Cream sauce had just started to thaw and seep out of the swollen, crumpled box. The first drop landed just to the left of his fly.

"I don't know shit," he said. There wasn't really much else to say, or time to say it before the scheduling meeting.

Ursula seemed to be considering his honesty before she nodded, one quick jerk of the chin. She turned towards the door. As she opened the door she tried to toss the flesh-toned wad of pantyhose over her shoulder into the bin, but it slid down the stainless-steel onto the tile and stray crumpled paper towels. Her shoes were quiet as she strode out.

ii. Support

AS IT TURNED OUT, Trinity was not only real but beautiful. All spangled green dress, upswept hair, lipgloss smile – all for Luddock, with three inches of wrist and ankle jutting out of his brother's suit, a row of open-bar cocktails in front of him. Luddock introduced Clint with a sweeping arm flourish. "This is Clint. This morning I hit him with a calculator. Now he's plotting my death."

"I'm Trinity." She had a wide, white-toothed smile, a firm handshake.

"Welcome to our Holiday Celebration, Trinity." *Trinity* had sounded so made-up. Clint had expected to spend the evening listening to Luddock pretend to talk on his turned-off cellphone, telling this imaginary girl it didn't matter if she was late, later, missed the party.

"Hello, Clint. Oh, little Christmas tree centrepieces. How non-denominational. Please don't kill my date." Her gaze flipped away without waiting for an answer.

Clint glanced around the ballroom, too. He spotted Ursula alone by the bar in a long black gown, wild white-blond curls. Anna was nowhere in sight. His nose throbbed.

They settled down to drink Luddock's hoard of drinks ("Never know when they're going to get even chintzier!") and mock the decorations and wait for Anna. There were half a dozen tables of IT, but the support team was cornered by the kitchen door. Sitting down, it was hard to see the bar, or the creative table where Ursula was seated.

Anna's voice drifted from behind him. "There is a stranger in our midst." Everybody turned. "I'm Anna. You must be Trinity." She reached out a hand. The day before, she'd bet Clint a granola bar that Luddock got her name from *The Matrix*.

"Hello, Anna. Luddock says you're my main competition."

"He's lying to make you jealous." Anna flopped into the chair beside Clint.

"Is it working?"

"Oh, I'm furious." Trinity leaned over and bit Luddock just beside the Adam's apple. Luddock winced, and smiled.

Anna wore a blue dress, shiny blue and wide-necked, revealing clavicles, sternum, initial rises of breasts. When she reached out her right hand to shake Trinity's, the neck shifted, clinging to the right side of her neck and baring her left shoulder. There was a flash of white-blond hair moving from bar to table. Clint caught it; Anna, as far as he could tell, didn't.

Clint had anticipated a miserable Holiday Celebration: chafing in his necktie, squirming in humiliation for Luddock's imaginary girl, averting his gaze every time Anna looked at Ursula, making sure Ursula never noticed him at all. Blood still clotting at the edges of his nostrils, pounding migraine. But over the stacked Portobello salad, Trinity said, "You know, certain people in the sixties thought orgies would have become de rigueur by now, replacing parties like this entirely. Isn't it weird that after all this time, we're still repressed? This evening doesn't even have orgiastic *elements*."

The whole table was entertained right through the chicken supreme. Anna never even looked towards Ursula, silent and grim, her fork neatly by the side of her plate.

Dessert was a wafer cup filled with mango mousse. Luddock tried his first, and quickly spat mousse back into his cup, wiped his mouth with his sleeve. Trinity stared. "It tasted like toothpaste."

"The party favour is chocolate truffles," she said. "Eat those."

"I ate mine at cocktail hour."

"Me, too. Clint?"

"Eaten."

"I'm keeping mine as a souvenir!" Anna hugged her purse, the same fabric as her dress. Clint wondered if she'd made them herself.

Luddock pushed his chair back. "You know, some hotshots have *left* already, without their free truffles. C'mon, Clinty, before the servers get them."

Trinity scooted closer to Luddock. "Actually, I was hoping we could have . . . an early night."

"Oh?" He swung around. "You want to go?"

"Well, unless you really wanted to stay . . . ?"

Luddock's eyebrows shot up. "No: *No*. What the lady says goes. Let's go."

They went. Clint and Anna, shoulders brushing in silence, were the only two at the table – the rest of the Tech proles long gone or drunkenly doing some dance with arm motions. Anna was deconstructing the centrepiece, watching Ursula's bare pale shoulders and the long curve of her back. Clint watched Anna watching, her pink mouth slightly ajar. She twisted two pine twigs together. Ursula folded her matchstick arms below her breasts, glared at the dancers. Anna only shrugged when Clint announced, "Right back."

He'd noticed a couple of fullish wine bottles had been abandoned on the next table. Finance. Clint went over to the empty table and plucked them from among the stained napkins and truffle boxes. Those were empty, for some reason. No one spoke to him; he didn't know anyone outside Tech. Anna was stuck with him. Poor Anna.

While he got back to the table, Anna had built a little man out of bits of greenery from the centrepiece. Clint had three wine bottles clutched in his hands.

Anna looked at him, bright-faced. "You planning on a long night?"

"Never hurts to be prepared."

She thrust out her glass. "Red, please."

Someone asked Ursula to dance; Clint was sure Anna saw. Ursula uncrossed her arms and held them out stiffly, her face trying to animate. At that moment, it was hard for Clint to believe in Ursula's attractiveness, that the man in the tux (probably not rented) could want anything with her other than the professional connection.

Clint sloshed wine into their glasses as they watched the couple spin. Ursula's skirt sloshed like the wine. One revolution, she faced the tech table, and Clint saw her big cyan eyes rest on Anna, and for a moment she was gorgeous.

He drank his medicine-flavoured wine and turned to Anna's lovelit face. "So – "

She startled, dropped her gaze and her smile. "How's your nose?"

"It's not broken, I keep telling you, it just looks bad."

"Luddock is *such* a fucker." She smiled a little, but it wasn't very realistic. Her irises looked again at the dance floor. Something ABBA was playing.

Then Trinity reappeared by the bar, breathless and flushed. She caught Clint's eye and waved like a semaphore. Clint stood up slowly.

"Hmm?" Anna purred as if waking.

Clint pointed at Trinity, and gathered the bottles.

Anna got up. "I wonder what's wrong."

Clint shrugged. "Only one way to find out." He extended his arm towards her, the hand without the wine, and Anna hooked on, warm and close. Trinity met them on the edge of the dance floor, now radiating Steve Winwood. Ursula was at the bar, but Anna focused on Trinity's cold-flushed face.

"D'you guys know how to jimmy open a window?" she blurted as soon as they got within earshot.

"Maybe . . . not really . . . Why?"

"We were – " Trinity's face flushed even more. If Clint hadn't liked her before, he did now. "I started the car but there was snow over the windows, so Luddock got out to brush, but he wasn't, wasn't *doing* it right. He was leaving streaks."

Clint nodded – that seemed plausible.

"So I got out, to show him."

"And locked your keys in the car," Anna added.

"With the motor running! We've been trying to break in for twenty minutes. Luddock's standing guard. Do you have *any* ideas?" Trinity put hand to forehead, faux-swoon, but she looked miserable under her irony.

"No, but we'll come help. Or look. Or just stand around your car with you."

"Absolutely," said Anna, and did not look behind her.

"Oh, thank you," Trinity wailed. "I'll go wait with Luddock."

Trinity rushed off. Clint pulled his mouth to one side. "She's awfully grateful. I wonder if she realizes what Tech Support actually does."

Anna shrugged. "I think it's a moral support thing."

They unchecked their coats and stole a hanger and went into the snowthick parking lot. Clint felt like he had won something: he was still near Anna, yet not listening to "Jingle Bell Rock" in sad silence. The wet snow felt perfect on his face after the hot dry party. His nose didn't hurt much at all.

Anna was trying to unbend her hanger as they headed for Luddock's headlamp silhouette. She walked awkwardly through the slush, even though her shoes were low, sensible. The big snowflakes wet her hair, curling it around her face. She might've been cold, but Clint knew she'd never take out her toque from deep in her big parka pocket. The toque had a pompom on the tip, and said Edmonton Oilers. She wore it on the way to work, but took it off before she came near the office. If Clint caught the right morning bus, he saw her with her head dipped over a book, the blue pompom bobbing with the bumps. If he sat with her, she'd be glad, but she'd take off the hat and fluff her hair, as if he were anyone. As if he had to be impressed. He almost never let her know he was there.

Luddock threw up his arms at their approach, cawing, "Clint, wine, Anna, a hanger! Thank *God.*"

Clint set the bottles in a snowbank, except one. Anna handed Luddock her almost-straightened hanger. "Now what?"

More snow fell.

Luddock slumped forward. "Everyone knows that wire hangers open car doors but – let me guess – no one actually knows *how*, right?"

"Right," said Anna, sadly.

"We're hardly car thieves," said Trinity, more hysterical than sad.

Clint blinked snowflakes off his eyelashes. "Pull out the rubber at the bottom of the window and slip the hanger in above the lock. Use the tip to move the tumblers."

Everyone looked at the hanger with new affection; at Clint too. "All right . . . rubber part . . ." Luddock turned to the car, muttering.

Clint had no idea how to jimmy a lock, but what he'd said seemed logical. He heard the scrape of wire on glass and took a sip of wine. It really was cheap stuff.

Trinity went over to the snowdrift. "It's like an open bar!" She plucked a bottle. "Thanks, Clinty."

"Clinty is *my* name for him. Clinty is my creation!" Luddock yelled, thrashing at the window. "Anna, come try this. Your delicate hands will do better."

Trinity glared. "*My* hands are delicate."

"She's the best – " Luddock held up his own giant hand " – at some things. You're best at others." He handed Anna the wire.

Trinity didn't smile, but Luddock just kissed her mouth and took her wine.

"Don't worry. Tech Support can fix anything."

Anna froze. "We're not *fix*ing it. A lock that's locked is working fine. We're trying to *break* it."

"Well, you can do that, too."

Trinity reached for the wine but Luddock pulled back. "You can't drink too much. I don't know how to drive."

Trinity spun towards the car, laughing, sort of. Ludduck threw his arm around Clint, bottle bruising his biceps. They started walking down the aisle of cars. "Holding up, old man?"

"I'm all right."

"You're dying. Why are you dying? It's not your car."

"I'm not – "

"Ya *are*."

"*Fuck!*" Anna's voice, quite clear. Something about the snow made voices carry.

"I'm fine . . . You don't drive?"

"You don't date." Couples moved in the distance, arguing or cuddling. "Everyone knows you want Anna. Do something already."

"She doesn't want anything done."

"Chickenshit."

"She's not into it." Clint looked up. The sky was starless, brown: low clouds reflecting suburban light. The snow was thickening, but it didn't seem cold, just damp. He felt sweaty beneath his coat, suit, halo of wine.

"You haven't told her *you're* into it."

"That's not the problem." He almost blew his stupid secrets, for the warm weight of Luddock's arm and the ozone smell of snowflakes and how much better a person Clint was than Ursula.

"You two should be together. Look at her."

They turned to still-sealed car. Anna was scrambling up onto the hood, frizzy wet curls flopping into her face. Trinity was already standing on the roof, peering down, a bottle in each hand. Her disintegrating updo looked regal above her big-shouldered coat.

Luddock muttered, "Oh, she's trashed. We're never getting home."

A flash of blond caught Clint's eye. Ursula crossing the icy lot, her heels tipping her heavy on the arm of the tuxedo man.

Clint flinched for Anna, but he still wanted her to turn and see. He wanted her to turn from where she was digging heel marks in the hood of Trinity's car, and see. Anna was watching Trinity slither off the trunk. If she just turned her head . . .

Trinity skittered out of the sodium glare of the light-pole, into the thick dark on the other side of the car, where the snowplows threw dirty snow and rocks and garbage. "Where's she . . . going . . ." said Luddock.

Ursula and her man were between Clint and Anna, oblivious to all the Tech drama. Ursula probably had power locks, keyless entry. She had everything, but if Clint called, "Hey, Anna!" Anna would pivot and see blond and dark approaching a single car. Maybe she wouldn't care, maybe things were like that. Or maybe they were with Anna the way they were with Clint: when she saw the one she wanted wanting someone else, it would be a cold bolt sliding shut in the bottom of her stomach.

Clint didn't yell, or whistle, or even let Luddock follow his gaze. He just whispered to himself, Luddock, the world, "No." He looked at the car. Anna was alone now yelling into the dark where Trinity must have stood. Anna was standing on the hood, laughing, snow on her hair.

He drank some more wine. Luddock's grip tightened on his shoulders. Something dark and heavy flew out of the parking-lot night, and smashed Trinity's car window.

Solidarity/Who is Christine?

I THOUGHT IN THE FIRST PERSON PLURAL FOR YEARS, until I finally passed the driving exam. When I tell stories from before that, it's *we saw, our house, gave us,* with no mention of who else. I try to be clear, but in my head, my family was always just extra limbs. If I bought a new skirt, if the cat threw up, if alien spacecraft lit the field across from us, who would see it but my parents and my younger brother Ted? My family moved as a unit, thought that way, and thought also that that's what good families did.

Until I could drive, how would I ever be singular? Even the park in the town was an exhausting bike ride away. When we finally arrived, we couldn't do much more than lie on the grass and sweat, then go buy gummi worms at the store, called The Store. And who'd want to do that all alone? Once I bought a gummi snake and tied it round my neck like a necklace. It was dusted in some special sugar to make it not sticky, even with sweat.

On the way: cornfields, sod fields, houses, farm stands. I sometimes biked past these things without Teddy or anyone, but if I never got off my bike or spoke a word aloud, was I ever really anywhere at all? On the wind-whistle road, I worried about pitching into the high grass of the ditch, breaking a necessary limb, being found in a week by someone's lost dog. I got home every time without a story, pronoun-less in any person.

As soon as I managed to pass my exam, I was allowed to take the car out unsupervised whenever no one else needed it. The first thing I did was drive around with the radio turned up very loud. Sliding the station wagon over the crest of a hill at 75 km/hr, I felt I could fly. Over the county line: cornfields, sod fields, houses, farm stands. Gas stations that were the same price as at the one in our town, restaurants I'd been taken to on special occasions since birth.

The second thing I did, the next day, was drive my brother to work. Teddy was working nights that summer, cleaning shops, offices, locker rooms at the potash mines. His start was dusk, when all respectable souls were at home in the flickering screen light. Every evening, my dad had been taking him to the Freshtastic one town over to meet Milonski's van.

133

My dad picked him up there after midnight, too, when most souls were under their duvets. (My parents didn't know the word *duvet*. They said *bedspread* as if we ran a hotel.) Now I was taking over the early drive.

For me that was the summer of the box factory. My father dropped me off on his way to the office. At first, I just sat in the sunrise on the warming concrete until my boss opened the door at 8:30, but after a few days he noticed me lurking and let me start early. All summer, my clothes and hair were always lightly powdered with the dust that rises when you slice through cardboard with an exacto. When my father picked me up in the afternoons, a beige haze drifted onto the car upholstery.

It never occurred to us to thank each other for these lifts, nor to complain about giving them. Good families had one car and shared it appropriately. I just took the keys at 5:10 and went out the door, Ted following in his coveralls. The sky was grayish, the sunset invisible, trees blowing hard. My parents were pale spots in the dark front window. Teddy pointed his thumb back, I turned, everybody waved. "C'mon," I said.

We'd been given no rules for the drive. We never were, exactly. Good kids left parties early because parties were silly, got As because school was interesting, drove defensively because other drivers were lunatics. No one said, "No stops" or "Stick to the main road." Just "Watch for drunks, it's cocktail hour." As if anyone we might pass called it *cocktail hour* when they got drunk after work. Besides them.

As we crossed the bridge, it started to rain, drops digging thick gray pits in the river. By the time we arrived, the Freshtastic parking lot looked flooded with only a thin sheet of water reflecting the creamy orange sunset.

I turned the ignition halfway, let REM and the heater stay on. Ted unwrapped his sandwich. Summer sausage. We rolled our eyes. Michael Stipe and everybody hurt, rain drummed on the roof. Summer sausage was good, salty-sweet and chewy. But that was the thing, it was chewier than gum. The mayonnaise dissolved the bread in our mouths and we were left gnawing on a round red disk of meat. I wouldn't eat those sandwiches in public anymore. I made trail mix – nuts, raisins, dusty-gray chocolate chips-easier, less embarrassing to eat in the school caf or on the factory steps.

Ted was less of a complainer, so I wound up feeling bad on his behalf. Of course I felt sorry for myself covered in thick-scabbed cardboard cuts and dust, memorizing German so I could talk to my boss. But I felt sorrier for my nocturnal brother, slumped in the passenger seat in the glowing wet dusk, chewing cold sausage out of his sandwich. At least I could sleep nights. At least cardboard dust was clean dirt. Ted said he'd never seen anything like the men's locker room at the mine.

Milonski's van splashed into the lot. "You want the umbrella from the trunk?"

"S'all right. You ok to drive home through this?"

I hadn't thought of that. The shower was becoming storm. There was little he could've done, though, save taking me along in the van. "M'all right. Good shift."

"Sure. Bye."

I shivered in the damp before Ted slammed his door. I watched the van pull out sure and steady. I pictured our car skidding off the bridge, splashing into the river. It happened every winter. I could be the first summer casualty.

I clenched my hands on the wheel, ten and two, going nowhere. I didn't know if I was capable of driving in heavy weather or not; the driving examiner hadn't mentioned that, one way or another. I had to decide what to do next.

This was first person singular.

I drove half a minute down the road and then stopped at the Hop Stop. I wanted to go home before the rain got worse, but I didn't want to drive in the rain. I wasn't enjoying independence but I didn't want to give up.

Hop Stop was a grayed plank building barely larger than a school bus, the sort of place you never entered unless you lived around the corner or were lost. The cashier had laid napkins over the clear plastic lotto case, and was carefully dabbing blue nail polish onto her right hand. "Heya." She didn't look up.

Magazines of glossy skin girls, wild blond hair the same colour as their faces. Spongy Twinkies also the same pale bronze. Light bulbs Triscuits tampons carpet-deodorizer coughdrops hand-warmers ice teas of various brewings. Plastic slushie urns with their spinning churns. One red cherry, one brown-beige coke, one blue raspberry. They had to dye the raspberry blue so you wouldn't confuse it with the cherry.

I watched the churns, but also I watched the counter-girl flick excess polish off her pinky. Somehow we were regarding each other without making any eye contact.

"Don't get the coke. Something's wrong with the thing." The brown one was frosty pale at the top, muddier near the bottom. I took the smallest clear plastic Dixie.

"I like red better anyway." I was fairly certain that that was true. My last slushie had been several summers ago, when someone else's parents had taken me to the beach.

"It *is* better. But you never know with people." That was a long enough sentence that I felt I could look at her. She was pretty, very pretty in a way I could never even try for: eggshell skin and thick red lipstick, black beaded choker and dyed red hair sliding from a waterfall ponytail.

With an audience, it seemed very unlikely that I would get the slushie into the cup without spilling, but I did it. I stabbed a straw through the lid and headed towards the register, already drinking. It tasted like cold sweet red. So would the blue have done.

Around the napkins on the lottery ticket glass were the scratch marks of a million keys and coins. She was still painting, gleaming blue.

"Nice colour." I pointed, idiotically. What else could I have meant?

"Thanks. Smooth sapphire, like the jewel." She finished her left hand and lifted it awkwardly, palm up. "That's a buck twenty-five. The red all right?"

"Yeah, good." I passed her the change, drank more. I wasn't sure if the interaction was done or not. It should've been, but she was finally regarding me, and I could hear the rain steady on the roof. Then she said, "I just put the syrup in – too sweet?"

I smiled, closed-mouthed, sure my teeth were red. "Nothing's too sweet for me."

"Yeah, me neither. I like them, uh, Laffy Taffy things. Now that I got my braces off." She smiled wide – her teeth were very straight. "I'm Christine." She reached out her hand and sort of petted my palm, fingertips carefully splayed.

"I'm Lynn."

"You work around here?"

I drank more. It was easier to drink than speak – her choker looked goth, not something you could buy at Claire's. "Dropping my brother off for work." I jerked my head sideways towards the Freshtastic.

"Oh, yeah, everyone works at Freshtastic. My boyfriend's at the meat counter."

I was too startled by my accidental lie to correct it.

"What about you? You work?"

"Of course." Who didn't work? Kings? Mermaids? "Factory. We make boxes."

We caught eyes and she asked me the question I asked everybody I met, on the rare occasions when I met anybody. "Is that a good job?"

"Not really. Is yours?"

"No." She shook her head so hard her ponytail broke free of its waterfall.

DID MY PARENTS KNOW that our dinnertime was exactly when other people were leaving their tables, free and ready to chat? When the good reruns were on? When the last light was fading in the yard?

Yes and no. We could all see out the window. We could all read the TV Guide. We could reorchestrate the whole meal for 5:30 when a guest was expected. Days before, my mother knotting her narrow hands carefully in front of her belly: "What do you think it would be nice to eat with your friend?" Clearly the meal, the entire evening, would have to be very different from what my parents preferred. For guests, hamburgers (shaped from ground beef and bakery bread crumbs), pizza (thrown dough, a long discussion about spices in the sauce), ice cream we'd tried to make ourselves all afternoon, stirring ice-cube trays of sugary milk, ending up with hard white pucks.

My mother was serving perch when she noticed my nails. She looked at them, then at my father, then at the salt cellar. Terrifying indefiniteness: there was no rule against applying strangers' nail polish. And yet it was strange, even I could acknowledge, to wave goodbye blank-fingered and return Smooth Sapphire.

A mushroom fell onto the table as my mother spatula'd fish onto my plate. My father grabbed it, stuck it in his mouth and napkined the damp. I looked at my garlic green beans and saffron rice, thinking about Twinkies, Twizzlers, gum in pellets.

My father swallowed the mushroom, said, "What's on your hand?"

"Nail polish." I spoke through fish.

It was a hard question to formulate, but he did. "Where'd you get it?"

"It's Christine's."

"Who's Christine?"

The lack of anything at all to lie about made me want to lie. I wished Christine had sold me drugs or had sex with me or at the very least that I had hit her in the face.

"She's my friend." Surely, faced with a judge, or God, or my parents, she'd agree.

My father's head jerked up and a particle of vinaigrette clung to his chin. "Friend?"

"Don't worry, she's not coming here."

I had exactly three friends who lived close enough that it was not deemed dangerous for me to drive myself home from their places late at night. Deena picked apples at the orchard, Helen painted houses, Tess waited tables out by the highway. We never did much but watch movies and eat popsicles, flopped in someone else's family room. Having friends to my house was an extractable favour: if I *really* wanted. I rarely did. Any visits left my parents with memories of disrespectful attitudes, sloppy demeanors, silly answers. My friends rarely asked for the privilege either. We couldn't watch R-rated movies in our den. Everything tasted strange and overcomplicated at our table. No one else called the TV room a den.

When Milonski was late, I told my brother plot lines from the movies I'd watched with my friends, the only thing other than work I did without him. Often Milonski was late. Ted got docked pay for being late, but there was nothing to do if the boss was stuck in traffic. My own boss paid everyone the same every week, no matter who stayed late or left early. Extra math might've pushed him over the edge. Fridays he came back from the bank with a burlap bag filled with a tiny stack of twenties to distribute. He wasn't trying to avoid taxes, just hated cheques in strange angular English, remembering everybody's name and how to spell it.

Every weeknight, my brother and I waited in the hot car, filthy and about-to-be filthy, respectively, while I recounted the narrative of *Top Secret* and Ted ate and we both sweated. Our parents told us to get jobs, to save for University. University, 14 months and counting for me. I was counting. I didn't know where or even what subject, but not to go was as untenable as flight, free love, a boxing career. Whenever I tried to imagine schoollessness, I was unable to get further than more boxes, gradually turning gray with dust until an inevitable accident with the exacto, a life on disability.

Our parents said get jobs. They never said get good ones. The idea of decisions was a ways off for country kids. Neighbours, teachers, other kids were always eager to point out that we weren't *really* country. For practical purposes, we didn't get far on that. Just because you didn't know how to milk a cow didn't mean you knew how to read a subway map. I could count on my fingers the times I'd ordered for myself in a restaurant.

Milonski parked across the darkening lot. Ted crumpled his napkin inside an old Freshtastic bag (small town operation – logo-less). *Good night, Lynnie.* He cast a long shadow along the parking grid, dipping the shopping ladies into gray as they pushed their buggies of ice cream, chips, pudding cups, freezies.

Then he ducked awkward into the big mud-coloured van and they pulled out of the parking lot. In the window against the sunset, Milonski was a mustached silhouette.

It was hot, I was tired and dusty. But I had a car and I could do what I wanted. As long as I showed up at the table at seven and ate in convivial conversation. As long as I wanted to eat whatever was served. As long as no friends called during the meal. I had an hour to kill.

All the slushie churns were in working order this time, and Christine had a hand of solitaire spread out on the lotto case this time. "Lynn! You're back! Guess what my boyfriend did, the prick." I felt as though I'd won a prize.

If the only things you are good at are getting good grades and being a good listener to other people's problems, summer is a pointless season. No one would give me an A on a box, no matter how neatly trimmed and folded. My boss sometimes said *gut* to me, but usually while he was talking on the phone and not looking at all. And he certainly didn't tell me his problems. My colleagues were dirty-skinned men in their thirties who made the same money as a stupid teenage girl, cutting squares out of cardboard all day. Technically they spoke English, but it wasn't my English, and they would never have told me anything, anyway.

All the people with problems worth telling were doing overtime or stuck in traffic or in the barn or in Muskoka. Only Christine, sitting pretty behind her counter, wasn't too sweaty sticky to have stories. I drank five slushies a week as June crashed and July crested, and Christine always had something to tell: her boyfriend getting tickets for dragging on the highway. A certain twisted leather belt she'd bought in Buffalo making her wonder, was it wrong to wear cows? Christine was painting the mouldings in her mother's house dove gray, but then the Home Hardware ran out of that shade. June. July.

CHRISTINE WAS MAD. She slammed the cash register door, which you always have to slam, but I could tell she was doing it with rage. The man was just standing in front of the counter, emanating silent anger rays. I recognized them from home. "In my day we called it *service*."

The door jingled so I couldn't slink out.

"Yeah. Well." She was holding out a palmful of change, calmly waiting for him to take it. Not calmly, but with the appearance of calm.

He didn't. Then he did. "I'd like to speak to your manager."

She whipped her head back and forth, hair flying. "Do you see my manager?"

"Jesus. Jesus." His back was tight and skinny under his thin cotton T-shirt. "Jesus." He stomped out, workboots heavy on the tile even though he was small and old.

I looked down at what I had in my hands: green apple licorice, Clorox-infused Brillo pads, OFF, Chiclets. I circled the store, putting things back. "What's up?" I yelled from the bug spray section.

"Nothing. You see that? What a fucker. Unbelievable."

"I just . . . heard the end." I went to the counter with the licorice.

"Well, trust me, he was being a fucking dipshit. Really. That's $2.25." Her nails were deep orange now, like a sunset or cafeteria chairs.

Some part of me wanted to ask inappropriate questions – what did he say, what did you say – to try to intuit whether he had in fact been a dipshit. This was the part of me that thought that good cashiers didn't paint their nails at work, thought that if all the syrup is sinking to the bottom of the slushie machine good cashiers did something other than warn people not to use it. If Christine had been a box I would not have let my boss see her until I'd taken the exacto and evened out her edges.

"Are you going to open that?"

"Um . . . sure." It took me a minute to rip the slippery licorice plastic.

She pulled out a slip of green with her orange nails. "You gotta stick up for yourself. It's not a big deal when one guy pushes you around a little, but it makes it easier the next time. My boyfriend, he works at the meat counter of the Freshtastic, right?"

"Right."

"So this guy was getting spareribs, like, so many spareribs, six or seven pounds at least, maybe more. And he says, he says he doesn't want too much *fat* if you can believe it, you know what spareribs are like." She was taking everything out of her purse, makeup and hair stuff and receipts spread on the lotto top.

The time for questions had passed. There was one appropriate answer. "Yeah."

JULY. THEN AUGUST. I had shallow exacto cuts all over my palms, and one that was deep on the thigh. My boss looked at me with wild rabbit eyes when he saw all the blood on my jeans. My parents said they weren't angry, just alarmed, but they said it loudly, often. They hadn't made me quit. Yet. Everyone said to be careful. As if I wasn't – if I hadn't been careful, I wouldn't have any fingers at all.

August. Careful August, but also winding down. The promise of grammar, geometry, badminton – things that, with grim effort, I could master. People to talk to who weren't blood relatives or miserable or German-speakers.

I came in and Christine had nothing on the lotto case but her folded hands. I called, "Hey, Christine," before going to the slushie churns. It was a nice night – the wind off the river had blown off most of the yellow from the mines. My friend Helen had permission to drive her company van up north camping for the weekend, and somehow, I had permission to go, too. If they hadn't let me, I would've had nine weeks straight of boxes and rental movies. Even my parents knew that would be terrible.

I wanted to hear about what Christine and her boyfriend had gotten up to when they'd gone to the fair on the weekend. Maybe someday I'd need to know these things. As I'd crossed the parking lot, a man had whistled at my dusty legs. The slushie churns were all spinning smoothly. Tonight: blue.

"You'll never believe what happened." The chip rack was between us, so her voice seemed to be coming from the hickory sticks and pretzels. "I got ar*rest*ed."

"Really?" I was startled enough that I let blue slush mound above the cup lip.

"Not actually with handcuffs and everything. But the cops came and I got in shit."

I doubted that I could get the lid on now – it seemed like it might squirt sticky. I crouched until my face was parallel with the crystal meniscus above the rim.

"Aren't you gonna ask what happened?"

I did want to know, but she always told whether I asked or not. So I just said, "Yeah," then put my mouth carefully over the edge of the cup and sucked up blue. There was silence under the slurping. "So what happened?" Still silence. There seemed to be sufficient room then to put the lid on. *Snap.* I straightened up and peered over the chip rack. Tears leached kohl in tarry streaks to her jaw, onto her pale neck and throat.

"Um, are you ok?" I carried the cup to the front. Her pale hands knotted up tight above the orange Kenos, the foil green scratchoffs. "What happened?"

A hiccup in her voice. "Fuckers said I was selling cigarettes to underagers. Fucking inch of makeup, padded bras, hoop earrings, they look thirty, how'm I supposed to know? You can't card everybody, not with a fuckin' line to the door."

I had never seen more than one other customer in Hop Stop. "It gets that busy?"

She looked at me through her clotty lashes.

"What did they do to you?"

"Fine. Five-hundred bucks. Fuckers. One stupid kid who's just gonna bum'em off her boyfriend, how's that worth five-hundred bucks?"

"Whoa. That's a lot." That would take me more than two weeks to earn, if I didn't ask my boss to start taking off taxes like my parents wanted. "How can you pay it?"

"Well, like, they fine the store, not the person, you know? Except, of course, my boss says since it's my fault, I have to come up with half. Plus I think I'm gonna get fired. Especially if I can't get the money."

"He'll take it off your pay, right?" I'd forgotten to get a straw but I couldn't see it being appropriate to go back.

"Dunno. Maybe. But what'll I do for money, then?"

"Um." This was not a question that made a lot of sense to me. You earned money so that you had money to pay tuition in 14 months, not so that you could do anything with it *now*. The money my boss brought me from the bank on Fridays mainly went back there on Saturdays.

"My mom's gonna fucking kill me."

I pointed out what I imagined to be her secret weapon in all times of crisis: "What does your boyfriend say?"

"Oh, *that* fucker. What the fuck does *he* know? Stoned all the time. I think I should fight this in court. What do you think?"

I was confounded by that – she *knew* she'd broken the law – but I knew the right answer. "Yeah, totally. You should totally stick up for yourself."

She sniffed a gray tear into her nose. "Yeah, maybe I will. Maybe my boss will back me up if he can get out of paying that way."

It went on like that for a while, what her mom would say, where the courthouse was located in the closest city. Probably way downtown, nearly an hour away. Someone – boss, boyfriend, mother – would have to drive her. Christine didn't have her driver's license, it turned out.

I told the story over dinner, and got back the quiet roar over the butter dish that I was expecting. They didn't like this messy illegal person, who-ever she was, and I could see where they would slowly begin commenting on how I was wasting my time and perhaps damaging my character by hanging around her. I chewed on grilled peppers and nodded without thinking, without arguing.

I was picturing Christine's dinner throughout ours. I could see it clearly, though she'd never described her house except for the mouldings. It would look like the McKenzie's place. When I was in grade one, the McKenzie kids lived near us. If their parents called and invited us for a specific time, we could walk over. Not on the gravel shoulder, that was dangerous, but carefully across lawns. We always went there, because our flower beds were delicate and we mainly played yard-games: forts, nerf darts, whatever we could come up with. But once the McKenzie kids asked us in for supper. We were under a bush when Danny said, "I'm hungry, let's go eat," and Lou answered, "Yeah. Ok." Then they both looked at us, frozen with our tree-branch-and-newspaper swords. They said, "Come on."

It was five o'clock in the afternoon. There was endless sun in the green bush, endless time to play. Pavlovian, we weren't hungry, but this was interesting and we weren't expected home for hours. I nodded, since I was the oldest. I took Teddy's hand – when he was small he was always sticky, but I was the oldest – and we went in.

Their lino was a different pattern from ours, but that was all right. There was a cat on the drier, that was all right. There were clothes, not folded, under the cat. The couch in the living room looked as though people had been reading magazines there and been suddenly called away. Then other people – the same people? – had come and, not seeing the magazines, sat down on them. The television was on loud, for no one.

The dining room table was not set, and there was nothing on the stove. There were no adults in evidence. Lou started taking things from the fridge and putting them on the counter. The mustard bottle tipped and rolled towards the microwave.

"Are you – are you allowed?" I whispered.

"Sure." Danny jabbed me with a box that said *graham crackers*. "Have an appi-tizer."

"Oh." I had to let go of Teddy to get one out. He sat down on the lino. I handed him one, unsure this wasn't a terrible idea. Our mother rarely gave us food out of boxes.

I watched Teddy eat, test balloon. "It's sweet," he said through crumbs.

Lou was spreading the jelly on the crackers. Danny was smearing mustard on slices of bologna and rolling them into tubes. Mrs. McKenzie entered, buttoning up her blouse. "Hey, kids. Hey, Teddy and Lynn. Good, you're eating. You need anything?"

"Nah." Danny put the jelly knife down sticky on the counter. "You want some?"

"Your dad and I are going out for supper tonight, sweet, remember? Just one." She took the cracker with her pink-polished fingernails widespread. "Sitter'll be here in a sec." A gob of jelly slid down her hand, and she licked it just before it touched her sleeve. Then she screamed. "Steve! You gotta go get the sitter!"

"What?"

"The sitter!"

"What? I'm in the bathroom, Jen!"

"Well, Jesus." She licked her wrist again.

"What sitter?" Lou put a whole piece of bologna in his mouth.

Mrs. McKenzie shrugged. "I dunno, Alexandra? The younger one."

I looked down and Teddy was all covered in crumbs. It looked like he hadn't eaten any graham crackers at all, just smushed them on his face. No one else was looking at us. I put the box of crackers very carefully on the edge of the stove. After I checked that it was off. I reached my hand towards my brother and we crept out together while no one was looking. In our own yard, I used a leaf to brush the crumbs off his face and neck before we went in.

I missed Christine, but I never saw her again. I passed the Hop Stop every time I drove Teddy to work, though. We could've approached the Freshtastic from the other side to avoid it, but it would've meant taking the highway. I wasn't really a good enough driver for that yet.

Zoom

THE HOUSE WAS TIDY BRICK, dormered windows and white-painted trim, but the roof shingles were green-gray, pond scum ugly. Nobody complained or even remarked on them, though. A roof is above what happens, above what matters. Under the shingles were struts and load-bearing walls, candy-pink insulation and chipped paint in a shade called Almond Frost. Under all that, it was almost suppertime.

Theo held his hand over the baby's eyes, illustrating and shielding, both.

"That's all?" Rae asked, still by the front door. She looked at Theo's hand, a couple inches from Marley's small face.

"If that, doctor said. Said there's not an exact measure for a baby's vision. Exactly." Theo felt like he could guess, though: her sight was probably no more than a colourful blur, the windshield world at a car wash.

Marley kicked a sleepered foot into the hollow of his elbow. Her eyes were the same pretty cobalt as Rae's.

Now Rae lowered hers sadly, or in a way Theo knew to recognize as sad – to a stranger, she'd merely look pouty.

"Jesus." Rae finally put down her briefcase and shrugged out of her coat, gaze to the gritty floor. Jake ran past, chasing something invisible, ignoring his family. "That one all right?" She flopped onto the shoe-tying chair, legs kicking straight out. Theo saw the chair jolt backwards with her weight, the back legs scratching off the rug.

"Sure. Certainly. *That* one? What is he, a squirrel?" He saw the wet curve around Rae's eyes. Theo saw a hawk circling above the backyard.

"You'd tell me if the boy developed squirrel-like tendencies, wouldn't you?"

He set Marley on Rae's lap. He wanted to look at Rae as a not-bad mother right then. She didn't flinch at the damp body on her pale wool skirt. That was something. She met Marley's blank gaze. "Ok day, baby? Anything to report?" She couldn't coo, neither of them could. They just talked, dull post office chatter, water-cooler banality. Kids mainly liked the sound of their parents' voices, anyway. Probably.

"Raaaaae." Jake was back, spooky-high-strung and charging towards Rae's knees. He tried to cuddle in, despite the boniness of knees and the baby there, despite Theo's own accessible knees passed en route. But Raeanne had been an unanswered question all afternoon, Theo as common as a daisy and grouchy, cursing at his laptop. Of course she was better.

"The Decepticons were attacking on the basement floor and then Marley ate the wheel off my truck but Thee found the wheel under her tongue she hadn't swallowed it and then we went to Marley's doctor and then at the drugstore it was seniors days but not for kids but they let us have Danishes because there weren't any seniors around and the subway got stuck in a tunnel and Thee said not to make a sound or we'd tip off the tracks and be lost in the dark forever and ever."

Jake had not yet learned to pronounce the O in his father's name, or punctuate his sentences with breath, or identify what shouldn't be repeated.

"Wow, really? You totally look like a senior citizen. I wouldn't put you a day under sixty-five." Rae raised her eyebrows at Theo, tears in check, subway lies unquestioned. Dismissed, he faded into the kitchen. He needed some small silence anyway.

HE THOUGHT of chopping vegetables the way that sculptors think of carving – the true form needing to be separated from everything else. He wasn't sure about the articles he wrote, how much he was making up about pet care and city politics and the best brand of mattresses, but he was sure about the turnips. Each slice was truth as it fell. And the next next next. *Chunk chunk chunk*. Turnips are tough; he had to put his whole weight above the blade. *Chunk*. The water approaching a boil, the hunch of his spine under the fluorescent light, his T-shirt hammocked between his tense shoulder blades. *Chunk*. Boiling now.

He was knocking slices into the pot when Rae came in. Marley was flopped over her shoulder, babbling quietly. Downstairs, the TV came on, bark of commercials.

Rae announced, "If I were a Transformer, I'd be Roboticon."

"Noo-o. You think you can be evil but you can't even speak in a monotone."

"You're right, I can't. Do you want help?"

"S'ok. You guys play."

Rae flipped the baby around onto her chest, then collapsed to the floor in almost one motion. They lay chest to chest while Theo peered through the greasy oven window at the chicken.

"Touch my eyes. Rae's eyes. Eyes. That's my nose. Ok, feel nose: cartilage, nostrils, blackheads, *nose*. Mouth – mrmmph. Inside feels wet, outside feels soft. Mouth."

Theo wanted to turn, watch her lick the baby's palm. He didn't. Rae was smiling through Marley's fingers smearing her lipstick. Rae was gazing at the ceiling as she dangled Marley above her. "Rae's mouth. It's there, I promise you. It's real, even if you can't see it."

EVERY DAY the shingles were the same swamp colour, no matter the sunshine on them, red-orange leaves, bird shit, haze of smog. Most days were the same indoors, too, with more action: Theo in the kitchen bouncing the baby like a jackhammer, Rae locked in the bathroom with the shower-radio, traffic report loud, the glittering spray off her soft white shoulders tense with highway possibilities. Rush hour made distance flex and bend; today an hour for six exits, tomorrow fifteen minutes, as if the curve of the earth had tightened. Jake flurrying through the newspaper for a picture of an animal he could describe in twenty-five words or more. He never knew what he was learning, just that he must. School was an arbitrary destination; having to go each day seemed to make as much sense to Jake as daily pilgrimages to the cemetery, the shoe store, Mars.

Mornings were hysterical, vital – the location of his rain boots and the part in her hair, the brownness of the toast and location of the car keys, the number of words in Jake's cow description. Theo manned the toaster, yelling: "The elastics might be in the top drawer of my desk!" "Jake, another word for *great* is *awesome*!" "Y'know, Marley, I don't like oatmeal either. Maybe it's time for *solids*, eh?"

Marley was planted in her high chair, beaming raspberry bright. Her tolerance for noise and chaos was stellar. Noise and chaos were her only access to the world until she could walk into it. He sponged oats from her fingers. Marley said, *Flawahahaha*.

Whirl and tumult, Jake and Rae searching for their shoes. Theo and Marley stayed barefoot. Their day was less urgent: an article on emergent architects, playtime, game shows, transcribing tiny tapes, writing about glass façades, surfaces. Of course he would shower and dress, bathe and dress her, eventually. But they didn't *have* to, no one would have seen. No appointments today, no trip to the post office planned. Even his daughter couldn't see him. Theo was invisible, double-sighted.

A doubling up of vision, a gift of outside. If it was a gift. He and Jake had been walking towards the hospital to retrieve Rae and newborn Marley when Theo had first noticed the top of his own head. The summer sun had bleached his blond hair even lighter. He noticed with pride that the spikes and swirls of hair were still thick, though a glimpse of sunburnt scalp was visible.

And then he realized he was seeing the spot on the back of his head that he could never see. He saw everything: his own red-tabbed jeans and sweaty back, the curve of fat on either side of his waist, the way from a distance Jake's small hand disappeared in his, tapering into one body. He was glad to see all of it, as happy as a dream-self discovering an unknown window in the house. But he didn't think too much about it. He was a father, and then a father again. He tugged Jake up the small grassy hill towards the doors, in pursuit of this new person. Two children, a boy and a girl, his. A son and a daughter. He'd won all the prizes. Blind daughter, he knew later.

And she was now here, against the fingerprinted wall, crowing rows of *n*s: "Nahanie nally nah nah. Bah. *Bah.*"

"Yes, Marls, I know what you mean." He tucked the corner of a toast triangle into her mouth. She tugged back, startled goose. She gazed at the left side of his face, at nothing, the imaginary world of Marleyness.

"Did you, did you see that folder, the blue one? That was on the table?" Rae rustled into the kitchen, breathless. "Did you? Toast?"

He passed her plated triangles, heaped with jam. "Purple?"

"Blue. Thank you. Dark blue." She stuck a corner into her mouth, chewed just as Marley wouldn't. "Like Royal-Bank blue, I guess almost purple."

"Ah, on the stereo, I think." He licked his fingers, went out to check and came back with it fingerprinted only in spit. "This is clearly purple."

Rae, chewing ardently, nodded, then shook her head, then shrugged.

Jake came in. "Toast?"

Theo handed him a plate. "Your sister won't eat toast, Jake. Weird, eh?"

"She's a baby, she *can't* eat toast. She doesn't have enough teeth."

"She's got *sev*eral teeth in there. She should try. We're a toast-eating family."

Now Jake was eating, and couldn't answer, and Rae didn't find the toast-riff funny, clearly. Theo put his own toast into his mouth. No one sat down at the table.

In the midst of Rae's red-brown bob, her part was pale, white as the snow on the roof. He liked looking at the places she didn't see herself. It made it easier to be tender, this aerial view. She seemed so vulnerable not to see what he saw, even though it was *her*. Even Rae had her blind spots.

He turned back to the stove to pour more coffee, watching her from above. She never looked at him when his back was turned; did she ever think of him when he wasn't around? He'd noticed in the past eight months, since he was able to notice such things, that she only gazed at him when he was gazing back. As he poured, she could have examined the pattern the pillow had smashed in his hair, but she didn't. She looked down at Marley, though, caressing her soft blond hair. That was something. Marley's hair was like his, just slightly darker. "Like mine, you think?"

Silence, stroking, a quirked eyebrow, her gaze finally lifted to Theo's turned-away back, her hand just above the chubby crease of Marley's neck. "Her hair? It's darker. Close, though."

"Or the shape of her head."

"Um, dunno. I don't think head shapes are that unique, really."

Theo was startled – maybe this was something he thought too much about. Skulls like snowflakes, like PIN numbers, fingerprints, diamonds. Every one unique. But maybe only since he had nothing better to think about, interviews about flat sheets of glass not taking much space in his mind.

Rae hauled Marley into her arms, touched her head gently, curiously. After a moment she murmured, "At least we remembered about the soft skull thing."

". . . I don't, actually. What?"

"When they were real small, the skulls were still hardening. Remember? We had to always set them on a different side so their heads would form round."

"Oh, yeah." Theo hadn't actually believed that, had thought roundness was just in the DNA. But Rae was touching Marley's head so very delicately, jammy fingers on curls. He went to touch the baby's head too – or to brush his fingertips against Rae's. "Nice and round."

Jake had disappeared; TV shouts were audible. The TV was a vortex: if a parent didn't intervene soon Jake would take off his shoes and the morning would be lost. But Theo had to ask – "What about me?"

Rae blinked, confused, but she was still looking at him, willing to follow the conversation a little farther. "You . . ."

"My skull? Are you implying that it isn't round? That my parents neglected me?"

"Hmm." Rae's laugh was just a rush of air through her nose, never more than that. All her reactions were moderate. She passed the baby into his arms and put her sticky fingers to his head. She was so casual about making the housebound sticky. She wouldn't have touched her own shiny hair. "Well, maybe life wears on the bones a little." She slid her palm under his jaw, up the other side to his eye. "No adult's head is really round."

"And the back?"

Rae smiled, a raspberry seed between her top front teeth. "What's the point in vanity about the bits you can't see?"

He shrugged, hugging Marley, who squawked. "It's just weird not to be sure – " which was a lie, since he was " – what part of your own body looks like."

"Damn, has he got the TV on? *Jake! Get your cow and put your coat on. You hear me? Jake?*"

"Yeah. Umunnadoit."

"*Now.*" A pause. "Well, turn around if you want to know. I'll tell you."

This was as he'd feared, but as he'd also known. And yet he still had to ask: "You've never looked?"

Rae smiled, wide and pretty, his lovely wife, trying to be charming. "Your face is what interests me . . . usually. But if you want . . . turn."

"Ok." And he did, felt and watched her big smooth hand with the slender wedding band, fingers probing hard under his hair – so thick, at thirty-four! Sometimes, sitting with a stack of untranscribed interview tapes and unwashed laundry, he would imagine how it would be if they split up. When. No, *if* for now. He could picture strange women liking his hair and smile, smiling back. He couldn't picture anything beyond that, though.

Jake stomped in, sulky because he'd had to turn off the television and now he was hot in his coat and they weren't going anywhere. Turning, Rae whispered, "Round enough for all normal purposes."

Theo could still feel the warm imprint of her hand in his hair, see the new tangles, no worse than what sleep had done, just different. He could see their snowy rooftop, less snow where the insulation was falling away.

He should go up to the attic and check. He should go pick up the fallen branches by the road, knocked by last night's snowplow. Marley nestled against his chest, closing her big cobalt eyes.

He watched Rae put on her coat. It was thick black wool, same as his. It broadened her shoulders, squared her waist. Her dark toque covered her hair, just like his, two for $10. He pressed his lips on Marley's warm head. Rae led Jake down the driveway. He thought her back looked much like his would, from a distance. From a distance, whoever wound up leaving would look pretty much the same.

Blood Ties

ROXY IS WAY OUT OF CONTEXT on the limp beige couch in my residence lounge. When she called from the airport, I feared some drama, but as I approach, she's sitting quite undramatically, for Roxy. Rosebud-patterned blouse buttoned to her throat; hands clasped in her lap. Her hair is still dyed navy, shiny as a shoe and clipped back above her right ear. The blouse, the clip: she's in costume as usual. Today she's the intimidated-outsider-at-an-impressive-university, which is just a little entertainment. Roxy's mind is as good as anyone's, and so is her degree. She looks childish, so much that her game trumps itself: she looks like any punk student tidied up for dinner with her parents. You can barely tell she's an adult with a good job. She's only out of context for me.

"Hey, Roxy."

She bounces off the couch, hands to her face. *"Colleen!"*

The *N* is nice and clear. My father's friends have a habit of dropping it. Roxy retrained when I hit high school, better than my dad, at least. She reaches to hug me.

"What are you doing in town?"

Her arms freeze halfway out. "Oh, work. It's a layover, from Halifax. I wasn't sure I'd get one, so I didn't call before, just got your dad to tell me your address."

"Ok." I'm not convinced – Roxy gets sent in for problems and bad news – but I'm ready to accept the hug. She's still talking, though, high and quick, her hands still frozen.

"I wanted to see where you live. It's been so weird having you far away."

"Sure," I say, but she isn't really listening.

"Now that I've seen it, you, though, I could go. Away. Now. If you were busy."

"I'm not."

She ignores me. "But I'd buy you dinner, if you were free."

Subjunctive. As if it's impossible. I finally hug her, and she startles, catches herself, settles her hands on my shoulders, her chest on mine. When I pull away, she's smiling so joyfully I feel a tug of guilt for the email I never answered.

"I'll have dinner with you, Roxy."

She smiles, thin lips a tight frame for big teeth.

Roxy isn't my friend. She's my father's friend. She's like a cupboard or a window – something inescapable and almost, but not quite, necessary. Just now, though, I don't want her to go. It is strange being so far from home.

We cut across campus in silence except when a gust of wind blows a bunch of dead leaves in our faces. Roxy draws up her hands and says, "Oh, how collegiate." Whoever she's being today, she's twittery.

I wonder if she wants a drink. I do. She probably doesn't want to eat anywhere with tablecloths and a wine list, but Ollo's is close and unlikely to contain anyone I know, and she says ok when I stop at the doorway. She stays in character past the hostess, all the way to the table: picking up the votive, smiling at all the forks, getting excited about the prospect of appetizers. It's less convincing than some of her other performances, or maybe I'm just getting older.

But I never entirely bought Roxy anyway. I knew what she was long before our first real encounter. At my father's parties, she was usually swimming in gauzy shirts and patched jeans, skipping around the apartment – our apartment. Then she was being the radical hippie chick. When I asked about the blue-haired one, Joe said – absent-mindedly, concentrating on not dropping the groceries he was carrying – Roxy was a girl with too much smart. She'd just graduated from a university program for becoming an opera singer, with a minor in Women Studies. There wasn't much of a job market for either of those things, though, so she temped about a thousand hours a week. Joe said he felt lucky she hung around with him.

I was eleven and my mother had been dead a few months, so I'd been living at my dad's place long enough that Roxy's blue hair by itself wasn't interesting to me. It was the way she watched my father, a face full of looking, even when she was yelling about injustice, or slouching on the couch with a strange little cigarette. I was always supposed to be asleep during parties but I saw most things. I think Joe confused childhood with a coma. Of course, he wasn't all that much older than Roxy, and he worked those thousand hours, too, without the smart. He did things like planting trees, teaching ice-skating, playing guitar in bars, organizing fancy salads at wedding receptions: things I hadn't really known were jobs.

He knew what he was and wasn't good at – I guess that's something.

He sent Roxy to talk to me without so much as an introduction, but at least he sent her.

It was a few months after I'd first noticed her hair, somewhere in the depths of fifth grade. Roxy appeared at the street-gate of the community centre where they taught us golf and cribbage and knitting and martial arts all in one room. I didn't hate it. Roxy wore white cotton sneakers with nylons, a green shirt-dress, a cardigan – some sort of bad-catalogue version of a mom. All the interesting mysteries about Roxy, except her hair, her sleep-deprived eyes and her tattoos, had disappeared. She didn't act so smart.

She said we were going for dinner and "girly chat." Though I didn't know what that meant, though she was a near stranger, I like to eat in restaurants, so I followed her. I imagined my father wouldn't notice my absence, and it didn't occur to Roxy until we were almost there to mention that the meal was his suggestion. That made no sense, and she said *your father* strangely, too gently.

Then I was distracted by the diner, the best thing I could've hoped for, in Joe's circles: moulded-plastic booths and cakes under glass, tub of stripy mints by the till, smell of bacon and vinegar. When my mother wasn't dead, I had eaten bacon every Sunday morning. Now everyone told me I was a vegetarian.

Roxy didn't notice the nonsmoking sign and took out a cigarette as soon as we sat down. That was Joe's sort of sloppiness – it didn't go with her dress and made me stop listening to her. So when she said, "I was wondering if you wanted to ask me about menstruation, Collie?" I didn't catch the nickname or even the question, really.

"No." I wanted the chicken fingers. Roxy probably wouldn't have argued, but her allegiances were other: she might have told.

I looked up and she was watching me intently, her Pepsi-can blue eyes and hair gleaming. Apparently her question had been important.

"What's that?" I said finally.

"What's what?" She exhaled thin gray smoke.

"Menstruation?" I knew I'd pronounced it right only because the stringy-haired waitress twitched before telling Roxy to put her cigarette out. Of course there was no ashtray on a nonsmoking table. Roxy shrugged apologetically and took another drag as the waitress stormed off. I gave a little cough of disapproval.

Roxy ducked, shoulders to ears. "Periods. Menstruation is the fancy word."

I thought maybe grilled cheese, at least it came with fries. I thought I'd heard grade-eight girls whispering *period*, giggling and turning red, but I didn't know why. Not for sure. I only knew the grammar lesson. "Punctuation?"

"Your, um, you didn't – " The waitress smacked down a glass ashtray. Sighing, Roxy stabbed out two inches of unsmoked white.

"You girls know what you want?"

It seemed funny to me that we could both be girls: my gray flannel school tunic with lunchtime's mustard over my heart, Roxy's shapeless green shirt-dress with just the wing of her butterfly tattoo visible over the collar.

Roxy snapped shut her menu. "Perogies, please."

No chance would I ask her what a perogy was, not when I was already one down vocabulary-wise. I had my clue though – I could find a p-word on the menu spelled like perogy sounded and see that it cost $4.25. Grilled cheese was only $3.75, so that was ok.

When the waitress left, Roxy rummaged through her string bag and pulled out a battered library hardcover. She didn't look at it or pass it to me, just held it to her belly, half above the tabletop and half below.

"Menstruation . . . periods . . . is, um, something that every girl starts to have around twelve, thirteen. Some girls develop earlier and you're tall . . ." Roxy trailed off when the waitress plonked down our glasses of water.

"I'm not that tall."

She looked stymied by that, pressing her fingers to her mouth.

If Roxy had been happier, had gotten what she wanted – some sort of imaginary job singing all day, some sort of imaginary relationship with my father where he looked down and noticed her, maybe she would've stopped with all the twitches and costumes, finally relaxed. Maybe Joe would stop staying out all night and getting fired from all his jobs. I didn't much like Roxy's smoking, or lovingly gazing, but the butterfly tattoo was so pretty and I wanted to go to university, too, someday. I was willing to make an effort. A small one, like "So what's menstruation?"

My effort did not pay off. Six years later, Joe still drinks too much, and works in restaurants, and ignores people who try to like him. Roxy has an office job now and is still a ball of gestures, though she mainly looks at Joe straight and clear. Now I'm almost as old as she was then – we're all grown-ups together. I can order a bottle of wine, fish and asparagus, three things the cafeteria lacks.

Roxy smiles weakly and orders something primavera, taps her fingertips at her jaw. A new twitch. Her left hand, her painted gray fingernails, glint of a small-carat stone on her third finger. Part of her costume? Would Roxy actually get engaged like someone from the fifties, or the suburbs? Does Roxy even believe in marriage like that, with jewellery and mothers-of-the-bride dresses, and chicken or fish on rented china?

She fiddles with the breadbasket. Who would she marry? Someone from work, someone from her gym or a bar or her choir? Joe wasn't seeing anyone I knew of in the summertime. I've been gone three months; even before that, I'd finally learned to sleep through the parties.

The wine is a ping in the back of my throat, nice, better than I would've ordered if Roxy weren't paying, weren't doing well these days, weren't a strange success story in the strange world of artists and repertoire. If Roxy married my father, he'd finally have dental insurance.

Roxy isn't drinking wine or eating bread, but she hasn't noticed me staring at her ring, either – she's spinning her glass in between her palms, watching the yellow splash reflecting the votive. I wonder if she could be in character for a whole wedding. I wonder if that would make her really married. I've always thought *real* for Roxy was less than it was for me. Everything she says seems to have quotation marks.

Even as a kid, I could hear them: "Well, Collie, menstrual blood is a signal that you're 'becoming a woman.' It's – "

"Blood? What bleeds?" I already sort of knew: some girls whispered pretty loud, plus there were rumours about grade six health class. But I was hoping they were wrong.

"Um, your vagina," Roxy whispered as the waitress collected the smoldering ashtray without slowing her stride. Roxy pulled the book away from her belly and opened it while I writhed.

"That's *hor*rible."

"No, no, Colleen, it's very natural. I'm just not explaining well." She flipped pages fast. "Here, look at this picture."

I wanted to say no. I recognized only the curve of a bum on one side of the picture and the juncture of belly and thigh on the other. The middle part was X-ray incomprehensible: green and orange tubes swirling like carnival rides.

The waitress put down my grilled cheese and fries, Roxy's platter of rubbery white and onions. I grabbed the ketchup bottle – we didn't have red dye products in our house. "What cuts you? What keeps you from bleeding to death?"

"It isn't – it isn't actually bleeding. It's just . . . extra blood." Roxy tried to hold the book over her plate, but the spine hooked the onions. She flicked them off and pointed. "See the green bit? This is your uterus. That's where a baby would go, if you were pregnant. Did your mother talk to you about where babies come from?"

I started eating the fries, which betrayed my dignity, but they were only good hot. "My mom was busy dying," I said with my mouth full of potato and tomato. "We talked about other stuff." I had learned that acting tough about my mother could end any conversation. Terrible, but handy. When I thought about my mother, who never cried and didn't have much patience when I did, it seemed she wouldn't have minded.

"Oh," Roxy said. "Oh." She stared at the neon green uterus. "Well, yeah, Joe figured it was something like that. He thought maybe you should learn this, you know – woman to woman. So. Here." She pointed to the picture's belly button, drew up her shoulders. "When a woman is old enough to have a baby, her body gets ready just in case, by – " she exhaled blue hair and flicked the pages forward, then back " – thickening the uterine lining."

And it went on like that, on and on. The whole sandwich, the whole book. By the end, I was aching for menopause. I hated her. She probably hated me. I certainly hated my father, for inflicting this on me. On us.

Of course, I had to know. When I got my period a year later, I used the pink-wrapped Always pads that Roxy gave me that night. She took them out of her bag in the foyer of our building. The super looked up from his mopping, but he didn't seem appalled. Maybe he didn't know what they were. I hadn't.

I smiled at Roxy, as fake as I could manage, and she walked me up. That was the whole point for her, I figured.

Joe was lying on his back in the corner, trying to fix the radiator, again. He lifted his head to look at me. "Hey, Collie, how was dinner?" Since he knew exactly how dinner had been, I just went to my room, which had been his room before I came. I left Roxy to narrate.

Even through the slammed door, I knew what was happening: Roxy was tucked up in a neat lotus on the floor beside my father's hip, recounting for him the gory details of our dinner, the tragedy of my motherless state, her theories for my future. My father would keep tightening and loosening until the effort made him sweat and he assumed the heat was up, or else until he hurt himself. This would take all his concentration. He would not listen to Roxy.

In my room, I tossed a single wrapped pad at the ceiling like a tennis ball, listening to the soft murmur of Roxy's voice, the clank of pipes. Roxy was doomed to be ignored, and both of us were doomed to bleed for no reason. It was like stigmata, except grosser and without symbolism. There was no point in being a woman if this was how it was going to go.

And yet it did go that way, and kept going, and here I am with Roxy in a fancy restaurant and she's just this person that I know with her funny clothes and sparkly ring. Maybe we really are just eating dinner for old times' sake, not for her to fish information on my dad, or for me to find out that all young women grow scales at twenty-one. Maybe. I take a piece of the sole and eat it.

"So, are you coming home for the holidays?"

I swallow the fish, feeling only the grit of bread crumbs in my throat. "I'm not speaking to my dad right now."

Roxy's dish is coated in cheese that clings and stretches from plate to mouth. She plucks it with her fork. "Well, from what he said, you're not *not* speaking, just . . . haven't in a while. You could come, he wouldn't give you a hard time."

I can't imagine what a hard time from Joe would constitute – arguing with him is boxing with water. If I stayed in the apartment, he might not even comment, or notice. Even if I argued, yelled, Joe would just let me run down like a music box, before he put on his coat and shoes and went out.

After the menstrual dinner, I didn't even want to fight. Being barely civil with my father worked ok – as long as I ate and went to school and came home – well, he was usually working, anyway. I lasted six weeks, until my mom's birthday and the jellyfish-sting of nearly forgotting it. Only in the late afternoon, when the traffic report said, "It's a summery ·November 30, folks, but the QEW is no picnic, let me tell you."

Joe was never home afternoons, but I didn't ask why he appeared in my doorway, only embarrassed to be caught crying. I found out later that he had been fired from his latest kitchen job.

"What?" I slurped tears up my nose. No fooling anyone.

"Want to tell me what's wrong?"

"No." Hiccup-sob, sigh. "No."

"Ok." He was out of place in his former room, looking sad and uncomfortable. And tired. "Can I – can I come in anyway? I'll be quiet."

"Um." Sniff. "Ok." I was trying to use short words, because sobs were still in my voice. I didn't want him there, but it would've been too hard to argue.

He slid into the room, looking at the Bon Jovi posters as if they were art. He tripped over my backpack and since that brought him halfway to his knees anyway, he just sat down on the dirty rug. We didn't have a vacuum cleaner.

Joe took off his grayed sneakers, and rubbed his ankles, from the long day or the fall, I wasn't sure. Even without speaking you could still hear tears in my throat with each inhale. It was annoying. I hated being the annoying one. I was glad when Joe said something stupid.

"I'm a pretty bad driver." His white sock was speckled with tomato, or blood. "Accidents up the insurance, do you know what that is?"

"Ye-ah." The short vowels were easier to say. "Of course."

"And even without . . . hitting stuff, the car would still need a lot of repairs." Joe owned an ancient Malibu that had mice living in the dashboard. "Think I oughta sell it?"

When normal adults wanted to sell vehicles they did not ask their children. My mother would no more have asked my advice about a car than about God or sex. I hated him for not being a better adult. I wanted to embarrass him, this useless parent. And I wanted to bargain for a better parent, too.

"Roxy loves you, you know."

"Um!" His gaze jerked up from his sock. "What?"

"She looks at you like she's melting. You should pay attention."

"No. Colleen, no. Roxy's my friend, *our* friend."

"She isn't. She just does stuff for me because she wants to make you happy."

"Roxy likes hanging out with you."

"*Roxy does not want to show me the period book!* Neither do you, I know, but it's *your* job. She's a volunteer, and the reason that she is is . . ." I sounded all young and wail-y and stupid. I hated that.

Joe always looks as if he hasn't eaten enough, quite enough, in quite a while, and when he's angry the skin tightens over bones even more, until he's all stretch and hollow. "Colleen. Leave it alone."

"Leave *me* alone." I was furious suddenly. I was always about to be furious at my father. It was like tossing bread crumbs to pigeons, just one crumb of agitation brought a fluttering flock of rage. "If you don't want to do things for me, *don't do things for me*. But don't send your groupies."

"*Group*ies?" He tucked his feet under him and sprang suddenly vertical, towering. "I don't, she's not, I just *men*tioned to her, without your mother . . ."

"You can say her name, you know." I stood up, too, to be even, except there wasn't really floor space for that, and he wound up stepping deferentially aside. He'd been mad for a second there, but I could see he was dissolving again. "Unless you forgot, you can say it."

"I'd . . . rather not." He blinked, longer than a blink, eyelashes resting on tight cheekbones. "I'll talk to Roxy. I didn't know you didn't like her." He opened his eyes and fixed his gaze on my face, which is bony like his but olive-skinned, like my mother's. He nodded once, firmly, as if he'd completed some simple math in his head. "I'm sorry." He went out, gently pulling the door half-closed.

I sat down on the bed. I felt as if everything would change now, one way or another. I'd never see Roxy again, or else they'd hook up and I'd always see her. I guess I was hoping for Roxy's funny clothes and bent cigarettes and earnest books. My father's clothes and cigarettes and books were irritating, because they were his. She would've diluted things to a tolerable strength, maybe.

That didn't happen. Nothing happened. I skipped dinner and spent the night in my room. When I woke up he was out and when he would've got home I was at a friend's. When I got home he was asleep and so it went. When I finally saw him on the weekend we were done arguing, for that round, as done as we ever were. At some point, he handed me the remote control, and I asked him to sign a field trip form. At some point, he admitted that he didn't work at Fellini's anymore. And life went on.

Roxy still came to parties. At the Christmas one (no Jesus carols), she asked me if I wanted to have coffee sometime and, in Second Cup she asked me if I liked any boys. I told her about Andy. A year later she helped me pick out my grade eight formal gown. How to drink without puking, how to study for high school exams. In grade eleven she asked me if I wanted to go on the pill. I said no; she brought me condoms the next time she came by to pick Joe up for tennis. When I called her and said yes three months after that, she made an appointment with her gyno and sat with me in the waiting room. And life went on. And on and on.

Until I left the city, I saw Roxy at our house or somewhere nearly every week. No one ever told me what Joe had told her. When he hugged her it seemed real and warm even if it was awkward, the same way it was when she hugged me. Joe and I never touched each other voluntarily.

The evening at Ollo's is meandering on. We tell each other the food's good, we compliment the waiter. Has every other meal I've ever eaten with Roxy had a thesis? I think so. I think this one does, too. It's not unpleasant, talking about the music piped into the airplane armrest headsets, but I point towards her slender finger holding the dessert menu. "Are we going to talk about that?"

She looks down with a little smile, as if the ring were a baby smiling back. "I was just – I was waiting – I'm getting married."

"It's lovely." I try to picture my father in a jewellery store. I put out my hand and she puts hers on top. Her fingers are damp.

We watch the glitter of her tiny diamond for a while.

"What do you think?"

"I'm thrilled. So, um. This is . . . sudden? Like, is he . . ."

"No, it's not, it's not really *sudden*. Like, a year? I think?"

"Oh. Um?"

"From work. You never met him, you've been so busy, and then away, and . . ."

If I order dessert tonight, it'll be something huge and gross, a hunk of chocolate brownie with ice cream, syrup, dyed-red cherries.

"Hey, listen, would you want to be a bridesmaid?" Her eyes are huge and serious. She smiles at me across the flickering votive and her smile is like something you'd offer a little kid with a bad dream, a comfort that means nothing.

I guess I've believed in Roxy more than I thought. I guess I am a little heartbroken.

Cal is Helpful

THE BOOKSTORE WAS DIZZY WITH CHRISTMAS, and Cal got called every five minutes to authorize voids for scared teenaged cashiers. He tried to look relaxed and cheerful, to goof around with the shakiest ones so they wouldn't cry through their mascara and go home early. "You just double-charge people 'cause you want to talk to me, I know," he said. They laughed happily at that, at Cal's sweaty hair and ability to remember their names. *NSYNC crooned carols, Harry Potter ephemera sold out, babies vomited on the carpet. Cal had already been there three extra hours, smiling at rageful customers, sprinting to the backroom, imagining lovable things he could've said to Mira before it was too late. He finally left at close, asking, "What would you *do* without me? I'm the best manager *ever!*" as he shepherded everyone out into a thick curtain of snow.

He didn't want to check his cell. He had Canadian Modernism papers to mark, and a presentation on "Lycidas" to write, both by Friday. No more Mira: no answering her apologetic texts, no picturing her face, no anything. Absolutely not.

But the screen said *four missed calls.* He strode through the snow-thick wind, phone pushed up under his toque and listened while he tried to light a cigarette. Telemarketer, Mira, hangup, Mira: just checking to see how he was. Her voice was very soft, very gentle. He absolutely didn't have the time or strength to call her. He slipped on ice, smoking and dialing at the same time. He righted himself listening to the rings. Two and a half rings. So much snow.

After *hello,* it took Mira a moment to ask – quietly, gently – "How are you?"

"Good. Well, ok. Work, marking, presentation Friday, so – "

"All that must be tough with . . . everything."

"I'm ok."

"I'm sorry, Cal. I'm just really sorry."

"It's cool. Well, not *cool,* but. But – "

"I'm working on a paper tonight too. Wanna come over?"

"I'm really ok. Really."

"Just because we aren't together anymore doesn't mean we can't talk."

"We are talking . . ." Sitting on Mira's crappy futon, his thighs parallel to hers, being pitied, would sap the strength right of him, he knew. "Ok."

He hit End, and stared at the halo of falling flakes around the street light. He hit Talk to tell Mira no, he didn't have time to go over it all again, even if he wanted to. *One new message.* He listened to the message. It was for Alan.

Alan didn't answer his phone much, and few people cared. Those who did knew who his roommate was.

Cal was only a block from home, and Mira's a block beyond that. He sloshed on, ran up the stairs, kicked Alan's door with his dripping boot. "C'min."

Alan was under a faded black duvet with a thick white hardback propped on his chest. "What's up?" Alan didn't look away from the book.

"I'm, ah, I'm going to Mira's. Just for a minute."

Alan did look at him then, even turned his head on the pillow and pushed the book flat on his belly, but he didn't say anything.

So Cal did. "How's the marking going?"

"Nearly done. You?"

"Not really. I took extra."

"Don't you present on Friday?"

"Don't you?"

"Yeah, but where am I going?"

Cal smiled with all his teeth. "Hey, you never know. Sarah called."

Alan closed his eyes longer than a blink. "What'd she say?"

"Just for you to call her. You gonna call her?"

"I dunno. I guess." Alan pulled up his book again. "See you Friday."

"I'm not staying over. Too much to do."

Alan didn't answer, already reading.

MIRA OPENED THE DOOR in a little pink tank top and plaid boxer shorts, a slice of stomach in between. They sat on the couch, her thighs parallel with his, not touching. "Aren't you cold?" He pointed at her shoulder, fingertip close to bare skin.

"No way. The heat's on – you'll feel when you've been in for a sec. God, you're a popsicle." She pressed her hot palm to his snow-clammy face, fingertips in his hair, wrist on his nose. "Kinney's a hydro miser, but he's gone for the holidays."

Cal stared at the creases in her fingers until she took her hand away. Then he stared at their reflection in the TV screen. Even across the room and reflected in shiny gray, he could see his unbrushed hair, wrinkles in his uniform vest, pockets of dark under his eyes. The unravelling hem of Mira's top, pink thread on her soft belly.

He fished for something to say that wasn't *why?* "What're you working on?"

"Umm . . . Romantics . . . Shelley . . . creative license allowing . . . sexual license." She was pleating the fabric of her shorts, hiking them higher. "What's yours?"

Sometimes Cal pretended he just worked in a bookstore. Sometimes, briefly, almost accidentally, he forgot about Milton's lament for a stranger, the closed book on his desk, the unmarked essays, the capped red pen. But then he'd see an undergrad he was supposed to be marking, or a friend he would grieve for if he died.

"Friendship, death, sheep. Milton. 'Lycidas' – you know it?"

Mira shrugged, sliding the tiny pink strap farther down her left arm, the one closest to Cal. "'Paradise Lost'?"

"Same guy. Different poem."

"Oh, yeah. Yeah, obviously."

Mira was in fourth year undergrad. Anthro. She took Lit electives to keep Cal company. She had short dark rotini curls, a small face full of tight angles, a short tight body that made a cheerleader she'd met once at a party say, "Wow, you'd be easy to throw." She said she treasured that comment.

"It's about how you could miss someone you almost never saw, just miss having them there . . . somewhere." Kinney'd kill him if he smoked in the apartment, but his head buzzed for a cigarette.

"I'll always be there for you, Cal. Not just somewhere. Whatever you need. You can tell me."

Cal flopped back on the futon, which didn't have a real back, just a hump of cushion. He was almost horizontal. "I know, Mir." The smokes were in his coat by the door anyway. Certainly not worth the walk, let alone Kinney's wrath.

"Really? Yeah?" She leaned over him. Her small dark eyes were wet.

"Oh. Oh. And I'll be there for you, too, Mir."

"You don't really owe me that, Cal. Actually. I've been. I haven't been so good." She crossed the far leg over the near one, drawing closer. She seemed to want to rescue him from his pages and papers, his undergrads and cashiers. "I really am sorry for being so. I think I'm. Better now."

"Better than what? You're always pretty good."

"Don't I seem freer? More relaxed, less . . . I dunno, nervous?"

"Are you nervous? Were you? I never noticed."

"I was. Now I feel . . . bolder? You have a strong personality and I felt in the – "

"You've always been pretty strong of personality." Cal closed his eyes.

"That sounded . . . what did you mean by that?"

"What time is it?"

"Ten. Well, just after."

He pressed his skull back hard into the futon.

"Strong of personality? Cal? Why did you say that?"

"Listen, Mira, I've got to go home and work," Cal said without opening his eyes.

Shifting legs on the futon. Closer perhaps, but still not touching. Did he feel the halo of her warmth?

"You're not *sleeping*, are you? Cal, I'm trying to get to something major here."

"Mira, today a man tried to return a broken-spined copy of *The Da Vinci Code* because it was bad. I'd been at work so long that I gave him the money. I have to mark dozens of Red-Bull-fuelled undergrad papers that are supposed to be about Canadian poetry but are in fact about Red Bull. I can't *do* this."

"*You* could use one."

"Red Bull?" Cal hadn't showered that morning, and he hadn't done laundry in a couple weeks. He'd sweated through his rayon uniform shirt hauling boxes, sprinting to get orders, defusing fights. Mira was right, the apartment was warm, too warm. He was sweating and everything itched: spine, armpits, balls. He opened his eyes. Mira was still coiled above him, so pretty, nearly naked. "Ok."

He didn't even wait until she turned before scratching through his pants, but the fabric was too thick and slippery for it to be satisfying. He knew he couldn't escape until he told Mira what she wanted to know, but he didn't know what that was. She seemed to want to be told why she'd broken up with him. And he didn't know.

That's why he'd taken it so hard, sprawled in the shoes and crumpled cigarette packs beside Alan's bed, sketching in the air above his face the way Mira arched her body up to catch a Frisbee, flung tea bags off her spoon into the trash.

Alan curled on the mattress above, his book hooked in the curve of his belly, peering down at poor prostrate Cal. "So you loved her?"

"*Love,* present tense. You can't just stop when they tell you to stop. You know this." Alan flinched as he did whenever Sarah's shadow loomed. Cal hurried on, "When Mira walked, she didn't bounce at all. Her spine stayed so straight." Cal made his fingers walk smoothly across the air.

"Walks, present tense. You aren't with her, but she's still walking somewhere."

Cal flattened his fingers onto his face. "That's hard to accept."

"That God didn't punish her for dumping you by making her a paraplegic?"

"That she's doing interesting things and I'm not seeing it." Even with his eyes closed, Cal recognized the scrabble of Alan picking library tape off his book. "What?"

"Well."

"What?"

But he knew. Cal knew it, on Alan's floor, on Mira's futon, wherever he collapsed, that Mira's interesting bits, her complicated jokes and puzzles and brilliance, had been fading for some time. Lately she was all A-papers and analysis of her mother in terms like "psychological warfare." Especially lately.

Something clanked in the kitchen, but Mira did not re-emerge. Cal drew his knees towards his face, then back a little; the slacks smelled like sweat and fog and rayon. Mira had been interesting, he knew, but then she hid her best mind, like a hot body in a baggy dress. He didn't know why.

Still, sometimes she said things like, "I can bend how I want to bend, nobody bends me. It's not good as a transitive verb." Even better, sometimes she *did* things like throw herself across Cal in bed when she came in sweaty and limp from her morning run. Her damp clothes would be almost frictionless. Cal learned to be above the covers then, to feel her. It was one of the only times she was ever limp, and he loved the curved weight, still panting against his chest.

What she loved was the hard bone in his sternum, how he was so skinny – fatless, muscleless – that when she pressed her face there, there was nothing to press into. Space always remained between her eyes and his skin, or space beneath her nose, unless she pressed hard enough to bend cartilage, sucked hard enough to leave a mark.

She came back, with mugs. "Kinney drank all the Red Bull. Coffee?"

"Sure." He put his arms out to jolt himself up. He hated this futon.

Mira set down the cups, set herself down on curled legs beside him.

"Wait – you had time to make coffee? Was I sleeping? Did I sleep?"

"I dunno. Your eyes were closed. Any dreams?"

"Um . . ."

Now their thighs weren't parallel, because her feet were tucked sideways, arrowing her knees towards him. Her rucked up shorts.

"Mira, I gotta get some work done or I'll fail."

"Have you ever actually failed anything, Cal?" She squinted through her hair, and tiny creases formed around her eyes. He'd been there so long, they were both aging.

"But I don't understand 'Lycidas' yet. But I think I could. I *could* do well if I worked at it."

Mira wiped the curls from her face. They immediately flopped down again. "Oh my goodness, Cal, you're Type-A."

His pants were catching the hair on his legs, he was sweating up and down. It was too fucking hot in these clothes, in this apartment. Where was Kinney with his violent metabolism to turn off the thermostat, open windows on the blizzard? "Of course I am. I want, want to succeed at things."

Suddenly, he thought about Alan: Alan building himself a nest out of old papers and duvets, getting Cs for doing assignments that he liked, not the ones assigned, letting his girlfriend disappear like a glove in the snow.

"So, you didn't want me to end us because you wanted to succeed at that too?"

"You said. You didn't. Jesus, Mira, what do you want from me?"

"I – " She fell on his chest as if she had been pushed. Cal almost glanced behind her for Kinney before he felt the full weight of her mouth, the strength of her tongue, the cool of her skin above the tank top. He longed to rub her cool skin along his sweating back, throat, legs.

She kissed him hard, the bruise of teeth through lips, the sudden sucking away of breath. Her fingers dug into his hair and attempted to drag through, got stuck and rested halfway to his left ear.

Oh, the beautiful body of Mira now resting fully on his lap and what was Cal doing? Nothing. He was rocked back, pinned helpless against the futon. He'd always known Mira was stronger than him, and now he was utterly overpowered by her small dense form. Cal was surprised that he was hard, wanting her, when he didn't think he had the energy to want anything. Mira shifted silkily, sighed, bit his lip softly but not – not gently. She reached down and tugged at the zip of his cheap rayon uniform pants. It stuck a little, it always did, but then she got it open. Thank god.

HE WENT DIRECTLY from Mira's to the library, sleep still crusting his eyes, the buzz of his cell on his hip. He had left as soon as he woke up, close to noon. He had gone while she was sleeping, the only way he could. It was still snowing.

He was in a transition stage: he didn't listen to his messages but he didn't turn the phone off – he didn't cry, but he didn't wash his face, either. He just wrote up grief and sheep and poetry as best he could on three hours sleep. The afternoon went on and on and the snow came down and down. To keep awake, he did pushups in the men's room, phone clipped tight to his belly. When the sunset started to tip in the windows and colour his notes yellow-gray, the words spun out over the page and drifted away.

Oh heavy change now thou art gone gone and never to return. He went outside to breathe cold air and stare at the pure white of the empty parking lot. He stood in the fading blizzard and thought about Milton and Edward King, and about how the worst loss is something you never really had in the first place. His cell vibrated again, horrible against his already jittery flesh, so he took it out and flung it across the still pond of snow. He was nearly surprised it didn't skip on the white surface.

HE GOT HOME at snow-gray dawn. Cal put Nescafé crystals, sugar, and eggnog in a cup, started the kettle and kicked Alan's door yelling, "Coffee?"

There was no answer. Cal poured, stirred the beigey sludge, and left it to cool while he opened the hall closet. "*Alan!* Did you borrow my good coat?" Really Cal just wanted the company. Mira had said she truly loved him, but she thought it was the love of a friend. She thought.

Alan didn't come out of his room, and the coat didn't surface, so Cal gave up and went looking through the bottom cupboard for Corn Pops.

A girl's voice said, "Alan had an early class." Sarah was looking down over the counter. Cal hadn't seen her in months, but she looked the same, a pile of sweatshirts with frayed cuffs, face pillow-creased, hair tangled ginger-brown down her back.

"I have the same class." Cal wasn't sure if he was glad to see her. They had once been friends, friends-in-law anyway, before she stopped opening her door when Alan knocked. "That's why I need the jacket."

She shrugged through her layers of fleece. There was no cereal, but he found a tin of Pringles. He put a stack of chips into his mouth and chewed, Sarah's gray eyes on him. Finally, he had to ask, "So, what brings you by?"

Sarah fidgeted her bare feet on the dirty tile. "I got evicted."

"I see." Cal had not budgeted time for this conversation, and he still hadn't found a jacket without soup stains. He would already have to skip a shower. He'd be late if Sarah continued to speak slowly. But she blurted out, "Can I stay here?"

Cal ate and Sarah watched. He wondered if she was hungry; she used to be skinny, but it was hard to tell under all the sweatshirts. "Chip? Salt and vinegar, very invigorating in the morning." He waved the canister at her.

Sarah rolled her eyes, but took two and chewed obediently.

While her mouth was full, Cal suggested softly, "Maybe you should ask your ex-boyfriend about staying here."

She swallowed. "He says it's your apartment, too."

Walking towards his room, shirt already over his head, Cal muttered, "Well, ok, if you think it's a good idea." He didn't know if she'd heard or not.

WHAT WAS INTERESTING about Sarah was the way she didn't want anything, or at least not much. She'd sit in a bar and not order a drink, she'd stand up on an empty bus, she'd disappear if someone said, "Hey, you'll like this." Sarah had stayed at their place for days at a time fairly often, but Cal was hard pressed to think of a time he'd seen her eat. He was startled that morning to see her back molars working on the Pringles, strangely muscular through the flimsy skin of her face.

Cal could not intuit Sarah, but he had liked her. Once he'd stormed home after a fight with Mira, thrown his coat into the sink and yelled, "Girls are stupid." Sarah, reading at the kitchen table, had raised her gaze and asked, "And contagious?"

That last time he'd seen her had been at the student centre caf. After that, Sarah had started evaporating, stopped coming to their place, finally stopped letting Alan into hers. But once they'd gone to the cafeteria together, the three of them. Alan had asked Cal to come.

"Hey, what're you doing later?"

Cal had been bolting yoghurt, late for something. He'd grunted through Strawberry Crème, motioned with his spoon for Alan to continue.

"Me and Sar are going to eat at the student centre. They have nachos now."

Cal choked on a pulverized strawberry, coughed and dribbled pink. Alan watched absently, as if Cal were a bird outside the window.

Finally Cal swallowed. "Why?" He wiped his chin with a paper towel.

"Sarah's, well, you know how she is."

"Not really." She was just the girl Alan loved too much. Cal liked her but he had no idea how she was.

Alan hugged his arms around his soft ribs. "I'm trying to help her be . . . less nervous. I could use backup." Alan never asked for favours, Alan rarely said multiple sentences in a row. Alan was leaning against the fridge in his boxers. His pale hairy legs stuck out, bird-skinny.

"Well, ok, if you think it's a good idea."

THE CAFETERIA was bright enough – you could see everything clearly – but the light was gray. The ceiling was an enormous tinted glass dome, colouring everything dusk.

"Well, here we are, then." The place was crowded and Alan's voice was loud over the chatter of undergrads. "Seems all right."

It didn't seem all right to Sarah, obviously. She was shaking, Cal could see it in her arms and shoulders, even through all those layers. "How you doing, Sar?"

No answer. Alan took her arm firmly and gestured for Cal to take the other. In his free hand, Alan had a notebook. He gestured with the notebook. They hadn't left the doorway yet.

Cal thought he'd probably never touched Sarah. She took pains to avoid even brushing against him in their narrow hallway. He thought she probably wouldn't like it if he touched her now, but her teeth were chattering – clearly she needed some sort of help. The grasp of his fingers took an instant to get through fabric to flesh. Of course, her arms were thin, but he was surprised by the hardness of bone there: no muscle, no fat, nothing.

Alan was staring at the notebook. "We'll walk a bit." He looked up.

He took a step on the tiled floor, and Sarah didn't move. Alan breathed so deeply that Cal could hear it a body away. Cal took a step too, his sneaker parallel to Alan's loafer. Sarah was wearing dirty pink Keds. When Cal looked up, he saw her eyes were filled with tears.

He had no idea what could misfire in her head to make the girls in diamond-patterned sweaters, the orange-glazed sign of the Pizza Pizza, the cry of "It's asymptotic, you douche," so terrifying. But she was. Terrified.

"Sarah." Alan had quieted his voice, speaking as he sometimes did when he and Sarah were alone in the kitchen, Cal in his bedroom overhearing the tone without the words. Now he heard the words: "This is fine. You're fine. I've got you. Cal's got you."

If Sarah had ever wanted anything, Cal would've offered it then. Chicken-pesto pizza, a diamond-patterned sweater, actual diamonds. Even if she never wanted, he wondered if he ought to try. In their kitchen, she sometimes laughed at his jokes.

All these stretch-cotton teenagers and bolted-down loop-backed chairs. Three minutes – it had been at least that long – seemed interminable to Cal, but it must've felt worse to poor shaking Sarah. Cal had once been a punk trying to skateboard at the mall, after all. He was inured to the oregano-and-fake cheese smell, the pushing-shoving girls, their sexy horseplay, even the gray light.

How long did it seem to Alan, who was from a mall-less town, who also didn't love the world, who had to put on a supreme force of will to address a class, buy groceries, attend a meeting. Alan did, though, grimly, one foot in front of the other, eyes sharp and quick and forbidding.

Now he was anguished, Cal could see it over Sarah's frizzy hair. Alan was flipping notebook pages with one hand, face tipped down, other arm slowly creeping around her waist. "Tell me what you are afraid of here, Sarah. Tell me the worst-case scenario here, before we go forward."

Still silence, teary gaze on the bins of plastic cutlery, the gray glass, the swoosh on a Nike shoe striding past.

Cal joggled his arm against hers. "What we could do is, is run. The faster we go in, the faster we go through, the faster we get out."

Alan shook his head, watching a girl with bleached pigtails steal a footballer's pizza slice. "It doesn't help to be scared. This is a just a cafeteria, nothing to run from."

"Not running *from,* just running. For fun." The girl climbed a table, holding the cardboard triangle aloft. The big guy grabbed her knees. Cal hopped up on his toes, eager for the spring. "Let's run."

"I don't think that's . . ."

They weren't really making eye contact – Sarah was technically short enough to be talked over, but that seemed so rude, as if she were in a coma, insensible. Which she seemed almost to be, staring now at the pigtailed girl's pink moccasins.

"Running would be better than just standing here paralyzed," Cal said firmly.

"I'm not paralyzed." And yet her lips scarcely moved, and her eyes didn't slide in either direction.

Alan looked startled that she had spoken, but he finally shut the notebook. "Do you want to, then? Run? Or walk?"

"Go. . . ." Her voice was reedy, wavering, fading. "Can we go?"

Alan shut his eyes and tipped back on his heels, pressing the book lightly against his sternum. "Of course we can go if you want. I'm not in charge. You said you wanted to try, so . . ."

"I . . ."

Cal didn't mind being close to Sarah like he'd thought. She looked as though she would smell of hospital, disinfectant and unwashed hair, but in fact, she was sharp as cloves, a pine forest in winter. Such a bright strong smell close up, but nothing at all a few feet away. He leaned even closer, letting their arms press from elbow to shoulder. He knocked back some hair from her ear. "Run. Run."

She pulled away from him, huddling into Alan. "We'll fall."

"We won't," Alan said quickly, but she was still talking.

"I'll fall. I'm clumsy. Everyone would see . . ."

"So we'll walk, then." Alan flicked the notebook into his jacket pocket, looked purposeful. Cal put out his foot again.

"*No!*"

This was the loudest Cal had ever heard Sarah speak, bell-like and clear, but he couldn't appreciate it, because the edges of her nostrils were pink and her hair was sticking to her cheek in the tears.

Alan tightened his hold on his girlfriend's waist. His fingers brushed Cal's ribs as they clenched, so tightly were they all tucked into one another. They swung around, all three on one axis, and bonked back through the swing doors, and out into the fading sun. They marched in lockstep past boys wheeling their bikes, past the overflowing recycling bin. They crossed the roadway and Cal hoped someone had looked for traffic because he certainly hadn't. Above the whish of distant cars and click of bike wheels he couldn't hear Sarah's breath, but he could feel it through his palm, through her sweaters and her ribs. It was a sob.

When they reached the traffic median, Cal realized how far it was to the bus stop on the corner opposite the end of the long driveway. Sarah must have realized it too, because she stopped there and sank down on the sidewalk. When the men finally freed her arms, she scooted onto the thin dirty strip of grass on the verge and buried her head in her knees.

Cal and Alan were suddenly left with air between them, as they were used to. Alan seemed to have absorbed some of Sarah's shaking.

Cal couldn't think of anything other than that they were free to smoke since they weren't in a school building anymore. The weren't really free, of course, Sarah weeping at their feet, but he stepped to one side of her and Alan went to the other and they were guarding her, so long as they didn't drop any ash in her hair.

Cal shook the pack at Alan, who nodded, sidewalk-gray. Cal took out two and lit them both in his own mouth, like a movie gangster, then passed Alan one. Deep drags.

And then, having given her all the time and privacy they could on the verge, cars and bikes surging past, they crouched awkwardly.

Sarah lifted her face from her knees and looked at them, tear-bright but no longer actually crying. "I'm sorry."

Both at once, "It's all right."

Alan ran his nicotine fingers through her hair and she turned towards him and said, "I hate cognitive behaviour therapy."

"I'm sorry."

"I hate the cafeteria."

Cal palmed her back. "Everyone does, Sary."

She dropped her face onto Alan's chest then. Above the traffic Cal heard what could've been another sob, or chuckling.

CAL SLIPPED INTO CLASS as the prof said how she'd truly enjoyed their time together and there would be no extensions on the mid-January paper deadline. By the time Cal had his thin dirty jacket off, Alan was standing at the podium, his shoulders hunched in Cal's cashmere coat. Alan looked miserable, but he looked like that at the grocery store.

The talk, near as Cal could follow, was about verbal clauses in *Samson*

Agonistes. Alan seemed at least slightly interested in his own words by the conclusion, though he did lunge for his seat. He was made to stand back up for questions, but there weren't many. No one really understood, so what could they ask?

Cal felt delirious at the podium. Mira had said she would die if they weren't friends. When Edward King died, John Milton hadn't seen him in maybe five years; it was the knowledge of the death that wrecked him, not actual absence. Or not. Maybe Cal had misunderstood the poem utterly. Maybe it was about sheep.

Most of the class looked puzzled and tired, but Alan's eyes were bright on Cal, awaiting insightful poetic analysis as if there were no Sarah or Mira or undergraduate papers in all the seven seas. His blotted notes started with a lame-ass Miltonic joke: "Throw hither all your quaint enameld eyes," but everyone laughed, because at least they could understand. After that, he was fine. The material was mainly coherent, and people thought he was funny and it was the last day of term.

Afterwards everyone shuffled around, talking and eating the cookies someone brought. A few people congratulated Cal on his talk. Alan said nothing to anybody, just took a cookie and sat quietly by the door. Cal knew he wouldn't eat, just put the cookie into his jacket pocket – Cal's jacket pocket. As soon as it was civil, Cal disengaged from conversation and nodded and Alan nodded and they both walked out of the room.

Through the hallway, down some steps, out the front doors and down some more steps, they were silent. It was a shock to see the world blizzardless, the sun gleaming off the icy campus, bikes and cars and squirrels. They walked a hundred metres before Cal said quietly, through the throb of his headache, "You spoke well."

Alan shook his whole body. "I didn't." He headed towards the street and Cal followed. The doors of the cafeteria had holly and bows on them. "*You* spoke well."

Cal looked sideways. "I did, didn't I?"

"Really." Alan nodded. "Not even considering . . ."

"Considering . . . ?" They walked a few paces. "Considering . . . the night at Mira's?"

"What, you were reading over there?" Through the gates, breathing off-campus air, they stopped walking.

"*You* had an interesting night last night, too."

Alan patted his chest for cigarettes. "I didn't." He pulled one out, shook the pack at Cal, lit them both without saying anything. After his first drag: "Sarah got evicted."

Cal nodded, still waiting.

"I couldn't get you on your cell to ask before. Can she stay with us?" No duration mentioned, not even *for a while*.

Cal winced; despite his digging mittenless until his hands were raw, the phone would remain in the snowdrift until spring. "Where'll we put her?"

Alan shrugged, Cal's coat collar bending his earlobes. "With me."

"Good idea?"

Alan seemed to actually think about that. "It'll be ok." He huffed out a long breath of cold steam and nicotine, looked at the sky, and then back at Cal, who was bouncing on his toes and smoking down to the filter. "How's Mira?"

Cal chucked the butt down hard enough to put it out. "We're friends now. We'll see how it goes." He clamped his lips together, feeling the dig of teeth.

"Friends?" Alan stared at him for a moment. "*We're* friends. You and Mira are . . . something else."

"Yeah, I know, but that's what we're saying right now."

The corners of Alan's mouth curved up almost past the confines of his face. "Let's go eat. We haven't got anything at home." Alan took a step forward, then stopped when Cal didn't move.

"I can't today. Go get Sarah."

Alan looked at his dark shoes on the snow-white sidewalk. "Sarah won't come. You know how she is."

Cal twisted on the sidewalk. "Let's go home."

Alan watched him with narrowed eyes. "Why can't you go to lunch?"

Cal let himself slouch. The weight of last night, the nights before that, the headache of tears, everything was pushing his head down. "I didn't finish the marking. It's due . . . now, pretty much."

"How many you got left?" Alan looked like Cal felt – pale and blood-shot, shaky and sunless. Alan, however, was more used to it. "And how long are they?"

Cal no longer had the strength even to shrug. "Maybe thirty, eight pages each. I'm gonna . . . well, I can't do it. But, maybe I can get a day's reprieve. Or – "

"I can do half."

"You can't."

"What? I can do CanLit. I can sign your initials. Still little M inside a big C, like a teenage girl, right?"

"Yeah. Alan – "

"Yeah?" Alan held out his hand, the caffeine tremor and the bitten fingernails.

Cal took off his backpack and counted out a stack of fifteen stapled papers. His pride would refuse, let Alan go collapse or talk to Sarah about whatever undid them. But the part of him that hadn't slept properly in weeks was stronger than his pride. He handed Alan the pages.

"Good." Alan sat down on the steps outside the gate. He took a red pen from his briefcase and looked down at the first page. After a few moments, he drew a heavy slash through something and began to scribble in the margin.

"You going to do that here?"

Alan looked up and, just for a moment, was something less than deadpan. "I'm not . . . ready to go home."

Cal nodded, his heavy head swinging forward so hard he thought he might fall. "Gotcha." He sat down on the cement step next to Alan, the rest of the papers on his knees. He felt cold leaching through his cords, boxers, flesh. He rummaged in his pocket for a pen.

Steal Me

LIKE A REEF AT THE BOTTOM OF THE OCEAN, Aida stood still in the middle of the dance floor, clutching her Corona. A small man with a huge Japanese beer was dancing with her. Schools of tank-top girls passed, their gill-shiny hair fluttered by overhead fans. The music had a high, buzzing beat Aida could feel in the roof of her mouth, lyrics about what Nicole Scherzinger could offer a guy. The guy was minnowing around Aida, ducking and grinning. The laser lights turned his blond hair algae-coloured, and he would dance with her whether she danced or not. He grabbed her right hip and tugged hard. When she lurched forward, he lunged in, too, trying to lodge his thigh between hers. Her skirt was too long and tight for that; his knee trampolined, and he threw up his beer-hand for balance, which knocked her beer-hand, and her seven-dollar bottle went splashing onto the ankles of a girl who wavered like seaweed on her high heels as Aida backed away. The guy said something, but she couldn't hear what and she kept going. He was cute, but she didn't like being grabbed.

She found Samantha pinned between the wall and a guy in a pink Lacoste shirt, collar popped. His hair was thick and shiny, possibly brown though it was hard to tell under the lasers. He was talking earnestly to Sam's pale upturned profile, but Aida knew no one could hear earnestness over the pound and whistle of the music. His knee was between Sam's thighs.

Aida leaned against the wall beside them, but Sam didn't see, staring into the guy's eyes. *He* noticed Aida, and smiled when she grabbed Sam's hand.

Sam turned languorously. She spoke, but nothing was audible. On the video screen above the bar, a girl was running, ducking and kicking, running.

Aida yelled, "I have to go to the bathroom."

Sam shook her head, blank but trying, ignoring the guy kissing her neck. Nicole whispered something hot and incoherent.

Aida pressed her mouth against Sam's ear and shrieked, "Bathroom."

The cup of Sam's ear tasted like salt, with an edge of perfume-poison.

Still nothing. Finally Aida just pulled the hand she had. It took Sam a moment to disentangle her thighs from the man, whose mouth opened in dismay, or maybe words, before he turned to Aida looking as poisonous as perfume.

Sam waved goodbye.

Aida kept the hand all across the dance floor, her thumbnail firmly tracing Samantha's wedding ring.

In the bathroom, with the attendant folding tiny towels and all the tiny girls on tiny cellphones, Samantha beamed into the mirror at Aida. Her mascara'd lashes were black spikes, incongruous with the blond sweeping down her spine, but she looked glitter-polished and cheerful. Aida looked blurred, smeared, although she wasn't wearing makeup.

"Wasn't he cute?" Sam wet her hands and patted the electric hair around her face.

"Where's Terry?"

She either heard or did not – the music was only slightly quieter in the bathroom. Rhianna now. All Sam said was, "Can I crash at yours? I *cannot* face the Go-Bus drunk."

Aida said ok, though Samantha was the least drunk person she could see.

AIDA PULLED OFF HER TOP, kicked out of the clingy skirt she had grown to loathe, and flopped into bed, close to Steve but not touching. He was curled towards her, bare-chested, boxers twisted low. She squirmed onto her side to unhook her bra, and her elbow brushed his bare chest. Like a sea anemone closing, he wrapped around her, pressed his face between her breasts. She felt his eyelashes flutter on her skin.

It was almost morning anyway, pink under the curtains. She tossed her bra to the floor and pressed her lips to his hair, gelled spikes pillow-smashed.

Steve sounded underwater. "Hey. Mmm . . . where were you? I let myself in."

"Uh, an old friend called, wanted to go out." She moved her mouth down, trying to tongue the shiny silver ring circling the tip of his left eyebrow.

Steve put his leg over hers. "Fun? . . . so late."

"Yeah, fun."

He squeezed her hip, licked her lips. "You taste like beer." His eyes were still closed.

"Shhh . . ." She tugged on the elastic of his boxers. "Be quiet."

"Why?" He helped her tug, and they got the left side down to the thigh; the right was still hooked up where he was leaning on her.

"My friend's asleep in the living room. I think she's leaving her husband."

AIDA HUSTLED STEVE OUT before the sun was all up, Sam still a breathless lump on the couch. In the hallway, the door only half-shut, Steve whisper-yelled, "You're not going to even let me shower? I gotta go to work and I smell like . . ."

"Well." She arched her eyebrows, trying for sexy, but she felt groggy and dirty herself, sagging against the door frame in half of last night's clothes. She hadn't stayed up all night since – she never stayed up all night.

"I'll cover for you at the library. We aren't short this week, are we?"

Aida straightened. "It's not a crisis. I'll come to work."

"You gonna just leave her? Who is this girl?"

"High school friend, no one you know. She's fine. Just buy me an hour."

She kissed him, but didn't open her mouth; there was motion on the other side of the door. This turned out to be Samantha intuiting how the coffee maker worked, finding the bread Aida saved for the birds, apparently taking Splenda packets out of her purse, for Aida didn't have those. She didn't have makeup remover, either, but there was Sam, bright-eyed, clear-skinned, murmuring, "Hope you don't mind, can't get on with the day without coffee'n'shower, comfortable couch, thank you truly, old friends are the best," before she disappeared to the bathroom.

Aida took a cup of coffee before going to put on pants. She and Steve would smell the same at work.

STEVE WAS ON REFERENCE DESK with Jennifer – the one with heavy-framed glasses and honey-striped hair who said that Aida's story-hours were chaotic and that crafts involving glue shouldn't be permitted and also once asked Aida where she got her clogs in a voice that did not imply envy. Aida was going to go straight to the overflowing picture-book cart and her new Madeleine display, but Steve caught her hand, startling Aida and Jennifer both. They were supposed to be a secret at work.

"Aida. I'm due for a break. I'll make you a coffee."

"I just got here. And I already had – " Steve tugged her into the break room and, stupidly, shut the door. They weren't a secret anymore. Aida peered nervously out the tiny chicken-wire window.

He took a step towards her, put a hand on her hip and was suddenly, dizzily, the man in the club, dancing with her by grabbing her. Aida backed up to the counter, hopped up to sit. "Where's my coffee?"

Steve raised his eyebrow, the ringed one. "What'd you get up to last night?"

"A club."

Steve turned to rummage in the cupboard, shoulders flexing against the thin fabric of his shirt. "A *club*? You, Aida?"

Aida looked down at her painter jeans, her Mighty Mouse T-shirt. Even the tight skirt last night hadn't been sexy, just odd. She'd made it from remaindered Halloween fabric. "Sam wanted to. Things with her husband seem . . . I think she thinks clubs are what single people do."

A packet of ginger tea fell into the sink. Steve turned the kettle on, grabbed the tea and tossed it from hand to hand. "*You* aren't single people. Did you get scammed on?"

"Eh. I guess." Story hour was in thirteen minutes. She wondered if there would even be a place tidy enough to seat the kids. She wondered if Jennifer and the others were in the corridor, wondering aloud about how the only male under forty in the branch had ended up with a girl who wore cartoon-shirts and kept injuring herself with the staple gun.

"And, you, the scammers, Sam . . . ? How'd it go? Before you came home to . . . ravish me?" He tossed her the tea packet, but she was peering out at the hall. The package bounced off her left breast, Mighty Mouse's billowing cape.

"Entirely PG, except for you."

Steve abandoned the tea. "You aren't unhot, you know." He came to stand between her knees, which were braced apart to keep her from falling off the counter.

"Says you." She stuck out her tongue and he was close enough that it brushed his forehead; he was less salty than Samantha. The kettle screamed before he could say more; if it hadn't, she probably would have kissed him.

SIX YEARS SINCE SAM AND TERRY'S WEDDING. Aida had long lost her snapshot of the old gang jammed around a table of salmon and flowers. They'd promised fervently to stay in touch, but until yesterday they'd mainly just poked each other on Facebook. Yesterday Sam had called from the Go-Bus from Oakville, wanting to go clubbing. Today, Samantha was sprawled in Aida's foyer with the late afternoon sun, a tangle of Winners bags, and a fat Harry Potter book. She jumped up when Aida came in.

"Aida!" Sam hoped around with her bags, a rustle of plastic.

"Hey." Aida fumbled her keys. She'd assumed Sam was back in Oakville. She couldn't think of a single appropriate question. "C'mon up," she said finally.

In the living room, Samantha revealed her Winners treasure: a complicated blouse, labelled in French, silky but not silk, sixty percent off. Aida squinted. "It's awfully low."

"That's the back." Sam flipped the champagne-coloured cloth and showed a slightly more modest slit. "Shoulder blades are the new tits."

"I didn't know that."

"Yeah, you wouldn't waste your time watching *What Not to Wear*." Sam whipped her T-shirt over her head and tossed it onto the couch.

"It could help."

"Doesn't really. Look at me." Sam went towards the faux-fireplace in her lavender bra. They were both staring at Sam's breasts in the mirror over the mantle.

Aida opened Harry Potter — *murder, The Hanged Man, dark looks.* "Kids at my library love this, but it's too heavy for me."

Samantha came back to the couch and flopped down. "Let's go somewhere *fun* for dinner, ok? Girls night out."

"Sure." Aida couldn't concentrate. "You probably shouldn't go around . . ." She drew an infinity symbol in the air in front of Sam's breasts. "City windows, you know."

"Give'em a show." Sam grinned, picked up the blouse and put her arms through the right holes without looking, on the first try. The cloth slid around her like gift-wrap. "Hey, you work in a library?"

ON THE STREET, Aida had to adjust her stride to Sam's long legs, her mind to the stares they got. Sam's skirt was not particularly short, but even from mid-thigh to ankle was far on Sam. Walking beside her, Aida felt like a lion tamer.

Sam wanted a sidewalk patio, despite the heat, yelling teenagers, clutching couples, unleashed dogs. Aida didn't know if she was supposed to study the menu or ask if Sam had left her husband. She located something vegetarian – eggplant – then looked up. Sam was staring over the railing at a guy leaning against a parked car. He noticed. He had paint-spattered jeans, untied shoes.

A smile started at the corners of Sam's pink mouth.

"Sam?"

"Heeeyyy, pretty girl . . . ."

Aida doubted it was his car.

Sam tipped her menu down and smiled wider. The man came closer, dangling a beer bottle from two fingers.

"*Sam!*" Aida shot a narrow-eyed look over the rail and grabbed Sam's hand from her placemat. The man moved on.

"The cutest guy just smiled at me. People are so friendly in your neighbourhood, Aida. You must meet so many guys."

"Well, no, not . . . Sam, where's Terry?"

Sam freed her hand to pick up her menu. "What's rapini?"

"Little broccolis, I think."

"Funny. He's at home. Where he's supposed to be. Oh, you know how it is."

"Sure." But Aida didn't know a thing about how it was with Sam, nothing beyond the Christmas cards, the Facebook profile, the reunion barbeques.

"Terry's a fucker."

The waiter appeared, broad-shouldered, friendly, name-tagged Gary. Aida ordered eggplant, Sam said rapini, balked, said Bolognese.

Sam watched Gary stride back to the bar. He disappeared behind it and still Sam didn't turn her head. The silence was getting long. "He messed around? Terry?"

Colour flushed up Sam's pale neck.

Aida realized the difference between calling Terry a *fucker* and saying he fucked.

"I – I think – maybe. Yes. I think probably."

Sam looked at her placemat, the napkin, the street. Her eyes were red around the edges, her nose too. They sat in silence awhile.

"Here you ladies go." Gary set down their salads. He was about eighteen, heavy with muscle and gelled hair, a pepper grinder the length of his arm. Sam brightened, and he overspiced the salad because she didn't say *when*.

THE TEN-TO-SIX SHIFT: frayed taddle tape and the cart with the broken wheel, stolen *US Weekly*s and taking down a bulletin board without a staple remover. Seniors who bickered over the obituaries and insisted the Raffi tape was too loud. Jennifer asking if Aida was wearing Steve's pants.

At 6:13, the sun was a smog blur and the air was swamp-hot. Samantha was slouching beside the curb in a picnic-white linen dress.

"The girl wouldn't let me wait inside. But she asked me where I got my shoes." Aida could imagine Jennifer being envious for real of these: soles of thick light wood, raw fabric binding the ankles. Aida liked how Sam tip-tipped along on three inches of pine. But to ask where they were bought was silly – they were shoes for Sam alone. No other pair could exist.

"What did you do today?" Aida started walking, and Sam fell in stride. The smogged sun was white as the linen dress, so hot it felt like there would never be night.

"*Eve*rything. I bought a purse on *the street* in Chinatown, and then I started walking and before I knew it I was in front of this big museum with ugly tarps all over. I didn't even know what it was at first. There was an exhibit, though, all colours and shapes . . . Not pictures, just *things*."

"I went, too. Fantastic." Aida was pretty sure *fantastic*, but not positive. She had been overwhelmed by the bright echoing museum, by Steve's narration at her shoulder. The floors were so shiny and vast, let alone the things on the walls and pedestals. Everyone silently clutched the earpiece from the audio-tour, moved slowly, alone and on tiptoe. Except Steve, who had actually studied Abstract Expressionism, who scorned the formula tour and wouldn't let her take one. He whispered, pointed, saved them each the $10 and made them both a spectacle. Aida remembered nothing of what he'd said, almost nothing of the art, just his hot breath in her ear, the glaring silent masses, and the wide shiny floors as she stared down at them. One painting was so huge and blue, herself so tired and disoriented, it felt as if she'd collided with it while standing still. "Fantastic."

"Oh, abso*lute*ly." Sam swung her arms wide, fingertips brushing Aida's. "I wish I actually knew something about art."

"Me, too." They were almost at Queen's Park, and Aida was on the edge of mentioning Steve, Steve's knowledge of art and life and librarianship, the way Steve said he loved her and she wouldn't talk about it. She wouldn't talk about it. "I don't, either."

"I saw this game in a movie." Samantha stopped under a tree. "Should we sit? It's cooler here in the shade."

"Well, your dress."

Samantha looked so puzzled Aida pointed. "Oh, it's old." She brushed her palms down the white linen as if to brush it off, then crouched down into a ball and tipped off her shoes, hard onto her hip but modest, legs curled beside her, shoes stacked.

Aida sat down too, less elegant, even in jeans. "A movie?"

"Arty thing. Well, it took place in a gallery. The girl who worked there, from each exhibit she picked the one picture that she would steal."

"Like, an art-heist movie?" Aida was uprooting grass with her fingers, getting dirt under her nails. Sam's nails were perfectly round, smooth and unpolished.

"Not steal for real. Like, just the one she *would* take, if she could."

"Ah, sorry, I didn't get it." Aida kept digging until she had a hand-sized hollow, the soil crumbling and riddled with roots and cigarette butts. When she looked up, Sam was staring, waiting.

"So, which picture would *you* take?"

"Um. I." Aida hadn't realized she'd been supposed to consider. "The big blue one, maybe. I felt like it was falling on me when I was next to it."

Sam looked down at Aida's dirty hands in the flickering leaf-shadows. "You think it's weird, the game?"

"No, it's just . . . I can't imagine having floors that shiny."

"Shiny?"

Aida felt the dizziness that came from people not hearing her interior monologue. "The museum's floors are so polished, the rooms are so big and empty and beautiful." There was a breeze in the treetops, that was what the flickering shadows meant, but she couldn't feel it way down on the ground. "The stuff belongs there."

Samantha tapped the back of Aida's wrist and said, "You worry too much, Aida. Are you hungry? Where can we eat?"

"Dunno what's around here, really." Aida scrambled up, but she still couldn't even see Bloor Street for the trees. "We can eat at home . . . at my place, if you want."

"Sounds good." Samantha smiled and reached up. After a moment, Aida understood and took the hand, cool and smooth. Sam slid her toes towards hers, so Aida did what girls did, in gym class, on winter ice, at drunken parties: she stepped on Sam's toes, knotted their fingers and pulled her up.

Their chests grazed, fabric on fabric. Sam left her toes under Aida's.

"It just doesn't feel like art belongs somewhere where no one lives. Lonely. I can't imagine stealing, but then there'd always be someone to appreciate it, even all wrong, with the light from the street and hung next to the calendar."

Aida looked down and realized Sam's nails were in fact painted, one of those French manicures that look like nothing only better. "What would you steal, then?"

"The blue one, of course."

"Same as me?"

"Sure. I like blue you can fall into, too."

"I DON'T UNDERSTAND who this woman is or what she wants from you."

Around two o'clock. Aida was lying with her head on Steve's bare belly, waiting out the heat so she could sleep. She turned to face him, but his skin was too warm against her cheek, so she flipped back to the ceiling. "All she wants is to sleep on my couch."

"Aida. Did you sneak out tonight?"

"Not *sneak*. I waited. I couldn't ditch her." Sam had had endless energy for wine and confession, lotus-positioned on the folded-out couch. *He isn't such a prize that I should fight for him maybe. I should just let him fuck off to whatever, whoever, probably.* Sam was straight-spined even at the bottom of the bottle. *I could be like you, a single woman. People always like me, I could . . . could like someone back. Someone else.* That lie again. Aida hadn't wanted to bring up her own strange luck, but when Sam finally tipped over around four, Aida had put the bottles in the recycling and carried her shoes out the door to come lie naked on Steve's bed.

"Does she even know you have a boyfriend?"

"She's leaving her husband, Steve."

Their voices were like cigarette smoke, floating up in the dark.

"If you're sleeping with her . . ."

"Oh, jeez, c'mon." She flipped over again, dug her chin sharp into his hot skin.

"I wouldn't mind, I don't think." His palms brushed her neck, pulled her chin up. "It doesn't really count with a girl. As long as you tell me all about it, anyway."

"What movies have you been watching?"

"What have you got?"

He was sitting up, trying to lean down to kiss her, but she twisted sideways to lie beside him. "That's not what girls are for, Steve."

"Well, what am *I* for, then? Aida?" His voice had gone still as a pool, suddenly. She could not see his face. Her eyes were just parallel with his bare hip, and looking up was all shadows.

"If you knew, what'd be the fun?" She pretended the tone hadn't changed, that they were still just telling dirty jokes. But it wasn't sexy at all, and she couldn't make it any sexier. She was already naked and so was he, but it was too dark to see and they weren't touching, so everything was covered, anyway.

AS THE BARTENDER passed Sam her change, he seemed to stroke her hand just a little. Aida sipped her beer and stared at the door. Steve had said that morning, as she left his place, that he missed her. She said, "You don't miss me, I'm here," but she knew what he meant. Even pretending not to know was starting to mean something. She knew.

Aida had told Steve where they'd be tonight, because he'd asked her. She'd told the truth because lying would have been a whole other level of – something. She knew he'd come, but she still couldn't picture Steve and Sam meeting. It seemed that they would cancel each other somehow. They were the two most attractive people Aida knew.

Samantha pivoted towards Aida with her candy-pink drink.

"Do you miss Terry?"

"No."

"No?"

"I – " Aida suddenly saw something fiercer than pretty on Sam's pretty face. "I should go home. I need – "

Aida was so startled by the idea of the couch blank and empty, only dark hairs in her sink, that she could not have ended that sentence for anything. What Sam needed – money, counselling, more stable shoes, another drink – was beyond Aida.

" – a lawyer."

"Oh. Wow. I – I just gotta go to the bathroom." She set down her drink and jumped up. She would tell Sam that Steve was coming when she got back. She would tell Sam all about Steve, and see what she thought.

She was surprised and not surprised when she got back from the bathroom and found Samantha leaning across bar-spill to chat with the bartender, and the man beside her was Steve. They must've seen each other, people like them always saw each other, but Sam was talking, Steve watching bass-fishing on TV. Aida stood outside the circle of the bar space, and watched the bartender admire the criss-cross straps of Sam's tank top, watched a table of fortyish women ogling Steve's shirt-stretching chest.

Aida was wearing a posy-patterned apron with cloth stitched on the back. She'd seen the idea in a magazine but somehow her stitches came out crooked, and the apron was the wrong shape, binding in the breasts and sleeves, billowing over the belly. People brushed past her, a man, a women, a couple – touching without seeing her.

Aida stepped forward, and Steve and Sam turned to her. They said *Hey* in stereo, then turned to each other.

"*Oh*. This is Sam*anth*a. Hello, Samantha. I'm Steve."

Sam smiled blankly, and extended her hand.

"Aida's boyfriend." Even as he pumped her hand, his face collapsed a little.

"Oh, she's told me *all* about you." Aida wanted to apologize for making Sam lie. She'd meant to mention Steve, but Sam always had so much to say. Now, too: she admired Steve's shirt, pointed out a free table, smiled and smiled and didn't look at Aida.

At a table for three, everybody is beside everybody. Aida sipped Corona and Sam tried to summarize Toronto – streetcars, sidewalk chalk drawings, men peeing in alleys.

"It's so great to see Aida's crazy city life." Sam gripped Aida's arm with her icy fingertips, but she still wouldn't look at her. "I let way too much time go by."

"It's nice having you here. The city looks better with someone new seeing."

"*Yes*." Steve grinned too hard, eyes crinkling. He was looking down, though, at Aida's arm with Sam's hand on it. "Absolutely. What else have you been up to?"

"Well, a club, and shopping, of course. And to this art thing, *Colours and Shapes*." Sam ducked her gaze. Aida was surprised she wouldn't flirt a little, just a flutter of wings. But Sam just swigged her drink, bunched up her mouth on the swallow.

Steve reached out and touched Aida's other arm, his fingers hot and dry and paper cut. He stroked up and down, making the little hairs stand on end. "*The Shape of Colour*. I loved that exhibit. I took Aida to see it, to show it to her. Remember, Aida?"

THE NIGHT FELT LONG. They played pool, and laughed a lot, but not really at anything; they didn't talk much. The bar was badly air-conditioned, warm and damp near the window. Aida stood there, watching Sam line up her shot, watching Steve twirl the ball rack on his finger. They were talking about wheat-beers, she could half hear. Sam was looking at the yellow ball, and Steve was looking at the spinning triangle, but they were both all towards Aida, the bend of Sam's elbow, Steve's taut neck.

Aida sagged more deeply against the wall, almost sliding down it. Tomorrow, Samantha would go home to her cheating husband and tell him she was keeping the house, the cat, their nicer friends. Tomorrow, tomorrow, tomorrow Steve would ask Aida again if she was ashamed of him, if she was unhappy, if she knew what she really wanted. And she would say no and no and no, but not yes to anything, and this time he would probably go for good.

Samantha made her shot and straightened up, and Steve tossed and caught the triangle. They clinked their glasses and then, before they drank, turned and air-toasted Aida in her corner. The light above her had blown, so they probably couldn't tell that she was crying. All the light in the room, from the TV and the beer sign and headlights outside seemed to flash on Steve and Sam just then. White teeth glinting, the loop of silver in his eyebrow, the fall of gold down her back. They were so beautiful, these unloved ones. If she could've given them to each other, she would have.

Massacre Day

Let's Go, Team Obvious!

MY MOTHER WAS WATCHING THE NEWS with her back to me, but she turned when I said a dirty word. It'd be obvious to anyone normal that some guy who shot a bunch of kids *was* a fucktard, but all I could see in her eyes above her coffee cup was *watch your mouth*. She didn't say it out loud like usual, though. She just did it – glared at my mouth as if a slimy alien baby was going to squirt out any second.

My mother is always so fucking literal.

As soon as I got out on the mucky lawn, I shook the DuMauriers out of my sleeve and lit one. Usually, I'd wait to smoke till I got beyond the window, but she didn't deserve it when she just stood in front of the TV with her head tipped, like she was making up her mind about shooting kids, like maybe that'd be something she could understand. I took a drag right out front, and anyway after two steps I was of sight. Sometimes, I just wanted to breathe fire.

By the time I got to the filter, I was at Tariq's house. He came out right away like always and kissed me hard with tongue like always, too. I wanted to talk about the Virginia man and all those dead people, but not with Tariq. It was too mean to talk about stuff he couldn't understand, and there was nothing I could mime, nothing in his little Collins Gem dictionary, for what I wanted to say.

Teyla Eats Breakfast

"THE PHONE LINES ARE NOOOOW OPEN, so if you wanna see – "

She opened her eyes and stared at the pigeon-shitted window: the rattle seemed to be the loose balcony rail, not a home invasion. Probably.

" – the fantabulous Ms. Avril on tour – "

David had left behind a cheap plastic clock radio that she could only sometimes turn off – other times the button stuck and drive-time radio was unstoppable. She dug in her third fingernail, an unbitten one, tugged. " – word of a jackknifed produce truck – " Her nail bent – a sliver of pain. She dropped the clock, curled into sheets so long past their wash-by date that they were limp as silk. She was alone with the wind, the radio, possible home-invaders. David was gone, though he had forgotten some things.

All David's remainders were defective. When she made it to the kitchen, the stove clock said 9:48. The window here was clearer, the sun slanting high. The clock radio was not only unstoppable, but three hours behind.   ·

At 9:48, she should have been in front of a chalk-dusty room, lecturing about Louis Riel. By 9:48, unsupervised eleventh-graders would be cackling at their good fortune, sprinting for the woods. They would not wonder if she was sick or dead, or else they'd hope so. They'd imagine her gory car crash, snickering at the thought of her bleeding on the exams until the red ink of the marks couldn't be read, and they would all get As. Little did they know she hadn't marked the exams yet.

Teyla had to phone the assistant vice-principal, say she had choked to death on her own bitterness. Some hideous pretty secretary needed to tap down the hall to dismiss any remaining kids. Teyla's tragedy was wearing thin on the assistant vice-principal, who didn't think divorce before thirty counted. Teyla would call after breakfast.

Toaster waffles. In the public school price bracket, syrup bottles were all shaped like log cabins or slave women. Still, Teyla liked the sugar rush first thing.

Except it wasn't first thing – the stove clock now said 10:03.

Teyla watched the smudgy gray kitchen TV. Clock-radio pop music was mixing with the news. David disrupted everything. Even when he was living in an expensive one-room condo far west of her, she could sense him like a warm spot in the ocean. Him and *her,* whoever he was with.

A smudgy gray kid in a duffle coat had killed all these teenagers.

Images of trees and hills. Alanis wailing from the bedroom drowned out details.

Cheap TV with no remote – Teyla had to stand up to turn up the volume. David's old sweatshirt hung around her thighs and caught on the plastic slave bottle, spilling syrup on her bare ankle. Such a strange sensation, nearly erotic, really.

By the time she could hear properly, it was all "authorities decline to comment" and "more on this situation as it develops," the death-toll, then the five-day forecast.

She had no one to tell, so she didn't know how she felt. Beyoncé sang "To the left." Teyla went into the bedroom to smash the alarm clock with a shoe.

A is for Awesome

WE HELD HANDS and walked slow and Tariq stopped to look at any car along the curb that was halfway decent. He even thought spoilers were *très très cool.* I don't think there were a lot of cars wherever he came from.

It didn't matter how late we were because every teacher had given up on Tariq as Impossible ESL and were just letting him pass art and autoshop and family studies. I had history first period, a fuck-off class where they put bad kids and stupid kids indiscriminate, and then treated us all as if we were both. Today we were supposed to write stories about Louis Riel the night before he was executed. I never read the chapters because the assignments were all just what you thought people felt, so there was no way not to get an A if your paper had the right names. Ms. Murphy said what we wrote depended on whether we thought Louis Riel was crazy, but whether I was sane or not, I'd probably feel pretty bad if I knew I was going to get hanged.

When we got to school, Kaleigh was by the doors yelling at her mom on her cell, which always gaks everything she says, so calling Kaleigh is basically like not calling her. As soon as we came up the lawn, she yelled, "Bye, mom," and shoved it into her pocket. She was all, "You guys, you *guys,*" and pulling us into the caf.

Tariq was all, "What what, Kay?" but I sorta figured what. Poor Tariq.

I was right: someone had put the media studies TV in front of the ketchup and salad-dressing table, and a bunch of first-spare keeners were watching. There was pretty grass and trees, all shaky like in an action movie, people saying *more soon, stay tuned,* but also, in the background, you could hear bullets.

When he heard them shoot-shoot-shooting, Tariq squeezed me hard against his side. I wondered if he came from somewhere with guns. We watched for a long time. Kaleigh went by the recycle bin to call her mom back, and I could hear her yelling, *Like, with a gun. Yeah, ok,* exactly *with a gun.* Tariq just looked sadder and sadder. It wasn't easy to figure it out without words, but you could. I was pretty sure that in a language Tariq actually knew, he wasn't stupid.

It was loud in the caf, with the TV, principal on the PA, Kaleigh talking like a squeak toy, shoes squeaking like screams. Mainly, people got bored with weather, the truckers' strike, commercials for drugs and orange juice before they figured out why the TV was even there. But we three kept watching, with most everyone else yelling and throwing hats and eating half-baked caf cookies.

Of course we were supposed to be in class, but Kaleigh was all, "Louis Riel'll still be dead tomorrow." Really, so would all those students and the French teacher and everyone, but the period was almost over and it wasn't like Ms. Murphy gave a shit. Plus Kaleigh was crying tiny leaks out the corners of her eyes and I didn't want to mess with her. Kaleigh was little and cute, like the smallest puppy, but little puppies get their food stolen and their heads stepped on, so they're always hungry and scared of the vacuum cleaner. Kaleigh was sort of a high maintenance mess, but I couldn't not be nice to her.

The stoners watched with us for a while but they were only waiting on the weather reports to see if they could go get high in the woods tonight. People came in and out, bell bell, and we should've been in Mme. Brittard's French, but I was flunking it so bad that I could *still* only tell Tariq to close the door, and that I liked him, which was the same as *I love you,* which was a little weird. Plus Brittard sometimes threw chalk.

Bell bell. Kaleigh finally turned off her cell and the student council kids were talking about how they could still add "and Virginia Tech" to the Columbine Memorial posters. We were pretty ready to go: Tariq had eaten all the strange gray bread in his lunch and Kaleigh's eyes were drying sticky mascara gray. But then that video, the dead murderer talking. It finally got quiet, 'cause there was nothing to say after that. And then it was too quiet not to try.

that video was nuts, he was
because he wasn't talking to anyone
that guy didn't even know what he was mad about
or else he was mad about things that happened on TV, or
  to other people,
or else he just wanted a reason.

HE WASN'T LIKE MY LOUIS RIEL STORY. He was excited for the dying.

History was way over by then, French too, plus lunch. I should've gone to art, but like hell was I going to class when everybody felt dead.

Teyla Goes to a Bar

NEON BEER SIGNS IN THE AFTERNOON would have proved, if only to herself, that she was hitting new lows, so she went to a classy hotel bar. Fashion-photo lighting, thick-upholstered booths, flirtatious jazz. But flirtation, the hand of a stranger on her thigh, was a bilious thought. She had eyes only for mid-terms and her bowl of cashews. Teyla was not watching the men at the bar or the TV above it. If she was going to abandon the students in this time of heartache, as the veep had said on the phone, at least she would get her marking done.

For a crazy man killing strangers in another country, yeah, maybe they were heartbroken. They wore their blood so close to the surface, anything could cut them. She recalled, vaguely, living that way, bleeding all over the place any time she missed the ball, didn't get flowers for Valentine's Day, saw roadkill or the six o'clock news tragedy. She was all drama, fever pitch, passion and horror. She couldn't calm down, at that age.

No one had gotten the dates of Sir John A.'s first term. She flicked through – no one. They conspired to get the question wrong, to torment her. Mathematically, someone would have to guess right. She'd been guessing for weeks what sort of woman David wanted now. Red X, red X. She'd probably nailed the type by now and didn't even know.

The TV did not match the heavy cushions and rich nuts. The flash of news and cereal ads made it seem as if there were blinking beer signs after all, as if a kid with his boots outside his jeans might snap her bra strap, laughing through bad teeth.

The waitress was more appropriate: a nicer blouse than she'd need to teach history, immobile curls and breasts. She brought Teyla's martini and spun away before Teyla could ask why it was clear.

She wondered if she'd forgotten to say *apple* before *martini*, or if the waitress had ignored *apple* because neon green drinks were déclassé. Maybe they had clear apple liqueur here; maybe they had never heard of apple martinis and were just guessing. Maybe ironed blouses and propped-out breasts were what David wanted now.

Teyla drank and tasted throat lozenge and paint. She had never learned to like grown-up drinks and this was so grown-up it was elderly. She tried to spit it back into the glass but the coughing made her suck down instead. Whatever it was it was burned. A man in a narrow suit was alternating watching her and the TV.

Watching didn't help anything. Teyla wiped her chin, breathed deeply, took a smaller sip. No point wasting expensive liquor, no matter how foul. She scraped another *X* through "The Pacific scandal was about rich people wanting houses on the ocean." She wouldn't look at the screen. She could recite the whole story herself. Still, sound penetrated, an eyewitness, a thin-voiced girl, gaspy and high: "He just came in . . ."

A sham interview, making witnesses recite in their own words facts already known. Familiar as an essay question: Four primary industries dependent on rivers, two no longer fishable fish, three problems with smelters, *in your own words.*

More of the girl stammering, sobbing. Finally, Teyla had to look, just to see if the girl was pretty. It was hard to tell through tears, snot, microphone. Then she wiped her face on her sleeve: no, not pretty.

Two questions left blank – X X – and one THIS WASN'T IN THE UNIT!! ☹ Teyla drank again, braced for the solvent flavour now. She looked up again as she swallowed. On the screen, above the traffic crawl, a sullen still-frame shot of a boy a few years older than her students, a few years younger than herself. X

Thanks for Comin' Out

AFTER MR. BANGOR TOOK THE TV for some grade nine geography video on oceans, I could've gone to English, or with Tariq to the library – he liked *Popular Mechanics,* and the big dictionaries – to finish my history paper before the end of the day. But I couldn't deal with Louis Riel when we had just spent the whole morning on crazy. So I told Kaleigh we had to go see Hart and Samir, and Tariq just followed, like always.

As we walked down the dirt hill towards the old subdivision, I was wishing that Michael Cho had had a plan, that he hadn't actually thought he'd just kill everyone. I wanted him to have wanted to kill just certain people, even if they didn't even deserve it and it was actually random, as long as it wasn't random in his mind. Because then he would've, not had a reason, but he would've known there was such a thing as a reason. He would've lived in the world the way people live in the world.

At the squat, Hart was pissy. "If you're gonna use this place like the fucking local diner, you better start fucking tipping." Hart was just talking to talk, like usual. Samir laughed. I gave them the slimy caf cookies we'd brought and he laughed more.

We sorta had to listen to them if we wanted to hang out there. They were more hard core, had actually dropped out and took off from their folks' places, did squeegee and got stoned off their faces the rest of the time. They were lucky finding that place to live. A fire had taken out the kitchen, the roof leaked yellow water, it was damp-cold, there were bats, but it was a real whole house, nearly. They weren't that hard core – if they'd've had to sleep outside they would've gone back and been the same as anybody, carrying granola bars to school, wearing pajamas, going to church on Easter.

Tariq sat on the couch and patted his lap all, "Hey, baby," so I had to go sit there. His thighs were like narrow planks digging into my ass and he'd be feeling me up the whole time, but when you're somebody's girl-friend, you can't be disloyal.

I thought Kaleigh would tell about what happened, but she was just picking white threads out of the hole in her jeans, not saying. I felt bad for Samir and Hart laughing and bullshitting, not knowing what was really going on, but I couldn't talk, even once we started getting stoned. The three of us just watched Hart and Samir jumping off the back of the couch and punching each other. After a while, Kaleigh started rummag-ing in the sideboard thingy that some family had left when they ran away from the fire. On top and underneath was all shirts and dead leaves and grocery bags, but inside there was a pretty decent stuffed cat, a busy-bee, a bunch of board games.

Tariq started putting the cat in my face, going "Mowmowmow," which wasn't funny at all and I had to slap his hand really hard to make him stop. The cat was orange and stripy, with horrible hard googly eyes. Kaleigh had a game box in her hands. She said, "The fuck's this, yo?" trying to sound tough. But her skinny face was still blotchy pink and her voice wobbled on the *yo*. She blew on the box, a little fakey puff of air. When some dust blew back in her face, she jerked like it was a bullet. Samir grabbed the cat and put it on her shoulder: "It's a ccccaaattt for Kaaaaleigh," and she flinched again and the cat fell on the floor. Samir was way more stoned than the rest of us.

She knelt down and dipped her face real low to look at the box, the picture of smiling multicultural kids on the front. It was pretty obvious she was crying again, bits of leaf stuck in the wet on her face. Tariq looked sad, but he was also sort of rustling underneath me like he wanted to be away. Hart and even smoky-stoned Samir were looking like, "The fuck?" I should've said something, I was the only one who could. But how can anyone say, just say

    some guy

    this guy

    he thought people were raping his soul

    he shot them

Who?

    I don't know, people at his school

What did they do to him?

    nothing, it wasn't them, it was just people

What?

    he was crazy

I don't –

    crazy

So I just went and bent over the box with Kaleigh and together our hair sort of shielded her face so the boys couldn't see.

Teyla Walks Home from the Bus Stop

TEYLA WALKED FAST AT DUSK, head down, her bag rattling against her side. She didn't know where any of her students lived. They didn't bite on the "personal histories" she assigned when she was hungover. Teyla stepped in a sidewalk crack filled with slush. Gray sleet had fallen while she was in the bar, failing exams and watching heroic teachers who let their soft bodies catch bullets through the door so that students might live. Shot through painted plywood, an 8:30 French class. Teyla wondered, grammar or literature?

The handles of the Pottery Barn bag of failing papers dug into her fingers. Bullets through a door – did they enter the body slower for the friction? A less deadly wound? That French teacher was dead, door or not. Would Brittard have taken a bullet for a student? *Not bloody likely* was the thought Teyla wanted to think – and then again you never knew, ever. You'd never have known that Teyla never shopped at Pottery Barn, she carried the bag so naturally. Her mother had given her an old duvet rolled up inside it, when David had left with their wedding-gift one.

Teyla didn't live in a Pottery-Barn part of town, not even a smooth-sidewalk part. She didn't know where any of her students lived. She never saw them in the Mac's or Dominion, but then, she always kept her eyes on the bottom shelves of tomato paste and applesauce, so they might have been there. They might have been anywhere.

Teyla kept moving through the slush, through her martini haze. She didn't have stupid fears when she walked alone in the evening. She wasn't afraid of the stoop-shouldered man walking towards her, not of him turning, trailing her, twisting her into an ally, kicking the sack of papers, making her beg. She was not one of those women.

She was afraid of things worth fearing. She walked into the Dominion to buy Lean Cuisine for dinner and she was afraid of the twitch of blue eyeliner on the checkout girl. A man was yelling at the girl. Screaming at her, really, whiskers spittled, for not double bagging, no, *for* double bagging,

the denigration of the environment

without even asking him what he wanted

DE-NUH-GRAY-SHUN

the customer

what he wants

Wants!

That girl, sixteen and slight, her small twitch, her flaccid hand beside the conveyor belt: Teyla was terrified of her. That girl was about to . . . Teyla backed slowly through the door. That girl clearly had it in her to reach into the bristled bawling mouth, grip the pulpy muscle of his tongue and pull with a force Teyla had never possessed, or even reckoned. She walked faster now, watching shadows as she walked home with no dinner.

She was not a popular teacher and she did not know where they lived.

Three Cheers for Nothing

WE COULDN'T WATCH TV AT ANYONE'S HOUSE because parents hated kids like Hart and Samir – dirt on their shoes, smoke in their hair, seven-day T-shirts and gray teeth. So we were just smoking and eating crackers and not knowing what was going on in the world, trying to play that '80s game with dwarves and faeries. Some of the cards were lost, and the instruction manual was torn, and anyway Tariq couldn't understand and Hart and Samir were way stoned. Tariq probably just wanted to go make out in the shaky-floored bedrooms upstairs, but he rolled the dice and handed me scorecards when I said to, and didn't complain. He was happier not understanding when no one else did either.

It was Kaleigh that I was looking at, though, because I knew she was the other one wondering, while Hart and Samir spat cracker crumbs at each other, and Tariq ran his hand up my thigh. I didn't even know what we wondered, really: the kids who got shot were mainly dead before we skipped out. The ones that were just hurt, well, it wasn't like I was in suspense about anyone in particular.

Kaleigh finally said something. She was fiddling with the chart of life or whatever it was, and said, "Do you think they found any clues?"

Hart was so baked he looked at his cards, even though there was no such thing as a clue card and she wasn't even talking to him. She was really talking to the floor, but I answered her. "A clue to what? Everyone knows who did it."

"I meant about why? I mean, he said why, but really actually why."

Tariq was watching us, holding a card of a pretty little fairy. He looked worried.

Kaleigh hunched over the map of the enchanted wood and stared at me, eyes all blue and pink. "Wanna go watch TV at Sears?"

She wanted what I wanted: a newscaster with a fat microphone, touching his ear, saying, "We're just now getting word that Michael Cho's supposed killing spree was really an excellent defense against aliens' murderous invasion. His quick thinking has saved us from an unimaginable demise. Michael Cho is also not really dead somehow."

Teyla Orders in Dinner

TEYLA'S MAIL WAS ALL MENUS. Now you could order delivery from the Mandarin Buffet. It was expensive and the gothic/oriental fonted menu, the random buffet was truly bizarre – coleslaw, potato salad, egg rolls, spicy chicken, kiwi mussels in black bean sauce. That last one sounded so ridiculous she ordered it, with coleslaw. Who was going to laugh at this joke? The TV picture was fuzzing so badly she had to shut it off before the news. The kids on TV would manage without her, just like her students. She wondered if they knew anything had been unusual about the day. Or if they did, if they brushed it off or wept in gym class. Blasé or hysterical, their only settings.

She'd told David, back when she'd had David to tell, that her students were only a few cc's of dopamine away from mentally ill. She didn't know, anymore, if she'd really meant that. Anyway, there was no more David to tell.

She could remember, if she let herself, how many fuck-prefixed names she'd been called, and called others. She remembered having almost-sex out on the rooty wet ground in the woods, trying to, not making it, wanting to die. But playing board games in her basement made her want to live and die, too. Teyla remembered a game with cards and dice that lasted all of that winter when she'd almost lost her virginity. She'd spent every evening huddled in the basement with her friends, the deflowering boy, too. She didn't even get Christmas cards from him now. Then, they were the same shade of sunless pale.

She'd lost that game, humiliatingly. All her pieces run off the board. She hadn't, she didn't think, cried in front of him, but after everyone left, she'd broken all the windows. They were above her head, just below the low ceiling. The chair legs had smashed into the ceiling but finally she'd punched through. On the second window, the glass had cut her nose and chin, and on the third her mother had come down, and thrown her winter coat around Teyla's arms to stop her and she'd stopped.

When the delivery guy came with the kiwi mussels, Teyla was shaking and she didn't open the door. That delivery guy was a kid like the kids in her classroom and they were all all all without checks to their sadness, capable of anything, anything at all.

We Are Made of Win

WE ALWAYS ENDED UP AT THE MALL even though we knew they would kick us out because of the No Swarming rule. Even if you weren't loitering, even if you were actually shopping, they still hated too many kids together. Swarms, like bugs.

The whole mall seemed weird and fake on Massacre Day, like the way you think nylons are real skin until something cuts through and you see the real real skin. It was still slush and dead stick-trees outside, but inside the mall was decorated for spring, all these fake pink flowers that don't even grow here. "Just like a bunch of fucking *vulv*as hanging over the escalator," Hart said with this awful chest-deep laugh.

Tariq could see me glaring and he took my hand and whispered, "Nice, nice," all warm and wet in my ear. It was funny to think he didn't know what a vulva was and he was so interested in mine. There were vulva-flowers over the entrance to Sears, too.

"So *what* is happening, exactly?" Samir was muttering as we went past the glass perfume counters stinking like bathroom cleanser.

There was this silent moment as we all walked towards the flicker of TVs in the back. All the makeup ladies in their white jackets, purple and silver eyelids, were leaning over the counters and glaring at us. I was ready to tell what had happened, if I could, but for a second, staring at the back of Samir's messy hair as we walked along, I sort of loved him because he didn't know.

The End

TEYLA LET THE DELIVERY GUY knock and knock while she lay on the coffee table, hungry, head aching. She wished there were a cut on her body, a gory wound that would stun her every time she looked at it. Something she could feel she'd survived.

Teyla couldn't imagine ever again breathing that school air of asbestos and hair products and spreadable cheese. David had been surprised on their first date when she said she was in teachers' college. Said she didn't seem like the type. Teyla was going to puke soon, or else go eat a sandwich. David wasn't there and he didn't know anything.

The knocking stopped. Then a kick. Then a *Fuck you.* Then she was alone again.

Teyla didn't know anything. She should never have stood at the front of a classroom and said she knew things. She couldn't even stay steady on her back. She wished she had a remote, so she could turn on the TV and see those kids, what happened to those kids.

Once she had walked down the hall with a board-game box hooked under her arm, digging into wrist and biceps. Even in her own high school, she was just some fucking toaster with a headband and no time to hang out after school because she had to get her strategy cards in order. And now she was in charge, panting drunk on the coffee table, the windows birdshit and black night and she couldn't shut the drapes because David took them. Everything in her life was because of something or someone that wasn't.

She knew exactly how he felt, that television boy, the crazy one, Michael. No, she didn't – she knew how he wanted to feel. How he wanted to win every argument, to hold the weight of the room in the palm of his hand, to win the kiss and the love and the swooning allegiance of the most popular. Power and fire and every element on the periodic table. Teyla did know how Michael felt. She lay on her coffee table, burning in the back of her throat, knowing.

ACKNOWLEDGEMENTS

Some of these stories have been previously published in slightly altered form. I am indebted to the editors of these publications for their faith and guidance:

"Chilly Girl" in *Exile Quarterly* 30.3 (Toronto, 2006) and *Journey Prize Stories 19*. (Toronto: McClelland and Stewart, 2007).

"Fruit Factory" in *The New Quarterly* 102 (Waterloo, 2007), and *Best Canadian Stories 08* (Ottawa: Oberon Press, 2008).

"Wall of Sound" in *Exile Quarterly* 31.4 (Toronto, 2008).

"The House on Elsbeth," "Linn Lai," and "Zoom" in *The New Quarterly* 107 (Waterloo, 2008).

"Massacre Day" in *Maisonneuve* (Montreal, 2008).

"The House on Elsbeth," "Tech Support," and "ContEd" in *Coming Attractions* (Ottawa: Oberon Press, 2008).

I would like to acknowledge the Ontario Arts Council for financial support during some of the writing of this book.

Thanks must go to my classmates and professors at the University of Toronto English and Creative Writing Program, for helping me find the beginnings of this book. Beyond the classroom, these stories were read and improved by my tireless colleagues: S. Kennedy Sobol, Nadia Pestrak, Brahm Nathans, Emily Arvay, Lauren Kirshner, Lindsay Zier-Vogel, Kulsum Merchant, and especially Kerry Clare. As well, I owe much to the many friends who supported this endeavour in other ways, often with food.

Thank you to Dan Wells and everyone at Biblioasis, for helping make *Once* a real book. And for two very different versions of inspiration, instruction, humour, wisdom and endless patience, I am forever indebted to Leon Rooke and John Metcalf.

Finally, I must thank my family, who thought I was a writer long before I did, and who are always right about everything.

Rebecca Rosenblum just graduated from the English and Creative Writing Masters program at the University of Toronto. Her work has been published in *Exile Quarterly*, *The Danforth Review*, *echolocation*, *The New Quarterly*, *Maisonneuve*, *Qwerty*, *Ars Medica*, and *Journey Prize Stories 19*. *Once*, her first book, won the Metcalf-Rooke Award for fiction. Rebecca lives and writes in Toronto, Ontario.

Marquis Book Printing Inc.

Québec, Canada
2008